MW01171307

Punchin Yard

By

DONNA MILNER

Table of Contents

Dedication

My book is "livicated" to first the Most High Yah Rastafari who has made all things possible giving me the strength, faith and endurance to make this book a reality. Also giving thanks to my mother and father Mavis and Roy Parris who has nurtured me to be whom I am today throughout the years. Although gone, I thank them so much for their wisdom and ideologies about never looking down on someone and loving humanity whether race or creed. As for my twin sister Dawn Parris, I will forever also love and miss her too along with my aunt Millicent Fawcett Sumner who has been the 'cornerstone' of the content of my book and the source of strength before her transitioning. Through 'trials and tribulations,' she has endured it all and has proven to be my Sojourner Truth. Then to her daughter my Cousin Hazel Fawcett Sumner I give thanks also for all of her patience, understanding and love shown to me while writing this book as a true reference in concurring about some information about my Guyanese culture.

I am also livicating this book to my Yehudah Haile, my little angel who transitioned in 1999 and also my other yutes/offsprings Jahkeda Ayana, Yeshimabeit Iniyah, Jaherald Selassie, Anniyah Heralda, Safiyah Salama and Kebra Nagast along with my GranPrincesses Ruby Savannah Zewditu, Yehudit lily, Kaori

1

Amira, Luna Yehudit and GranPrince Izaiah Lee for overstanding that sometimes their Queen Mother and Grandmother was very busy when penning this book. Naima Parris is my great-niece whom I must also remember as she is also a budding artist alongside her father Jahfari and the granddaughter of my belated twin sister Dawn.

To my cousin Joseph Dookram who departed so quickly and for whom I will forever love for his consolations on my not so good days by deterring my down feelings. Cousin Hensley who transitioned the same day as my mother I had loved and appreciated so much as I concurred with him like his sister Cousin Hazel also as the man with the family's archives and other information. My aunt Dr. Myrna Fawcett who made it possible for most of the family migrating here in America I give my gratitude for this opportunity with also her encouragement while writing this book and to also my very lovely Aunt Norma Pollard whom I always am very elated to speak to from time to time as her wisdom is that of essence. Cousin Nichelle Beckles is my cousin but like little a sister who always check in with me and whom I also love dearly. To Windy Smith and Myra Smith; mother and grandmother of Naima Parris who has been more than kind to me over the years and my initial support and inspiration in initiating this book.

Also to Leemire Goldwire and my late King William Alfred Milner who always believed in me and my potentials. They always encouraged me to do the best that I can. Also, my cousin-in-law

2

Osmond Browne with his jovial ways when my day is not as good as it should be. Then to Lynne Miller who has been the best neighbor that I have ever had in Miami, Florida, and my ex-classmate Wendella Mahabir Britton whom I knew since I was about eight years old in Guyana. To her also I really appreciate for her encouragement like a counselor and the knowledge also that she imparted about Guyana. Then to also the entire Milner family in Guyana for being so awesome to myself and lineage.

Acknowledgement

Special acknowledgement must be made of my sistrens Maxine Headley, Roxanne Keith and Lynne Bouknight who has always been so caring and supportive since knowing them. Also to my professor Dr. Victor Wallen of the course Social and Cultural Foundations of Counseling whose class bought out the best writing in me and to the many others whose names I cannot remember because my transcripts are all packed away from all those years ago.

As for my book cover, I want to thank my nephew Jahfari Haile Parris for his   wonderful illustration of the tenement yard. Then to the many other friends and relatives whose belief in me has been never ending.

The Barrel

A walk alongside the lake with trees as my constant companions, while squirrels play hide-and-seek with wild flamingos. But just as I begin to think about how much I had liked those days in "the land of many waters," a plane hovers above. Patsy then comes to mind. Cinnamon complexioned with hips half as wide as the doorway, hair dark as molasses, and hands akimbo as if in defiance, she would rush outside to peruse the sky with blatant curiosity. After all, it's that time of the year. That time of the year when relatives come home; some announced and some unannounced. Her lips now pursed as if to almost recite her wishes for the holidays, she is becoming tachycardic with her heart racing with anxiety and worry.

Stanley peeps through the tattered curtains on his bedroom window and notices her. He grabs the opportunity to join this binnie1 that he has been sooring2 for a very long time now. Oh, how her fluffy body tantalizes him!!! He wants to make her his wife, but she tells him she is not interested which makes him loose sleep countless nights with a profuse longing for her. Says she loves Bertie who lives abroad in Strauffaus.3 He sometimes dreams of the kind of kids they would have with his color as dark as coffee. But, would this really be? He is outside now. Then A

---

[1] *Young woman*
[2] *When a young man romantically pursues a young woman*
[3] *A term used at that time in Guyana for "America"*

walk alongside the lake with trees as my constant companions, while squirrels play hide-and-seek with wild flamingos. But just as I begin to think about how much I had liked those days in "the land of many waters," a plane hovers above. Patsy then comes to mind. Cinnamon complexioned with hips half as wide as the doorway, hair dark   as molasses, and hands akimbo as if in defiance, she would rush outside to peruse the sky with blatant curiosity. After all, it's that time of the year. That time of the year when relatives come home; some announced and some unannounced. Her lips now pursed as if to almost recite her wishes for the holidays, she is becoming tachycardic with her heart racing with anxiety and worry.

Miss Cheryl from next door received one from her daughter in Canada earlier this afternoon. The whole yard see sheh tings. Emptied it out by sheh front door. Shared out candy to de lil chirren and some flour to de women fuh mek black cake. She even dig deeper aan gih them some cooking oil. She is so excited. Sheh get everything sheh want.

"Dis ain gon be no deh bad Crismus, ah swear,"[4] Cheryl boisterously yells. She is grinning now. Perched on her front step with teeth as white as pearls while two-faced and envious Doris whispers into Ethel ears on this hot afternoon.

Wonder what she saying?!! That Doris could never be trusted. Always a bag of confusion and "Miss Mouth ah Preh

---

[4] *"This is not going to be a financially bad Christmas with no food, I swear."*

Preh."[5] Always telling people business that they tell sheh behind closed doors, and in confidence. Fabricating by adding more to it. One just cannot confide in her. Not at all. Once Sandra did tell sheh that sheh was cheating on sheh chile fadda,[6] sheh tell he. Nearly mek he kill Sandra. Once Avril did tell sheh that sheh pick Hensley pocket after they come from de dance, sheh tell he. Once Wendell did tell sheh he choke and rob Bisnauth when he did drunk, sheh go to the police station and report he .... always running sheh mouth. Wonder what sheh got to say bout Miss Cheryl now?

Patsy is worried as sweat runs down her face, and mingles with the powder in her bosom. She is disgusted with the crowd in front of her neighbor's Cheryl is sharing out some splitpeas on sheh front step. Said her son just find a big, big bag of it in the bottom, bottom of the barrel.

"Allyuh cud mek some cook-up. Put some tripe inside,"[7] she yells, while her son Colin with enamel cup in hand, repetitively pours the peas in the neighbors' containers.

"Tikkay!!! Got to be careful not to drop some sweat in dem beans, Colin" [8].......

---

[5] *A woman who gossips a lot*
[6] *Her child's father*

[7] *"You all cud make some cook-up rice; peas and rice and put some tripe (animal stomach inside." It varies)*
[8] *"Watch out!! Be careful not to drop some sweat in those beans."*

I only teasing he. Ha, ha, ha!!! Wish ah could get some myself for dinner tonight.

"All dis commotion fuh ah barrel," Patsy mumbles to herself.

Her thoughts then rushed back to the plane that she saw four hours ago. Maybe Bertie was on it, and not here yet because he is clearing immigration. Taking longer because he has to find his own transportation since he didn't ask anyone to pick him up. Maybe his luggage plenty because he didn't send a barrel and decided to bring de tings in he suitcases. She had asked him, amongst other things, for some 'hard pants' or what we call 'denim jeans' overseas, some photo-print shirts, some psychedelic looking jerseys, a fat cap like de ones the Jackson Five wear, a pair of kickers,[9] a sexy slinky black dress and some black stilettos fuh Ole Year's Nite,[10] a pair of yachting boots or what they call sneakers nowadays, a pair of Clarks shoes for sheh goddaughter, some brassieres and other under clothes, a watch, a pressing comb for sheh hair, some hair dye fuh sheh Aunt Millie and some American hair grease to put inside to mek sheh hair in dripping jerry curls like sheh got "good hair" or what people refer to as hair that is not coarse.

She had also requested some flour, peas, cooking oil, garlic and other spices, peanut butter, jam, cereal, sugar, rice, sardines, tuna, mutton and other canned foods, powdered milk,

---

[9] *A pair of shoes with big heels*

[10] *The night before New Years Day; 31st of December*

toilet paper, tooth paste, mouthwash, soap powder to wash sheh clothes, soap to tek a bath, hair clips, lipstick, powder to suit sheh complexion, a tablecloth fuh sheh Christmas table, some decorations, and two blinds[11] fuh sheh one window that sheh could gather up thick and nice to leave the sunlight out. Then if sheh sweetheart bring more than two panels, sheh could save the extras for next year or send them to sheh family in de country[12] or in town. She specifically said "red" …….. red fuh keep out de bad eye[13] out sheh window from de neighbors, especially that Doris who always wishing people bad.

She is trying to remember what else she had asked for, but her memory becomes foggy. Sheh vex now. She had wanted some fruits to mek some black cake.[14] It's too late; time done pass, and she cannot set them in rum. So later for her cake-making this year. He would of had to send them fruits about one year ago. Miss Cheryl did get hers then, and tonite sheh baking sheh black cake with dem same cured fruits …… dried currants, raisins, cherries, prunes, cinnamon, cloves, nutmeg, eggs, cut up orange rind and nuts of her choice ……. all cured in rum, and ready to make the first fruitcake in the yard this year. Of course, without this cake, it does not feel like Christmas with its mouthwatering aroma.

Patsy is now grinding her teeth in disgust as if to say that her man is not coming back; not interested in her anymore. De

---

[11] *Curtains*

[12] *In the rural area*

[13] *Evil eye or what Jamaicans call "red eye"*

[14] *A fruit cake made specifically for the holidays and made black with burnt sugar*

same thing did happen to Oslyn. De man did promise sheh he would return. Didn't turn a straw, did promise to marry sheh and never looked back. Stopped communicating, and when she find out .... he mek ah ooman 'belly big'[15] in Brixton. Thank God sheh cousins find out bout he. Find out he whereabouts. Fix he snaggle teeth and turn sweet bai[16] in England. Then he write home and give sheh a 'Jim Cock bring Ram Goat Story' [17] about how sheh cousins telling lie pun he and that how he turn a Christian over there aan de otha aan de tarrah [18]........... and how he still love sheh.

Lie, dat is lie!!!

"*Oh Gawd, ah hope Bertie dhoan do mih duh,*" Patsy prays. "*Dem neighbas gon laff. Ah tell Tessa de otha day dat he comin. Thank Gawd sheh dhoan run sheh mouth. Sheh mite spare mih if he dhoan come.*"

She then closes her window and goes to sleep. A little too frustrated to go outside to draw some water from de standpipe and fetch de bucket to the makeshift bathroom in the far corner of the yard. It getting too dark now and de other day, she almost cut sheh right toe from one of the zinc sheets that was used to build that closed in make-believe bathroom outside. Hot and sweaty, she then comforts herself with the reflection of the fairy lights[19] on her

---

[15] *Made a woman pregnant*
[16] *Sweet boy or ladies man*
[17] *A very complicated and confusing story/explanation*
[18] *And so on, and so on*
[19] *Christmas lights*

bedroom wall from the house over the fence. She grins a little at the disobedience of her neighbor that dis always put her lights up early; not a true custom of people in this country.

Is Gertrude, who dhoan care bout no custom. Sheh like put dem up fuh sheh granchirren. For when they come over to visit. They dis get really excited and dis run up and down in sheh "lil two by four," [20] and keep nuff, nuff noise that does mek sheh happy. Sheh place small, but sheh also happy selling sheh flutey and custard blocks [21] to mek ends meet.

Gavin's husky voice awakens Patsy as usual the next morning. He lives just on the side of her with his common-law wife and seven kids. He works as a stevedore at a nearby wharf and although he boasts about how much he enjoys his job, it surely doesn't seem like he enjoys having to leave for work so early in the morning. The walls are not soundproof and every morning his galavanting next door at around 4 'o' clock would cause Patsy to jump out of sheh sleep.[22] Apparently his wife does not assist him to prepare breakfast and his take-away lunch, as she could hear him battling with the pots and pans to tek outside to the makeshift kitchen to heat up he water and mek some tea. Then also warm up the leftovers from the day before on the coalpot[23] perched up on **quartette** rocks outside in the yard. Or better yet, heat up he food

---

[20] *A little tiny living space*

[21] *Frozen juice from ice trays and custard block is made of evaporated milk, custard powder, sugar, cinnamon, nutmeg, almond or vanilla essence and then frozen*

[22] *Was awakened suddenly out of her sleep*

[23] *A metal receptacle used to cook on with coals in the bottom and a grit in the middle to hold pot*

up on the kerosene stove on the table on the far corner of the one room they call home.

The aforementioned; the little space has been made into two bedrooms ...... and only space that excludes the typical rooms in a normal house setting. In here there is supposedly a wall that is really a huge curtain as a line of demarcation between the two so-called rooms. This type of arrangement is customary so mommy and daddy could have their own privacy and the kids, the other side. Also, there are no beds, but blankets, pillows, and sheets on the floor while I must reiterate that there is no kitchen, living room or bathroom inside. This is atypical of most tenement yards around the country, as these conditions are self-explanatory of individuals experiencing profuse poverty, and whose landlords or landladies has broken up one house into tiny compartments. These kinds of rentals; with some having no windows, but made-up doors apart from the main door to enter the building, are excellent sources of income for these owners as they financially exploit these tenants with these impoverished dwelling places. Then some are most times of sub-human conditions.

Patsy could also never forget how Gavin seemed like he and his wife were arguing one morning, and a fight broke out. Then she heard the screaming and yelling of dey chirren. But above all, suddenly it appeared like Gavin punched Carol, and like they were coming through her wall. Oh, what a day!!! But .... this burly fellow always proclaims that he loves his woman and has the best job in the yard.

"Ah like mih jab. Ah dhoan only get ah paycheck. Ah dis get 'prags.' [24] *Ah dis get tings from farin aff dem ships, aan whuheva ah cyaan get aan dem sailors 'mek styles' fuh gih mih . . . . dem boys dis gih mih from dem otha ships . . . . . . from whuheva dey thief,"* this stevedore cunningly says.

He is right . . . . like if he don't thief tuh. Not a sound from anyone, since they know he is telling the truth because in a tenement yard, and elsewhere, a stevedore is a very important person. He has prags or goods that is much sought after. This is how Gavin makes his living. It is extra money on the side which enabled him to purchase a motorcycle to ride to work. He could walk, but he prefers not to. Must show off that he got some money, and as for Carol, his 'betta half' [25], she is always in style; wearing the latest fashions from abroad along with his kids. Then, this stevedore, when he gets really dressed up, you don't recognize he. It is as if he has just arrived from New York or some other place overseas. Man, yuh should see he footside with he Clarks shoes and how he be pripsin[26] with he kangol on he head looking "ustad" or what we may say, "very fashionable."

Thank God Patsy has no work today, and could roll over and go back to sleep. But first, she has to wait until "Mr. Stevedore" cranks up his bike and takes off. Lord, you should hear the noise!!!! Who don't sleep sound or is even deep asleep, it wakes up. This

---

[24] *Free goods*
[25] *Partner or soul mate*
[26] *Modelling*

is about a quarter to five and Phillip, another tenant is yelling for him to stop.

"*Mih nerves bad. Ah cyaan tek dis. Every mawnin yuh disturbin we. 'Every Tom, Dick aan Harry.'* [27] *Ah tell yuh ahready ... Stroll yuh bike outta heh aan rev it up ova suh.*" Phillip angrily yells.

Now God knows that this yard does not need this kind of commotion this time of morning cause people want to get dey sleep as most of them do not work on weekends. Patsy then peeps outside, peeping so skillfully that no one can see her. Oh Gawdo!!! [28] Doing this in Guyana is like minding somebody's business, so one has to be cautious. Some people feel triumphant when not caught peeping. But who says someone didn't see her!!! Bridget is outside. She is waving at Patsy as she is apparently seeing her shadow behind the window blind. Patsy feeling defeated, waves a weary right hand back at Bridget. She then once more seeks refuge in her bed, but again is being tormented this Saturday morning about whether Bertie will be coming home for the holidays or not.

"*It look like ah gon be heh alone,*" she sighs. "*Dis life ain ezee. Like ah gon haffa guh up tuh Berbice tuh mih family.*"

Bridget seeing her light off, hears Patsy's loud snoring outside her supposed bedroom window and decides not to call out her name. She has something to tell Patsy who is obviously fast

---

[27] *Everybody*
[28] *Oh God!!!*

asleep on the tiny cot that she had received from her ex-employers before they departed for Canada. This is indeed a novelty for this lovesick woman, as most of her neighbors does not have the privilege of sleeping in such comfort, but instead have to resort to the bare floors. Now amidst Bridget's anxiety this morning, it seems like Gavin's bike is not bothering her at all.

Just after midday, two men pull up in what appears to be a local shipping company's truck. They are attempting to undo the lock in the back door. They are taking what appears to be a barrel out of the vehicle and just rested it on the ground as one grabs a folder from the compartment, quickly looks inside as if he is double checking the address, and places the object on a dolly.

Doris, "Miss Mouth ah Preh Preh,"[29] just come out the latrine[30] and is walking towards the gate. Didn't even wash sheh hands; wash off dem microbes or germs with the water at the standpipe and handsoap left out for that purpose, but is now standing in front of them. From her gesticulations, one could see that she wants to know whose barrel it is. She is pointing now. Pointing towards Bridget's door. She is leading the way with the two men following her, and of course, with facial expressions that are green with envy. Her footsteps are quickening now as one could guess that she is eager to know the content of the barrel, and that the faster she gets to Bridget's doorway is the faster she will know what's inside.

---

[29] *A lady who gossips a lot*
[30] *An outside unflushable toilet*

Just then Bridget opens the door, and shouts, *"yuh know how laang ah did waitin? Ah waitin from since five dis mawnin. Ah cudden sleep. Ah cyaan wait fuh open it. Gawd, ah gat ah good brotha. Bless his heart!!! He keep he promise. He waan mek mih aan dem chirren happy, aan mih motha tuh."*

The men has now placed the barrel in her house, and one gives her a paper to sign. Then suddenly, without an invitation, Doris rushes pass Bridget through the open doorway, then walks down the hallway joining her children who are beaming with delight in their supposed living room. It appears like they are in heaven; as if life has become an instant utopia. By this time, both women are now attempting to open the barrel.

Doris is in anticipation since she is not only known for gossiping, but also for smooth talking her way to getting prags from people.

"Ah dhoan pay ah penny fuh nutten. Ah dis be real nice tuh de person. Ah gat ah good tongue in mih head," she boasts.

Of course, who didn't know that she is also a con-artist. De whole yard know that sheh ain't ezee!!! Conned a sailor on Main Street a few years ago. Walked away with he briefcase when she did young and pretty. Had over five thousand pounds inside. Left the hotel room when the Englishman was sleeping. He drunk like hell. Went back to de ghetto and had a party...... food cooking, beers drinking, dominoes playing, and the ice-cream van that was passing is now parked for over an hour in front of the yard. The children happy, the adults happy, and even the mangy boney-looking dog chewing on a chicken bone in the alley is happy, cause Doris buying through. Now the coolie[31] man smiling cause she is his best customer today for his ice-cream hustle. British pounds changed up into Guyana currency!!!!! Whoo hoo!!! Americans would say "Holy Cow!!!" Shevonne is smiling cause sheh good fren Doris got plenty money today and sheh fix sheh up.[32] Done get sheh small piece,[33] and enough fuh Christmas. That was the year 1966.

Now five years later, Doris ain't no spring chicken no moe.[34] Her daughter, Sharon, tek afta sheh motha footsteps[35] and doing the same thing. She has six children that sheh motha does watch when she out on the ships at nite or on Main street at the brothel.

"Sheh is ah good daughter. Nuff man fool sheh up. Two ah dem farin aan deh get sheh pregnant. De chirren nice aan gat good hair." [36]

Doris then pauses with tear-filled eyes, and adds ……..

"Deh light skin tuh. Sheh 'slip up' aan get four moe.[37] Dey fadda vanish laang time now. Sharon aan gat no education. Sheh leff school early fuh help mih wid sheh otha sistas aan brothas.

---

[31] *A man of Indian descent whose foreparents arrived in Guyana as indentured laborers from India*
[32] *Set her right financially*
[33] *Pocket change, more than a stipend*
[34] *Not young or youthful anymore*
[35] *Has some of her mother's traits and behaviors*
[36] *Hair that is of very soft and of straightish texture*
[37] *Made a mistake and got four more*

Dis is all we know. Living in dis yaad since deh born. Ai tuh aan had luck wid men fuh move mih out."

So this is her story that she repeats over and over, and over again to the whole, whole wide world. By this time, both women are just getting the barrel open with the children as their curious onlookers. Just then they hear a knock on the door; their room door and Terrence, Bridget's second child runs to open it.

"De barrel come, oh mih Gawd!!! Gary sen it? Ah din believe. He dis lie suh much. Gawd ah suh happy, suh happy. Ah waan see whuh inside. Ah tawt we wudda been 'out like south,'[38] but he ain leff we out dis year at all." Then again she lets out another .... *"Oh Gawd!!!"*

That was Granny Tinsy, Bridget's mother. She is back from her Saturday morning trip to Bourda market and is extremely ecstatic. So ecstatic that the bora, callaloo, karela or bitter melon and tomatoes at the top of her basket is about to fall out. Also, along with the mithai and pholourie [39] that sheh bring as snacks fuh sheh grandchildren.

Look out!!! She almost stumbled on the metal ring that was used to secure the barrel. Bridget had carelessly tossed it by the closed doorway, not expecting her mother to arrive home so soon. What you think? Think Grandma Tinsy had an intuition that her son had sent the barrel instead of doubting her daughter from the time he made the promise? Brainstorm!!!!! It easy. Ah only

---

[38] *We were left out*

[39] *Indian snacks made out of flour but the latter has peas inside*

'pulling y'all legs.' [40] She did know……. deep down inside. A mother's intuition. That's why she come home early.

Patsy heard the screams and wants to know if something happened. What is going on? Is something wrong with the old woman? Is someone bothering her? Is she feeling unwell and needs help? She hurriedly puts on her clothes and heads over there. Thinking that she was the only one to hear the outbursts at their neighbor's house, it wasn't so.

There are several people both inside the hallway by Bridget's room and outside the building's main door. Truly concerned about her elderly mother while demonstrating the kind of cohesiveness in the "ghetto" or 'hood' as Americans may call it, and a variable that sets itself apart from this country's very socially stratified society. Since they all have gotten there before her, and Patsy now sees the barrel, it is easy for her to make her deductions …… another barrel has arrived in the yard, and that its residents are going to be alright for the holidays. Ms. Cheryl own did come just yesterday and she did give them some oil, flour, split peas and candy. Now Bridget is giving them seasoning powders, rice, some canned meats and vegetables, dried beans, powdered drinks, some more Christmas candy for their children, and even soap.

"*Is ah pity he din sen some 'fugicle' aan hershey kisses. But dey wudda melt,*"[41] Bridget complains.

---

[40] '*Teasing you all.*
[41] *It's a pity he didn't send some fudgesicle/ice-cream bars and hershey kisses but they would*

19

The mentally challenged Daphney then replies, *"hershey kisses, ice-cream. Put in ……. as* she points to a plastic bag …… *sen dem."*

The crowd of more than thirty people laugh until dey belly buss [42] with Gwen joking, *"yuh stupity or whuh? Yuh is ah 'lamatha? Yuh cyaan sen no candy like duh. Dey gon melt. Aan de ice-cream!!! Duh gon melt tuh."* [43]

Grandma Tinsy starts to explain that the barrel took a month to arrive from Brooklyn, and that Gwen is right about her son not being able to include chocolate and ice-cream in the barrel. Some people start to disburse as it is now about 6 'o' clock in the afternoon while others remain put, drooling on the items both on Bridget's floor and her table top.

"Ah going home now," says a disheartened and very sad Patsy, while clenching on to the three plastic bags that her closest neighbor has given her.

"Dhoan throw dem bags away, save them fuh if yuh gaffuh guh to de store," Gwen shouts to her, since she knows too well that these were bags just acquired from America in which the food items came. Also something to show off as the names of stores in America are on them …… something to cherish.

Once more, a bewildered Patsy settles down in one of her two chairs, having ignored the invitation from Stanley to take her to a party in Barr Street, Kitty. After all, all she wants is to be with Bertie; her one and only love.

As usual, she could hear the music blasting from his jukebox on this Saturday night. It is a song by Dobby Dobson, and her favorite ………..

"This is My Story" I have no song, song. Just, just alone and brokenhearted because I fell in love. In love with you." Then continues ….. *"Yes, darling I love you and ……. "* as if he is both lyrically teasing, and trying to seduce her.

She is grimacing now. Oh, how brokenhearted she feels!!! Maybe Stanley does truly love her, she is thinking. Or maybe, he just wants carnal knowledge of her; something that Donna has always warned her about.

"Yuh gotta be careful gurl. Dem 'bannus'[44] not easy. All dey waan is fuh get in yuh drawers. Den dey 'big yuh belly up'[45] aan ……. dey gone. Gone with de wind, neva fuh see dem again. Blasted trickstas."

Patsy had always adhered to her friend's advice. Always did. That's why she is shunning Stanley. She also had other friends who has horrible stories of unrequited love. Shakespeare yuh hear that? This gentleman doesn't like 'love-given and not returned,'

---

[44] *Young men*
[45] *Get you pregnant*

21

and saying the same thing like whuh Rosie from de other yard did say ………..

"Dem bannus dis be like 'ah fifth wheel tuh ah jackass coach'[46] afta de baby born, aan when yuh ask dem fuh lil help fuh mine de pickney," yuh dhoan hear from dem again. They don't return the love you give them."

Sunday mornings in the yard is very quiet with some attending the Methodist Church a few blocks away, while some are recuperating from partying the night before. Some get up at about ten, and others after 1 or 2 'o' clock in the afternoon depending on how many drinks they had like Basil and Tony with they hangovers. Time elapses so very fast like in the case of Denise who has *'copped ah ting,'* [47] or as some may say, found a prospective boyfriend. She brought him home in the wee hours of the morning after meeting he at ah fete [48] on Durban street last night.

She is lying all wrapped up in the arms of the man who hardly knows her, or she …… him. Also, forgetting or ignoring the fact that she has taken her three children to her mother's house for her to babysit them, and always promising to get them soon after the party, but never does. After all, she has gained the reputation of being a "carry-off girl" or for some who does not know what this term means; a man who meets a girl at a party,

---

[46] *A wheel that is useless, hardly used because there are four others*
[47] *Caught a prospective lover*
[48] *A party*

dances with her, then eventually sweet talks her into leaving with him. Then he would 'carry' her to his house or a hotel for sexual pleasure.

This time around, Denise has brought this gentleman to her room or home. You see, he is a newly arrived seaman on vacation, and a great candidate for a boyfriend or 'sweetman.' He is from Guyana and is back home to have a good time for a month.

"If only ah cud get he as mih man, ah gon be ahrite. Mih life gon change. He gat ah good job aan he gon fix mih up[49]. Ah cud all move out tuh, aan ah gon get tings from Germany aan all ova. Plus Stanley aan he wife cyaan show off pun mih no more," she is saying in her mind.

She then snuggles up closer to the man she hardly knows with her naked body to keep warm. After all, she sees him as an excellent prospect, although she cannot remember his name. She ain't wrong, but better you than me girlfriend. You don't know his name, and 'giving it up?'[50]

Hey Stanley, listen up!!!! The seaman "stole yuh thunder," as my children would say. It mekkin mih[51] laugh now. Or betta yet …. it getting 'tun up' in here cause Denise *"canta"*[52] boyfriend running tings. Yes, he in control since I forget to tell y'all that a seaman got more status than a stevedore.

---

[49] *Going to look about my welfare*
[50] *Giving her body up sexually*
[51] *Making me*
[52] *Not real, make-believe imaginary boyfriend*

De otha day sheh was 'pahlaverin'[53] sheh self in de yard, and boasting about how much things sheh going to get from this man when he go back pun sea. Little do he know though, that sheh foot faas [54] and that she is one of dem ooman who dis 'blight yuh up,' aan yuh cud 'neva see yuh way' again becauz of all dem men sheh dis sleep with.

"Salt yuh up aan tek yuh luck."[55] I didn't say so. Is Percy and he friend dem by Big Market seh suh.

See, that girl known all over cause word is that apart from de parties, she trying now to do the same job like Sharon now pun de down low.[56]

Where's Patsy? We forgetting sheh? Can't get carried away!! Puh ting, is wheh sheh dey? [57] Ow, poor ting!!! Missing sheh man. No, no, no!! Can't hurt sheh feelings. What? What Doris 'sehing?'[58]...... Give her some handkerchiefs for Christmas to wipe away sheh tears? Laughing also that once Patsy aunty sent a barrel for the family from Brooklyn and she hurriedly went up to Berbice to see whuh sheh get. If you see how she get excited. Powder up sheh face like she competing with fish about to be fried, that's why ah saying so. The whole yard cudn't wait to see de things.

---

[53] *Showing off*
[54] *Very sexually promiscuous*
[55] *A term used in Guyana with emphasis on the word "salt" as it is said to hamper prosperity*
[56] *Secretly*
[57] *"Where is she at?" Poor thing!!!.*
[58] *'Saying'*

When she come back ….. a big bag full of winter clothes. My God!!! De aunty send sheh turtle-neck sweaters, corduroy pants, skirts, wool berets, and even some gloves. But …. No food. Now who dis wear [59] these kinda clothes in a weather like this? In a hot country like Guyana? Unheard of!!! But, word was that sheh aunty is working at a nursing home and cleans up people houses as a second job. So, she takes all de throw off clothes[60] and pack them in a nice little barrel and mail them. This lady they hear though, makes money in America but she spends it out. Ain't got enough to send a barrel full of things like Miss Cheryl and Bridget own. Sheh sport it out. Party de money out and gamble some.

Ain't got ah pot to piss in or ah window fuh throw it out" [61] and living donkey years [62] in America.

Then this puh niece walking around the yard last year this time and showing off on people in a brown corduroy skirt, and a green and white stripe turtle neck long-sleeved sweater with a red scarf like is winter. Then she got the nerve to put on some long black winter boots that wasn't even sheh size. She limping because the shoes hurting sheh toes. Sheh ain even know 'sheh head from sheh foot'[63] with how de pain got sheh. Well yuh know de utcome …… people did laugh so hysterically, that Sam chile

---

[59] *Now who wears*
[60] *Used clothes*
[61] *Doesn't have anything in life*
[62] *Multiple years*
[63] *Brain muddled up that she could not think sometimes*

motha did almost pee up sheh self. Even Jason who head din suh catholic [64] did understand that Patsy was acting like "ah neva see come fuh see." [65] Y'all waan hear more? Read on .... life in this South American country sweet, eh?

So now Daphne is rapping at Patsy's front door. Call her "slow" but she is very loving and compassionate. Ernest did rape sheh because she kind of little developmentally disabled, but that's another story!! She rapping harder, and harder, and harder. The fingers on sheh right hand hurting now, but no answer. Then Carol, Gavin woman, pushes her head through the doorway and says she did see Patsy leaving about twenty minutes ago. Nevertheless, Daphne continues to rap on the absent woman's door. This is a cottage split up in two and they both have separate front doors.

"Yuh aan hear whuh ah jus seh? Sheh nat dere." [66]

She de Carol always yelling at Daphne and mekkin sheh 'basidee.'[67] Confusing the girl, I mean. If only this young woman had gotten some mental health interventions earlier in life; something that has a stigma in this country, she might have coped better. She is 32 years old and her mental status has been deteriorating more and more every day. This has made her an easy sexual target for some inconsiderate men in the yard. Got pregnant about five times and she grandma take her to a 'quack' for illegal

---

[64] *A little deranged*
[65] *"Never had anything in life, and is unaccustomed"*
[66] *"You didn't hear what I just said? She is not there."*
[67] *Making her confused*

26

abortions. Now Miss Beulah does dey 'foot aan foot' behind sheh [68] so that sheh don't get no belly[69] again, and that none of dem boys dhoan feel sheh up.

Doris is now taking the young woman back to the house where her grandmother rents a room, but not before peeping into Denise's window to see which man is in her house today. Told y'all .... always minding people business!!! Anyway, back to Daphne ...... she has been living here with her grandmother; Miss Beulah after her biological mother; the elderly lady's daughter, abandoned her at the age of five. Word is that Daphne's mother supposedly fled to Saint Lucia with a 'pallawallah' man [70] as if free, single and disengaged, or "all by herself without responsibility," as some may say. Others would say, "she bare, but didn't rear" her daughter. Thank God Miss Beulah cooks black pudding and souse[71] every Saturday to sell to sheh neighbors. Outsiders patronize her too because word got around that sheh "haan sweet." [72] This money helps her to take care of herself and Daphne because the small pension she gets from the government is insufficient for them to survive on.

Time to play dominoes .... Phillip who been yelling at Gavin the other morning about he bike setting up the tables and chairs. They are usually buddies on "dominoes day" with Stanley

---

[68] *Constantly walks behind and monitors her*
[69] *Get pregnant*
[70] *A small island man*
[71] *Meat like mentioned above in vinegar with cucumbers, pepper, celery and wiri-wiri peppers*
[72] *Cooks tastily, her food is delicious*

fetching out some beers, and playing some music on he stereo by the fence. Dookram wife just mek some curry chicken, rice and choka fuh dem to eat. Anybody knows what choka is? There are three types .... It is roasted eggplant or boulanger by itself or mixed in with saltfish or smoked herring. Then yuh dis put garlic; plenty garlic mashed up inside with shallot or chives and onions.

"Bai, is wheh dem otha fellows? Dey comin?" [73] Terry, Bridget boyfriend asks.

Sam is just walking out the adjacent rooming house, and shouts, *"Ah comin,"* with a bowl of cow-heel souse in he right hand, and bottle of bush rum[74] in the other. The bush rum he buy from a friend from Troolie Island, Essequibo.

In the far corner of the yard, the children are playing games like hop-scotch and hide-and-seek, while the women are sitting under the tamarind tree gossiping. Don't tell me ah lying!! Ah come from Guyana too. They are doing exactly that ...... gossiping. But ...... Patsy missing, and is almost sundown.

Miss Cheryl is a little disengaged. She yells after her granddaughter, *"dhoan leh dem lil bai feel yuh up. All ah y'all as ah mattuh ah fact."* [75]

She has to fiercely delegate this to them after as a young girl, she could clearly remember how in the games of hide-and-

---

[73] *"Boy, where is the other fellows? They coming?"*

[74] *Illegal rum or bootleg liquor*

[75] *"Don't let those little boys feel/fondle you up. All of you as a matter of fact."*

seek, how the little boys would become manish,[76] and take the girls to a place where no one could see them. They would then put their hands into their underwears touching her and the other little girls' private parts. That's when they played "mommy and daddy." She doesn't tolerate such behaviors and is very, very stern. She continues to keep her eyes on Cyril who is the ringleader, and quite an aggressor. That's why when sheh was sharing out de candy from sheh barrel, she only give him one. One......only one!!! To show he that she don't like he, as opposed to giving the other children five apiece.

"He too wutless aan 'cammon place'[77] aan suh young. He is ah 'bad seed'[78] aan always molestin de lil gurls. Nat on mih dead body, he ain touchin mih granchile. De lil wretch ...... lil scallywag. He too boderation aan he motha does give he 'nuff spounce Ah dhoan like duh lil bai," she says to the other women.

"He too "Wutless" .... she really means to say "worthless."

Ladies, a word of warning!!! If you trying to find out about a man in Guyana, or Jamaica, or Trinidad, or Grenada, or Saint Vincent, or Barbados, or Saint Kitts, or Venezuela, or Panama, or Nevis, or Haiti, or Cuba, or Puerto Rico, or Guatemala, or Honduras, or Montserrat, or Guadeloupe, or Australia, or England, or America, or Brazil, or France, or Sweden, or Costa Rica, or

---

[76] *In trying to be a grown man*
[77] *"He is too worthless and vulgar.'*
[78] *Bad breed. Of kzjno proper quality through reproduction*

29

Serbia, or Germany, or Nigeria, or Ghana, or Tanzania, or Bermuda, or Surinam, or Senegal, or Antigua and Barbuda, or Grenada, or St. Croix, or Anguilla, or Spain, or Portugal, or Lebanon, or Costa Rica, or Belize, or Uganda, or Botswana, or Uruguay, or Turkey, or Italy, or Panama, or Denmark, or Switzerland, or Sweden, or India, or Pakistan, or Rajasthan, or China, or Nepal, or Belize, or wherever, and the people say he "wutless," leave he. Don't be with he. He "Wutless" ...... be in a relationship or not, he not no good. Ah no good man!!! These kind of men dis lie tuh ...... lies too.

That's why Miss Charlotte still waiting five years now for a barrel from sheh "wutless" son Ernest in New Jersey. He ain't 'fit ah shit'[79] and de thing is, she just tell the ladies that she expect a barrel from he on Thursday.....same ting last year and on the 23rd. Dat ain't rite!! Not rite!! Because de "wutless" boy lying. Rudy reported when he returned from vacation that Ernest not working 'no wey.'[80] Got a caucasian woman tekkin care of he. Bout he[81] sending a barrel with a fridge inside and other items. Now who would believe that? Poor ole lady!! But she still going to be looking out for sheh barrel day after tomorrow .... she and she neighbor mentally challenged Daphne. Cause nobody else in this tenement yard ain't buying he story!!! A barrel with a fridge inside? Hell no!!! .... stupitness!!!

---

[79] *He is 'no good'*
[80] *'No where'*
[81] *About he is sending a barrel*

You see how Patsy missing out? Missing out on some humour under de tamarind tree, and some food from dem fellows playing dominoes. The ladies; Cheryl and the others, were just saying that sheh wasting sheh time and energy with Bertie. If was Denise, de "carry off gurl," sheh wudda done 'gih he blow' [82]...... cheat on he and might of all gone and see sheh 'fresh ting' [83] in Buxton.

Lorna; Bridget step-daughter, hears the women discussing Patsy and mentions that it look like she went to church. Ms. Doris is questioning the little girl some more, and she just said that Patsy had a bible in sheh hand.

The women are all giggling now, then Gwen jokingly intervenes rather loudly, "*cyaan put it pass sheh. Mus be went tuh de obeah chuch fuh tye he up.*[84]

She just said that word in de real Guyanese creolese ..... "chuch." That's not the way it is spelt in the English dictionary, and plus, the real word is "church," but we ain

diggin nutten[85] cause we don't have to comply with the *"Brits"* who speak it the proper way ova yonder in England. I also want

---

[82] *Would of already 'cheated on him'*
[83] *'New prospective boyfriend'*
[84] *Cannot put it pass her. Must be went to the witchcraft church to spiritually control him/lock him.   in as her lover forever"*

to emphasize that it's not that we Guyanese are not smart, but it's just that we have a way with words. We dis tun dem up and tun dem   down[86] ……. all in de fun.

Ah dis seh it like duh tuh …… "chuch." Then mih chirren dis laff when I pronounce de word "x-ray." Dey dis say in their American accents,[87] *"mom, the word is not x-TRAY."*

Hahaha!!! Who cares!!! I live in America, but I is still a Guyanese. Ah doesn't pronounce some words right, just like I just wrote a grammatically incorrect sentence. Yep, sure did!!!

Then I say "pass me de ting" and they dis ask me *"which ting?"* Thing ….. a noun … all in de linguistic fun!!! Also, common among Guyanese and most English-speaking Caribbean countries.

But anyhow, in getting back to what we did just saying ……. about Patsy with ah bible in sheh haan, cause it looks like Patsy went to pray fuh sheh man.

"Sheh gat 'typee'[88] aan missin sheh man bad bad," Carol yells ….. as she and the others make their way to their separate domains, while hoping that Miss Charlotte "wutless" son keeps his word this time around … bout he sending sheh a barrel with among other things …….. a fridge inside.

---

[86] *We usually turn them up and turn them down*
[87] *They usually say in their American accents*
[88] *She is missing and longing for her man badly*

<u>Happenings</u>

"Look who ah buck up wid by Big Market?" [89] That was Sharon. She is pointing at Patsy who is reluctantly following her into the yard. Sharon who like a prodigal daughter is now appearing since Friday night. It's Monday morning and Doris understands because her half-way intoxicated daughter would not have left her kids so long if she wasn't making money. Hair disheveled, eyeliner streaking, lipstick dripping on each side of her mouth, and clothes unkept, but this young woman looks like she had 'ah ball.'[90] Had such a great time that sheh foot look like it hurting cause sheh limping. Shoes in hand and replaced with a pair of *"Bata neva done"*[91] rubber sandals. Anyhow, despite all this disarray, there is something that looks intact …….. her handbag that she is closely guarding because when Phillip just beg her to buy him a pack of cigarettes, she said *"ah gon gih yuh lateuh. Ahrite."* [92]

Then now she is seeming extremely cautious and paranoid in front of him, as he seems very curious to see how much money she has inside. She is also disgusted with him begging all the time.

---

[89] *"Look who I just found/walked into by Big Market;"* ... *the largest market place in town*
[90] *A great, great time*
[91] *A local shoe store with shoes that was said to be cheap but never outfinishes their wear*
[92] *"I am going to give you later. Alright."*

"Yuh cyaan get ah job? Crise man," she angrily says.

"Ah is ah ole tief man. Everybady know mih. Ah 'crass out.' [93] *Cyaan get ah jab. Deh frighten ah tief dey tings,"* he sadly replies.

She then staggers into her house to get the much needed rest she requires, while Doris begins to count the money her daughter brought home after spending four days and three nights on a Norwegian ship. She is snoring now, while her children will come home from school to a dinner of sardines from off the ship, with rice.

"Is wheh yuh went? Yuh disappear from we yestaday," says Ms. Cheryl to a disgusted looking Patsy.

"Ah went tuh mih Cousin Hazel in Meadow Brook." She means Meadow Brook Gardens behind Lodge.

"Ah went fuh use de fone fuh see if ah cud get on tuh Bertie. Ah waan know if he comin," Patsy lethargically replies.

"Oh, ah see," says Cheryl.

Then Doris joins them with hands akimbo while a cachectic cat runs towards the imitation kitchen apparently for scraps of food. Patsy wants to escape now, and forces a yawn because she knows too well that this very fast or inquisitive lady

---

[93] *Crossed out/ostracized from getting a job*

is waiting to hear why she was missing yesterday afternoon, where she went, and last of all ......with whom?

"Ah got ah headache. Wonda wheh mih limacol deh?" [94] Patsy complains, and bids her two neighbors goodbye, knowing too well that they weren't satisfied with her answers.

It's after lunch now and she has to rest up for a few hours, then head out to her job as a waitress at Brown Betty; a local and very popular restaurant. It is here that she met Bertie. He had been a very bashful customer there until one day he asked her out. They went out several times, and as the dates continued, they fell in love. All this time his aunt in New York had been trying to sponsor him, and one day he went home to find a large envelope with a letter inside from the U.S. Embassy. It was an appointment for his Permanent Residence Visa and hence, his Green Card and Social Security Cards after his arrival in the States..... the United States of America. Bertie was going to America; an event that has deeply saddened Patsy until today. Now she longs to see him, but what makes matters worse is that he nor his aunt did not answer the telephone either last night or early this morning.

"Ah tell yuh dey mus be out deh pun 14ᵗʰ Street aan China Town lookin fuh dem bargains. Deh is weh dem people dis mostly guh aan shop when dey comin home, ah hear. Cheap tings. Nuff, nuff bargains. Dhoan worry. He shoppin fuh come home. He mus

---

[94] *I have a headache. Wonder where my limacol – mentholated lotion) is?"*

be waan fuh suhprise yuh. Dey tired aan ain answerin. Dey faas asleep."

Those were Cousin Hazel's consoling words. But little do people know is that sometimes those 14th Street clothes in Manhattan cannot even stand up to a first wash; an attribute of the quality of some of the inexpensive clothes that arrives in Guyana. Although these clothes come from foreign, they do not outlast the three fuh 'D' or 'three yards for a dollar' cloth that is often sold on Regent Street. Mother Beulah could attest to the durability of the latter, as many of Daphne's clothing has survived all year due to the prolonged tugging and pulling on many of the pieces that her grandmother had her attired in.

Ask Miss Marva, the seamstress who lives down the street if y'all don't believe mih, because she also would tell allyuh that they even had seersucker[95] that had more quality to it. Then she even makes diapers for newborn infants because is a heavy cotton that got dimples on it fuh hold de baby urine. Coming back to the 'three fuh D' [96]... dem clothes dis last all year long ..... nothing like dem cheap clothes that Guyanese people does buy pun dat 14th street that they does bring home or send in barrels while they all dressed up in more expensive clothes when they laan up[97]

---

[95] *A light fabric of linen, cotton or rayon usually striped and slightly puckered*
[96] *'Three yards of cloth for a dollar'*
[97] *Arrive*

home. All because some of them don't want to spend plenty money pun they relatives and friends.

The loitering outside her bedroom window distracts Patsy from her overwhelming feelings of depression. Miss Cheryl has stimulated the salivary glands of many of her neighbors.

"*Ah bake it as ah did pramise Friday nite. Ah soak it wid some rum aan red wine. Ah bake nuff. Dis is jus ah lil taste. Y'all like it? Ah hope suh.*" Then goes and sit on the wooden bench outside her doorway.

They are now commenting on the cake she has just shared for them to taste. The men, women, and children are giving their opinions.

"*Lawd, it taste nice fuh so, Miss Cheryl. De fruits dem plenty yuh see, aan de cake nice and moise aan meltin in mih mouth,*" answers Sharon.

She is sober now after a few hours of rest and a nice bath. Let's pray the rum in it does not intoxicate her again like when she arrived home this morning cause she stale drunk. [98] Don't worry, if sheh get upset stomach, there is some gingerbeer [99] outside the house basking in the sun. She lucky that somebody

---

[98] *Residually drunk' or slightly drunk*

[99] *A drink made with ginger (blend or grate), brown sugar and fermented with a little rice. Optional - cut up in four two large green limes and add inside. Put in sun for 2 days. Strain it off on the third day. Then drop inside some cinnamom and a few cloves. Bottle and put in fridge.*

didn't take it after leaving it outside in the dew the other nite. Forgot it and went partying again. Gets wild this time of the year while she looking "mucho dinero" or "plenty money" and other things for she mother and children, other family members, friends, and sheh "lil piece ah man."[100]

Gavin has just arrived from work with his noisy motorcycle. He wants his neighbors to disburse and revs its up.

"Is whuh y'all doin? Ah waan pass. Move out mih way," [101] he curiously shouts.

His wife Carol quickly jumps in his path, and hands him a piece of her leftovers. He smiles and licks his fingers.

"It delishous, eh?[102] Miss Cheryl mek it aan sheh waan we taste it. Sheh is de fuss fuh mek black cake in de yard dis year, aan sheh gon soak it wid de rum every day suh it cud be nice aan strong on Crismus day," Carol tells her common-law husband, as she secretly romanticizes that he would marry her one day, and that their wedding cake will taste just as good as the piece she just savored.

---

[100] *A so-called man; a poor provider. Just fit for the bed*
[101] *"Is What you all doing? I what to pass. Move out of my way."*
[102] *"It is delicious, eh?*

"Could I kindly get a slice please mommy," says Orin, Bridget's eldest son, and Miss Cheryl quickly obliges him just as Rosie from the other yard screams ……….

"Gih he ah nice big piece. He deserve it. He dis do good in skool. He 'show we up'[103] not only y'all, but we ova heh tuh. Show we poor people up. Dat poor people chirren brite tuh. Dat we bless. Gawd ain fuhget we aan we chirren."

Of course, he is truly deserving since last year he passed his Common Entrance Exam to attend Queen's College which was a Grammar School first opened in Guyana in 1844 at Colony House as an Anglican School for British Colonists so that they could feel at home in British Guiana. These were the children of the expatriates and later eligible local students of married parents were admitted.

"Bai, ah tell yuh. When de results come out de whole yaad had ah party,"[104] his mother reminds us.

They were all so proud of him, not only in Punchin Yard, but also for blocks on end.

"He is ah 'brain box'[105] jus like he granfadda," Bridget declares. *"Ah wish de ole man was still alive fuh see he. He waan fuh be ah doctor, aan he cyaan wait fuh help me aan he brothas.*

---

[103] *"He makes us look good," a good example academically speaking*
[104] *"Boy, I tell you. When the results came out the whole yard had a party."*
[105] *"He is a 'very intelligent person' just like his grandfather."*

He seh he gon move we out." She then smiles in anticipation, then continues ......

"*He suh brite[106] aan dis tell mih why ah mek only man chirren. Someting bout chromo-someting. He suh intelligent dat ah dis waan cry. Cry with joy.*"

Just then Orin clarifies what the "chromo-someting" means, and is now giving a complete explanation about "chromosomes" and how a male carries an XY chromosome, and a female an XX. Then continues to explain that he and his brothers received a Y chromosome at conception from their fathers with an X from Bridget. So, that's why they are boys. Bridget is nodding her head while smiling, and although very proud of her son who surely has just demonstrated the ability to become a physician, all this information seems to be giving her a sensory overload.

Bridget's menial job as a maid at a local hotel is insufficient to earn her a livable wage. Plus Orin's father is in jail, and she could barely buy food for herself and five kids; all boys, much less move out of her very small place that got them all choked up and claustrophobic. Then unfortunately, de otha fella[107] that she has the other four chirren fuh marry another woman and hopscon.[108] She is also thinking about how lucky Orin is that the colonial days are over, where offsprings of unwed parents couldn't

---

[106] *Bright/smart/intelligent*
[107] *Then the other fellow*
[108] *Disappeared suddenly as in abandonment*

attend Queen's College, but instead to Cambridge High School and other schools. Thank God times has changed and those restricted opportunities has been abolished.

Orin is beaming with delight as he realizes how everyone in the yard favors him along with spoiling him rotten, and when the other kids don't have a clue as how to do some of their homework they rely on him to assist them. Never mind his brother, Trevor, and some of the neighborhood kids teasingly call him an "English Duck," as if there is anything wrong with speaking perfect English. He also remembers how everyone came outside to see him off on the first day of school.

"Ah like he uniform. De tye nice tuh," Dookram excitedly said, as he himself is secretly longing for his son Saheed to also attend that school if their papers don't come through in time to go overseas.

Orin was proudly wearing a white shirt and khaki trousers along with a canary colored matching tie with black stripes. Oh, yes!!!! Who says that some underprivileged youths in poor neighborhoods don't have potentials!!! Since time and time again, they have become some of the world's greatest leaders, doctors, lawyers, teachers, engineers, entrepreneurs, and other professionals, denoting that anything is possible despite where you came from or how poor you are, or were.

Bridget then continues, *"we is poor people, but 'whuh dhoan miss we dhoan pass we.'[109] Ah know mih son gon mek it. Miss Olga used tuh live in heh. Sheh raise eight chirren in heh in de front room ova suh, aan sheh punish suh till yuh see. But some of dem chirren 'brite.'[110] When ah move in heh, sheh did jus preparin fuh move out afta livin heh fuh almost fifteen years sheh tell mih. Sheh sista sen fuh sheh son in de States aan he went aan tun ah .... whuh yuh call it Dookram?"*

Her neighbor is now answering her question .... *"ah baby doctuh. He dis delivah babies Miss Olga seh."* [111]

Orin then chimes in .... *"mom, he is a gynecologist, and I want to become a cardiologist."*

Bridget smiles, then says, *"Yeah, Miss Olga son tun ah 'big shot'[112] aan buy ah big house in Bel Air Gardens fuh dem. Is duh rite Orin, ah pronouncing it rite? De area wheh sheh live now?"*

Her son nods his head in agreement, and his mother continues, *"eh heh, sheh move tuh wheh dem 'highfuhlutten'[113] people dis live. See how Gawd good? He dis mek poor people chirren brite. At lease some ah dem dis really be smart aan even if some ah dem turn out fuh be ungrateful, most ah dem dis help*

---

[109] *"What doesn't miss us, don't pass us" in terms of opportunities*
[110] *Very smart*
[111] *"A baby doctor. He delivers babies Miss Olga say."*
[112] *A high society lady, a person in higher socio-economic position*
[113] *Big shots, ruling upper middle or high class*

dey parents wen dey get big. "Puppy dis tun dawg"[114]*......... big, big aan help dey parents when dey get position,"* as she hugs Orin and begins to kiss him.

"Miss Olga even get lil 'hoity toity"[115] *tuh,"* she grins. *"But sheh deserve it. She aan dem lil ones who leff back in de house ain sufferin no moe. Ain 'haan to mouth"*[116] *no moe. Ah hear de otha son in England bout to join de Royal Air Force tuh. See whuh ah seh? Oh, aan ah fuhget ...... Is she who ah get mih kerosene stove from. Thank Gawd ah ain got tuh go out deh aan use no coal pot. Fanning dat ting all day long fuh cook ah pot ah food. De kero stove got two burners aan it fass. Ah cud cook two pots ah food one time. One wid rice aan de otha wid stew. Bless her heart. We ahrite now. All becauz ah she. Dat Miss Olga!!!"*

Mother Beulah then chimes in about how dangerous it is to be dwelling outside in de yard at night because a snake did nearly bite sheh a few months ago, and how lucky Miss Olga is to escape dem crappoes [117] that be hiding by de genip tree in de yard especially when de rain fall. Also, how she did almost fall down a rainy night trying to go to the latrine.

Sheh 'dotish' or whuh? Leffin sheh granddaughter Daphne alone in de house- when sheh cudda use sheh 'posey'[118] instead.

---

[114] *Children grow up and get big from a baby to an adult*
[115] *Acts better than other people with an attitude*
[116] *Barely getting by*
[117] *Those big frogs*
[118] *She could have used her 'potty'*

But only she knows cause that granddaughter of hers there did topple de thing over and no amount of jase fluid and dettol could of disinfected de place from the scent of the bodily excretions. So that's why she had resorted to going outside again. If only that damn girl could give sheh a little chance to relax. The old woman having too much stress all the time. Plus this extra cleaning to do.

As the afternoon lingers on and dark sets in, Patsy goes outside to collect water from the standpipe and then proceeds to the makeshift bathroom in the far left hand corner of the yard to take a bath, since she has to prepare for work. Having filled a few buckets at around noontime to wash her dishes outside and fetched some inside to scrub her floor, she feels somewhat tired, and again wishes that her living conditions will one day become better.

"Only Bertie cud help mih mek mih life betta," she resolves to thinking. *"Unless ah guh back in de country."*

She then decides that after work tonight, instead of Anita, her co-worker and boyfriend taking her home, that she will ask them to drive her to Cousin Hazel's house instead. Tomorrow is her day off any way, and plus she needs a break from the curious women around her to settle her head, especially Doris.

"Ah dhoan blame yuh," Anita agrees. *"Dat ooman Doris. Sheh too 'faas.' De otha day ah went by yuh aan when ah was*

44

leavin, sheh did 'corner mih'[119] askin mih bout yuh bizness. Asked mih when laas yuh hear from Bertie. Sheh too "quisitive."

She meant to really say "inquisitive" which denotes a knowledge deficit from a poor level of education because this young woman like Sharon also, had to leave school at an early age to financially assist her mother with the upkeep of her siblings. This is because of her father's death when she was eleven years old. If only her vocabulary was intact, maybe she could have gotten a better job at Bookers or Fogarty's as a salesgirl. She had once gone to Bettencourt store, and said that the woman who interviewed her didn't understand most of what she was saying. Said she had to repeat herself several times.

Could it have been because of her poor vocabulary, coupled with her rural accent? Then she black, and in those days mostly Portuguese, East Indian, Chinese, and mixed-race girls were hired here, and especially in banks. The banks, of course, preferred most graduated female and male students from the five top schools like Bishop's High, Queen's College, St. Roses High, St. Joseph's High, and St. Stanislaus College; denoting again how color and class played a part in upward mobility in this land of six races.

"Eh, eh, dat nat "truh" .... "true." Whah Anita talkin bout? Ah dis dhoan get no problem aan ah cudda work deh how

---

[119] *She prevented me from escaping in order to question me*

long ah want, but Gavin stop mih. Seh he waan mih home wid he chirren," Carol convincingly says.

That's Carol. She always emphasizes that. Says she has no problem getting hired anywhere. Said she used to work at Fogarty's and that she was hired immediately when she applied. She also emphasized too that she didn't even have to do an interview. Said the lady just smiled at her and asked when she wanted to start. But, what Carol doesn't realize is that she is light-skinned .... a red ooman [120] as some people would say in Guyana. Mixed with "Putugee" or Portuguese, East Indian and Black. Tall and slim with long hair reaching the middle of her back at the time while working at Fogarty's before getting dem kids .... now she appears much shorter, high belly [121] because she didn't tye it down [122] after each pregnancy, and sheh complexion looking orange. Wonder if she could still get hired at those stores now if some still exist? She ain't looking that hot anymore after giving birth to her children, but still confident, and blames her tarnished complexion on the iron tablets that the doctor gave her when pregnant.

"It mek mih look black."

No, no, no!!!! Don't you ever tell a red ooman in Guyana that she getting dark. Yuh kidding me!!! All hell will break loose.

---

[120] *A light-skinned woman*

[121] *A large abdomen obtained by a woman who has just given birth*

[122] *Place a piece of cloth on her stomach and tie it tight enough so that her belly will eventually get flat*

46

But, we going to keep this a secret from her …… she got black veins too at de back of sheh legs. Varicose veins. He, he!!!! Thinking that she sexier than Lorraine who moved out months now. Left over a year. Met a bakra[123] man from Barbados who 'fall head ova heels'[124] in love with her jet black skin because she "dark and lovely." Engaged her two months after meeting sheh. Married her six months later and she living in that "island of the flying fish." She is Bridget's cousin who helps her out with the kids. Is she who send money for Orin school clothes and books for Queen's College. Her husband is a police officer and shows her off to all he police friends and other people.

"Leh Carol carry sheh frowsy self suh." Is me, Donna Milner, sehing suh. Is I writing this book. I could seh anything that I want, and I mean it ….. Just some comic-relief, you know. My point …….. fuh we all laugh.

"Hello, hello, good nite Miss Avril, Bertie deh come?" the frustrated Patsy enquires.

She is now gluing her ears to the telephone, as there's a lot of noise in the background at her cousin's house. This is where she was taught about the "happenings" for the holidays as a small child until now. It is also this house that her entire family would visit when they come down from Berbice, and is here that Cousin Hazel, her mother and two brothers taught her how to get into the

---

[123] *A white person*
[124] *To fall madly in love with a person*

Christmas spirit. Also, how to make ends meet to acquire the things they need for this time of the year.

"Ah cyaan hear yuh, cud you seh dat again Miss Avril. Oh, ah see. Oh, he leff dis mawning early fuh wuk. Okay, okay. Ah gon call back lateah. Ahrite, thank yuh Miss Avril. Bye now. Oh, ah forget. Please tell he dat ah love he. Yuh hear mih Miss Avril? Aan dat ah miss he tuh."

Reluctant to hang up, Patsy then turns to an eavesdropping Hazel who is not only sandpapering the wooden chair in front of her, but also anxiously waiting to hear what her bewildered cousin has to say. Miss Avril said that Bertie is not at home, left early for work this morning and that she must call back. But, did Patsy ask that very important question? …… "Is Bertie coming home for Christmas?" No. Is she scared to do so, and why?

Doris did say that *"sheh fraid to ask. Fraid he leff sheh. Dat's why he ain comin. Got ah gurl in Brooklyn."*[125]

Hazel is thinking the same thing, but is afraid to mention it. Jacqueline is nodding her head in the far corner of the room, as if to say Patsy 'leff pun haan.'[126]

We have to pray now, pray for this young lady who Stanley sooring and sheh don't want he because sheh want a man abroad

---

[125] *"She is afraid to ask. Afraid he leave her. That's why he is not coming. Got a girl in Brooklyn maybe."*
[126] *'Left without a man or partner'*

who could buy her nice things, send her some U.S. dollars, and most of all, take her to America. Now sheh looking all giddy[127] and holding sheh head cause sheh couldn't speak to he just now. Good luck to that, cause most of dem bannus [128] don't come back, but again like "ah seh,"[129] we going to pray. We got to also go down on our knees and join in prayer cause only mostly the women return to marry the boyfriends they leave behind. Or send for they husbands and children. See why Patsy in such agony?

"Puh ting" ……. poor thing!!!!

Ask Shirley too. Wendell lied and said he was coming back to marry her, and all time now……. you could see he in some of dem Guyanese clubs and people yards hanging out with the fellows playing cards and dominoes. Done forget Shirley exist. Got a thick Yankee woman spoiling he.

"Eh, heh," [130] and I know he tuh. "Wutless" …… another one like Ernest. Don't want to wuk ….. work. Y'all leave mih alone. I could pronounce de word however ah want. Not because I writing this book ah have to always use standardized English. Ai is ah Guyanese tuh.[131]

---

127 *Dizzy-headed, confused*
128 *Those fellows or guys*
129 *"I say"*
130 *"Yes"*
131 *I am a Guyanese too*

That reminds me of my Jamaican friend in Florida who used to always wonder why I would bend down to the floor searching when sheh talk. She didn't realize that I was searching for the 'h' because she just said *"ouse."* She meant to say "house." Dropped the 'h' somewhere. Hehe!!! That's why I was searching for it. Then I would say, "ah jus tantalizing yuh .... teasing you." Then I had to tell her 'tantalize' is a word Guyanese people use meaning to 'tease' you. My people!!! You know de deal. It's a good thing that all of us express ourselves differently throughout the world. Very, very interesting indeed ..... in this world I call a "cultural mosaic."

Miss Millie just come home. Just bought a big, big, fat, fat, fat snapper with a big head and some other food items. Now she boasting about how she going to fry some in the morning for breakfast and save the balance to fry piece by piece for the holidays. Steam the part with the fish head also when sheh in de mood cause sheh boys like it. Patsy is glad to see her aunt and rushes to hug her as she is placing the items in the refrigerator. This; the fridge, is something she always wanted. That's why she has to buy ice from the "ice lady" Parbattie in the yard to mek sheh drinks cold and preserve od items.

Now, you see why she likes to visit Aunt Millie, Cousin Hazel, and her two other cousins. She could get her nice cold sorrel, mauby drink, gingerbeer, or swank [132] here with no worries

---

[132] *A popular homemade drink made in Guyana with water, limes and sugar*

of them spoiling, and could also use the inside toilet, and not a latrine in the yard like where she live. It is here too that she could get a really nice shower and don't have to worry about "peepin Tom" Harry who it is said got binoculars and gets on top of a shed in the alley way and peep at the women bathing. Ain't also got to worry if she going to see a snake at nite if sheh go to pee or 'do do,'[133] or the dogs in the yard barking at her.

So, there are many, many advantages of visiting this house in Meadow Brook Gardens where again, I say, is where "the happenings" or preparations take place for December 25th .... pepperpot cooking, black cake making, ham baking, fresh bread baking, sponge cake making, gingerbeer making, aunty Desmond wine making, sorrel drink making, rice wine making, plain rice making, provisions boiling, and anything else that a Guyanese want to eat for de holidays.

Even the walls are being painted this year in a nice light yellowish color since this very durable paint that Miss Millie nephew who is a seaman brought from abroad, and lasts for about five to six years. Cousin Lenny is high up on a ladder with brush in hand ensuring that he is catching the corners well, while Hazel continues to sandpaper one of their wooden living room chairs under their 'bottom house.'[134] Ulrick, her youngest brother, has completed the other three. Later tonight the three siblings will

---

[133] *'Defecate*
[134] *'The space under a house since it is built on tilts' where families relax*

51

lacquer them, while Gladstone, the neighborhood upholsterer is making new cushions to replace the old ones.

That Gladstone is a champion you know. He dis help people save money during this time of year. Makes they old chairs look like new with the fabrics or leatherette that he covers them up with ….. nice and new like yuh just buy de furniture from the store. He is much sought after that's why when he riding he bicycle on the street people be calling out to he.

"Eh Gladstone, ah waan yuh fuh cover mih chairs aan 'stick mih mattress.'[135] Is how much yuh gon charge mih fuh 'do over' mih two 'settees' wid dem nice cushions dat yuh dis mek?" several of his prospective customers would say.

Then goes another old customer of his …. *"tek mih address, Glatz. Ah waan yuh come roung by mih house aan see de wuk ah have fuh yuh. Dem lil granchirren mess up mih new chairs, aan piss up mih mattress even though ah tell mih daughta not fuh gih dem ovaltine or milo fuh drink late in de nite. Yuh know ah move out rite?"*

This champion upholsterer would just shake his head as to say "yes" as he is navigating his "roung belly nelly" ….. de bicycle with the half-circular bar that he grandmother 'dead aan leff he' [136] through the traffic, while that last customer almost

---

[135] *'Needle it up here and there ' with waxed twine and buttons from one side to the next so as to prevent the fiber or other material from shifting that would make the mattress bulky.*
[136] *Died and left for him*

52

knocked him down as he was handing him the piece of paper with his address. "Glatz" …. as most people know he by, and dey lookin fuh he from since September is most sought after around this time of the year.

"*Is whuh is duh?* Jacqueline, Hazel's friend who's sitting closest to their living room window yells. "*Ah feelin some water pun mih.*"[137]

A perturbed Miss Millie looks outside to see if her clothes on the line is getting wet. But, it isn't raining. It's Ulrick washing his mother's house with a brush which he is constantly dipping in a bucket with some bleach and liquid soap inside. He is now washing it down with a water hose like "pressure cleaning" to wash off the dirt and dust, and forgot to tell the others inside to close the windows ……. all of them in the entire house so that nothing gets wet. He apologizes to his mother as he becomes super excited to take on this job five days before "Santa Day," ……. but Jacqueline does not buy his excuse, as she is angry that the water will fade her photoprint shirt.

Sheh is an ass or what? Sheh ain't got no sense? The darn print is embedded in the material and the little drizzles of water from the water hose cannot fade the pictures on the slinky material which in any case was made to wash. Thinking she knows it all because she just come home too from Cayenne. Plus come to show

---

[137] *"I am feeling some water on me."*

53

off on Hazel, she ex-classmate, that 'sheh doing good now.' [138]
Get ah ole Frenchman; sixty-five years old and she twenty-three.
Is this something 'tuh show off bout?[139] And yuh think Ulrick
'tekkin sheh on?'[140] He outside whistling, and sometimes singing.

Even joining in with Little Orson next door .... *"all ah
waan fuh Crismus is mih two front teeth, mih two front teeth aan
ah have ah happy, happy Crismus."*[141]

The little kid is smiling now, revealing some missing teeth
or snaggle teeth at the top of his mouth .... they singing, they
laughing, as the man on the ladder now has to make sure that he
doesn't topple over and fall on the little four year old who has left
his yard, and is now over at Miss Millie, and standing just below
him. The boy is happy and wearing a buckta[142] on his buttocks
while imagining he swimming in the water coming from the hose
to the sunken in concrete here and there in the yard. He thinks they
are little swimming pools with de bleach inside that smelling like
chlorine, and tries to plunge into one of them.

"Tikkay yuh fall aan buss yuh head," [143] Ulrick shouts, and
the little boy hesitates, then stops.

---

[138] *She is prospering now.*
[139] *'To show off about'*
[140] *Paying her any attention'*
[141] *"All I want for my Christmas is my two front teeth, my two front teeth and I have a happy, happy Christmas."*
[142] *A boy or man's underwear that fitss below the waist*
[143] *"Be careful you fall and burst open your head."*

Last year this didn't happen because he was smaller and didn't have the sense to leave his yard as his mother, Eileen, laying up with sheh good friend husband….. aan ai ain gon call name.[144] Cheater!!! Thou shalt not commit adultery!!! In America she would have been charged for child neglect and sheh 'sweet man' [145] wife would of divorce he and get nuff; plenty alimony if he got money. "C'est la vie" ……… that's life," my French friends would say. But don't let me get carried away here!!! We talking about the house-washing and not Guyana where adultery is not heavily penalized. Then pun top ah duh,[146] word is that sheh only waan de man fuh he lowlee*147* because he is a "nutten …. nothing pocket man" with no money and that is only de sweet sex sheh does get from he. Nothing else!!! Like if yuh cud carry duh tuh de store.

Anyway, back to business …… Ulrick is almost done after moving the ladder some fifteen times. He loves the way his mother's house is looking. Hazel runs outside to inspect. Inspects all round the house, and smiles at her brother as all of the dust and dirt accumulated all year long has disappeared. She likes the way it looks. Like new but worries deep down inside that the paint will eventually fade away to nothing but bare wood as time goes by.

"Maybe it mite only gat anotha year," she is thinking.

---

144 *And I am not going to call name*
145 *Her boyfriend who is married and also has plenty women*
146 *Then on top of that*
147 *She only wants him for his penis*

Nevertheless, this is another Guyanese custom that must be practiced ...... 'do or die'..... must be practiced by homeowners like Miss Millie, as they also 'break up de house' about a month before "Father Christmas Day." Bruk up[148] de house by disarranging mostly the living room and packing away the chairs, tables, putting away the rugs, wall hangings, and all other items around so that the house could look immaculate later as they find ways to rearrange the furniture differently.

Back in the yard, Maxine .... remember Cyril? That's his mother. I mean the little boy who Miss Cheryl don't like, and she says is the ringleader that like play the 'mommy and daddy' game and molest the little girls. Duh lil wretch.[149] Well, he mother watching out for the postman because Cyril grandmother on he fadda side suppose to send a card. She is hoping that money is inside fuh she aan sheh lil bai she call "mammy nice chile." [150]

Stanley, as usual in the yard and watching out for Patsy says, *"is who yuh lookin fuh?"*

Maxine answers him, and he says that he has not noticed Noel, the mail carrier, as yet. Of course, he is being delayed with more mail for the holidays, and harassed if some people does not

---

[148] *Break up*

[149] *That little wretch or scamp*

[150] *'Mommy nice little child, 'obedient, etc.*

receive anything in the mail as the weekend is over with just a few days left to go shopping.

"*Yuh sure, Noel, dat yuh ain gat no mail? Yuh sure y'all aan misplace it in de post office or yuh ain drop it pun de road?*"[151] most would say.

"Monkey see, monkey do,"[152] I would say, as they all heckle the same remarks in 'copy cat' manner with regards to the possibility of lost mail.

They all be harassing Noel that sometimes he 'dhoan know he head from he foot.'[153] I personally could remember Andrew, my next door neighbor 'suckin he teeth,'[154] and who would sit on the bench outside the doorstep ranting and raving about not receiving anything today from his uncle in Maryland. He would become so furious that when he played cricket with the little fellows leading up to Christmas, he would play so ferociously, that the ball hit one of his team mates in he eye and give he a 'bonghee'[155] on he forehead too. That boy had to go to school for the new year with not only a bump on he head, but with bloodshot eyes after Andrew 'knack he'[156] in both.

---

[151] *"You sure, Noel, that you ain't have any mail? You sure you all ain't misplace it in the post office or you didn't drop it on the road?"*
[152] *Everyone doing what they see the other do, copy-cat behavior*
[153] *He Is very confused*
[154] *A way of using the teeth to show anger*
[155] *A bump or lump on the forehead sustained from an injury*
[156] *Knocked him*

You see what these holidays dis bring? All sorts of happiness, but yet all sorts of sadness. People want 'dis' and people want 'dat.' People want from far, and people want from near. All because of "the baby boy in the manger."

Miss Millie floor been stripped since the first week of December. Linoleum taken off by her two sons. All day long they scraped and scraped with metal tools until it was all off. Perspired but got every bit off the floor. They exhausted but they had to follow they mother instructions because like some people, she does not want them to put the new one over the old one. She wanted every bit off and now the time is approaching for a new replacement. Sheh been paying down little by little for some new linoleum and now just waiting to pay the last installment before having the boys bring it home.

"Yuh sure we cud fetch it pun de bicycle."[157] That's Ulrick questioning his brother, since he somehow can't figure out how that long piece of linoleum could fit on such a small flimsy bike.

"It gon fit man, yuh gon see when we guh fuh pick it up,"[158] answered an illogical sounding Lenny, while his brother was also enquiring as to if the weight was going to puncture the bicycle tires.

---

[157] *"You sure we could fetch it on the bicycle?"*
[158] *"It is going to fit okay, you are going to see when we go to pick it up."*

58

Just then he is distracted by Brenda; knock kneed, and about two hundred and ninety pounds, but to him, very sexy. She is waving to the two brothers who are having a cool drink of coconut water in their front yard after debating about the linoleum and another way of getting it there without the use of the bicycle. Lenny then fixes his eyes on this young woman who has just recently moved to their neighborhood from the bauxite mining town of Linden. Clad in a red halter top and white mini skirt, her so-called voluptuous body is perceived as arousing to this young man, and every time he sees her he thinks about the American song *"Tired of Being Alone"* by Al Green. Although he knows that this young lady does not know how much he is attracted to her, he wishes that he could be as brave as Stanley, and not so shy!!! If only he could disclose his adoration to her the way Stanley did to Patsy!!! But, all he could do is watch her until she fades into the distance.

His sister, Hazel, knows all about his feelings for this young woman and tantalizes him when she sees Brenda passing by.

"Look, look Lenny. Yuh gurl passin. When yuh gon tell sheh yuh 'check' fuh

sheh? [159] *Dhoan leh anotha bannuh get sheh. Hurry up!!!"*

---

[159] *That you truly admire her*

Lenny would just giggle and bow his head, hoping that one day he would overcome his shyness and 'rap' or reveal his feelings to her.

"Ah gon 'punche panch'[160] *till ah get shih. Is only time,"* he whispers to himself.

Hazel and she mother now in the kitchen checking the fridge because apparently Miss Millie pay the "Chinee" man for the Dutchman head cheese and he didn't put it in sheh bag. They checking de fridge…. all over. Shelf by shelf. Patsy checking the garbage, but it not there.

"Ah gon gat fuh guh bak tamarraw aan tell he. Ah cyaan afford fuh loose mih money," [161] Millie whines.

Of course, of course. After all, the holidays is not complete without this cheese in almost every household.

Oops!! Hazel mother and Patsy aunty look like she missing something else now!!! Sheh looking again!!!! Scratching sheh head and looking confused. Looks like she trying to remember 'dat something' but cyaan put sheh haan on it.

---

[160] *"I am going to take it easy one step at a time ."*
[161] *"I am going to have to go back tomorrow and tell him. I cannot afford to loose my money."*

"Is whuh happen mammy? Yuh lass someting else? Try aan rememba nuh," Hazel says very comfortingly while embracing her mother.

Patsy then chimes in, *"tek yuh time auntie, tek yuh time, tek yuh time,"*[162] with a very anxious look on her face.

But, what is it? What is it that this fifty-two years old woman cannot remember? She looks triumphant now as she is remembering the item.

"Mih garlic fuh mih garlic poke." [163] She means "pork," not *"poke."*

She is explaining to the two girls that she needs it for tomorrow morning. Maybe she left that too at Mr. Chung store earlier today. So much responsibility for Miss Millie; a single-parent mother of three children in their twenties. She is always busy, that's why tired and confused tonight. She washes and iron clothes for a 'big shot'[164] woman Miss Bruckner who came to this country as a youngster from England with her retired Guyanese parents. The pay is a little more than a stipend, outweighing her labor of besides laundry, cleaning also within the confines of her employer's home. Hazel mostly helps with the ironing as her mother's employer has no washing machine, and Miss Millie has

---

[162] *"Take your time aunty, take your time, take your time"*
[163] *"My garlic for my garlic pork."*
[164] *Upper class woman*

to tediously use a tub, scrubbing board and brush. Then their entire family walks with the finished product; thoroughly washed and freshly ironed clothes to Miss Bruckner's house a few miles away. Then take away the soiled clothes to be washed and ironed again on separate days, and the process repeats itself over and over again.

Domestic work was the 'thing of the day' for most of the local women while some with financially stable partners stayed at home to tend to and nurture their children. They were also able to escape the long lingering effects of "exploitation of man by man" which catapults as their workload increased during the holidays like in the case of this mother; Miss Millie, who by the way, also sold the poultry that she raised on her property. She also sometimes rented out her bottom house[165] to people who wanted to keep a birthday party or wedding reception.

"Haan wash haan, mek haan come clean,"[166] she says with a sigh of relief, as her older son is now able to contribute financially to the household by just acquiring a job at the Water Works a few weeks ago.

Patsy now wants to head back home, but she remembers that she had promised to assist with the polishing of the floors. She then quickly peruses the entire area of the living room, then estimates how long it would take her and Cousin Hazel to put the liquid polish on. Also, she goes to a familiar closet to look for the

---

[165] *The space underneath of a house because the house has been built high on blocks or stilts*
[166] *"Each one help each other" to acquire a goal*

"polisher" which they will take turns at using to shine the floor, but it appears like the neighbor did not bring it as yet to lend to the family.

Since she still has time, she departs by saying, "*ah gon guh now, aan ah gon come back pun Thursday. Yuh hear mih?*"

That's the day before Christmas eve; the day when most people polish they floors so it wouldn't become dull before the "big day." They then become very careful that water does not fall on the floor which alters its shine. In my own home I could still remember my parents delegating to myself and sisters as to who will, and where they will polish. Ours was a very large house with a huge living room, dining room and verandah downstairs.[167] So, by the time we got done, our nails were tarnished with that deep brown greasy substance called "floor polish" that every Guyanese household had depended on year after year to add a flair to their decor. This was after we had gone down on our knees, and putting the polish with a piece of cloth on the floor.

Remember shoe polish? Well think of what a large container of this looks like …… then it would melt sometimes into a liquid according to the room temperature of the house, or some people would take the chance of burning down they house by heating it on they stove top instead of allowing it to melt in a warm place. I hope nobody don't try this because I know a certain

---

[167] *A porch*

person who did try it and the darn thing ketch afire. [168] It flammable. Y'all hear mih? Don't ever try that. Yuh house could catch afire. Times change now. Lacquer yuh floors, hear me!!!

Anyhow, as I was telling allyuh,[169] we would have to get down on our knees and put the polish on inch by inch ...... by inch with a piece of cloth even though some stores did start to sell a polisher to put the polish on de floors. But mih motha did say that it wonta [170] be no good. That using the rag was better because it could catch every corner. Also, that you could put more layers of polish on. What a torture!!!

But, did you ask about the condition of our knees? Well, they got bruised even though some of ahwe dis[171] did wearing a knee pad, and the ones who didn't; leaving a darkened color to that area for many years, with cocoa butter not helping at all. That useless cocoa butter. Ah ain gon lie, mih knees was neva de same. Some people even got the nickname "black knees," and didn't like it because they didn't want the term "black" attached to them. Ah talking bout de people that ain't pure black, and "Valerie C" was one of them. Y'all laughing? Is true. Ah not lying. Good thing we had an electric polisher with some nice pads on the bottom to shine the floor, but for some people like in Millie house, they had to use a manual one.

---

[168] *Catch afire*
[169] *I was telling all of you*
[170] *Would not have been*
[171] *Some of us*

Good luck to that!!!   But, 'all in de fun'[172] with the forthcoming day that Santa Claus supposedly leaves gifts in stocking caps fuh de lil chirren aan de adults who really believe that he travels all the way from de North Pole to Guyana to bring them gifts. Then de thing is that me and mih siblings and we friends did believe 'duh stupitness'[173] until Miss Elaine who was a Jehovah Witness and didn't celebrate any holidays, did tell we ....

"*is not truh chirren. Not truh. Ain no Santa Claus comin down the chimney.*"

Anyway, in getting down to brass tops,[174] she wanted us to know that duh story was a lie.

Well fuh me ...... Ah did always suspect dat cause 'it din' sound rite. Jus din soung rite, but dem big people dis waan tuh seh dat yuh arguein when yuh ask dem ah question aan dat yuh rude. Bloody 'ole geesers'!!!*[175]*

I could give rudeness now. Dey cyaan beat me cuz ah big now, aan dat Miss Irene dat 'six feet down,' sheh was anotha miserable ole maid with no chirren who was always scolding we. Neva mining sheh business aan always comin outside aan actin

---

[172] *'Amidst all of the usual fun'*
[173] *That stupidiness*
[174] *In getting down to the real truth*
[175] *Well for me ..... I did always suspect that because 'it didn't' sound right. Just didn't sound right, but them   big people this want to say that you arguing when you ask them a question and that you rude. Bloody 'old folks'!!!*

65

like ah 'black cake'[176] when dem chirren waan fight afta school. Damn 'wagoness'[177] aan ah ole one tuh at dat'!!! Scolding de chirren like if she was they parents with ah 'wire cane' in sheh haan, and the school children better listen cause she was the neighborhood cachar[178] who did believe in the 'Santa Claus Story' tuh ...... Big belly Santa!!!

---

[176] *An intruder in someone's business*
[177] *Trouble maker*
[178] *Informer*

The Hustle and The Bustle

Patsy waiting for a 'hire car' to tek sheh home.[179] Ulrick and Cousin Hazel trying to flag down one on Princess Street. The East Indian driver say he could squeeze sheh in. He done got six passengers inside. They packed in like sardines and she don't know what to do, but Ulrick tells her to take it while Hazel nods her head in disgust.

"All dese hire cars suh pack up. Nat one wid lil bit passengas,"[180] she complains. Then helps to force her cousin into the car.

Patsy is almost sitting on the lap of another passenger. After all, it's Tuesday morning and just a few more days to shop. So, de hire cars full up …… full up like soooo!!!*[181]*

"Ouch, yuh hurtin mih leg," the female passenger murmurs while trying to minimize her already tiny body.

But this woman understands that like Patsy, it took almost an hour for this driver to stop for her. After all, everyone is trying to get their last minute shopping in. Plenty cars on the road racing one another. All trying to get to Regent Street and downtown to

---

[179] A 'multiple passenger taxi' to take her home
[180] "All these hire cars so packed up. Not one with a little bit of passengers."
[181] Filled with plenty, plenty passengers; very, very crowded

67

Bookers store, Fogarty's, Bettencourt, Demico House to get a little snack and other stores. Also Phillip used to watch a man store there in Big Market, Patsy remembers but he thief the man things ..... thief up jeans, thief some t-shirts, thief some tennis shoes, thief some perfumes, and almost all de women underwears and bring them to sell in the yard. Even thief some fairy lights[182] to sell all around town till de man fire he and he never get hired again. You see, because on the road amongst the hustlers, word gets around very quickly and if yuh mess up and yuh 'haan faas,'[183] them and you 'coo-coo dhoan boil.'[184] In other words, if you dishonest like "Thief Man Phillip," you and them wouldn't get along ever again. 'Plain aan strate,'[185] they would not want to associate with people they cannot trust like Phillip.

"Well, well. Is who ah seein?"[186] Patsy squinting her eyes from the gleaming Tuesday afternoon sun cannot believe who she is seeing.

But, she's correct. It's "Cousin Leslyn." She's Carol's eldest cousin and daughter of her favorite aunt. This woman is no stranger to the yard and is always a pleasure to see. You ask me why? Because without her input at this time of the year, life for the tenants in this yard seems incomplete. That is because not only is she the "champion cake baker," but brings a half of a pig from

---

[182] *Christmas tree lights*
[183] *Like to steal*
[184] *'Don't get along.'*
[185] *Straight up with no sugarcoating*
[186] *"Well, well. Is who I am seeing?"*

68

Hopetown, Berbice, to bake on Christmas Eve. Y'all think Miss Cheryl could bake? No, no, no!!! Leslyn 'tun up' in the make-believe kitchen with Carol and the children roung sheh. [187]

Y'all think Miss Millie house got action with the cake-making? You should see "Cousin Leslyn" performing .... apron on flouring pans, salt butter washed out over and over with water to take the salt out, then she adding sugar to make the mixture smooth and nice while ah lil bit moe[188] Demerara sugar burning on the coal pot outside to make the cake black along with some molasses. Then fruits that was set in rum all year round in a plate oneside to add in. Now eggs in as shell after shell she throwing in the old bucket they using as a garbage can, as the cake batter is about to be put into the box oven[189] outside in de yard.

Flour on Carol lil son face. Now how de hell did he get that on him? Eleven months old, and barely just start walking, but I know how he get it. He hiding under the table because he older siblings standing around Leslyn, and all Little Jason could do is crawl under there. So he pushing he head out from time to time like a turtle to check out de action and flour fall on he. But .... all in the "Fadda Crismus" fun.

---

[187] *And the children around her*

[188] *A little bit more*

[189] *A metal box with firewood under it in order to bake cakes on a rack. The door must be shut close.*

"Is how yuh look suh? Ah tell yuh stay away from deh,"[190] Carol yells to her youngest child while her cousin beckons to her that it's okay.

This is because very patient Cousin Leslyn only comes to this house twice a year and really enjoys the children's company. Plus, this forty-eight years old woman is ah ole maid[191] which means she never got married. Once Lincoln was tacklin sheh[192] but she wasn't interested because he was not a church-going man, and his height; "too short" according to this very tall and nice looking lady. Then the people in the village said that they might be related. Might be 'far away cousins.'[193] Well, oh lawd, that not going to fit well because if they did get married, it might have been a case of 'cousin aan cousin mek dozen,'[194] and maybe birth disorders.

See this wudda be 'ole house pun ole house'[195] with plenty chirren. Mih fren Junior seying use de word "piccaninnies" …….. that f-ing word that ah neva did like to use to describe black children. "NO, ah seh no!!![196]

---

[190] *"Is how you look so? I tell you to stay away from there"*
[191] *An unmarried woman*
[192] *Pursuing or courting her*
[193] *Might be cousins and were not told so*
[194] *The saying that if two cousins by chance gets married, they sometimes make lots of children*
[195] *Problems upon problems, worries upon worries*
[196] *"No, I say no"*

Tell mih if ah wrong nuh, tell mih nuh mih Guyanese people? [197] That word "pickaninny" is an old colonial term meaning "small black child." Now what dah heck!!! It is in the dictionary with an explanation that it is the way people of the West Indies used to call their offsprings. Nevertheless, ah think ah once heard that it came from the British.

Then Cousin Leslyn chirren would have a daddy who short like ah "baccoo or buckoo"[198] as ah just tell y'all that sheh say he too short for she height. De man who ah just mentioned wanted to be with her.

She's a legal secretary too at a law firm in New Amsterdam, that's why she can't come to town or as we say Georgetown, too often. Has to take vacation. Was taught to make the cakes, and other holiday foods by her mother who old now and gets "car sick" on the long journey here from Hopetown.

Me Donna, mih family from deh tuh, ah meant was to tell y'all. On mih 'motha side.' [199] They from Hopetown, West Coast Berbice."

Anyhow, Cousin Leslyn is following her mother's footsteps and keeping the promise to Carol. Oh, how they love her presence!!! She is very patient with the kids too, and teaching

---

[197] *Tell me if I wrong? Tell me if I am correct my Guyanese people?*
[198] *A legendary character from Guyanese and Surinamese folklore. He is also a short dwarf like creature who is kept and used by people in order to gain monetary success.*
[199] *My family from there too, I meant was to tell you all. On my 'mother side'*

Carol's eldest daughter how to cook and bake. Leslyn secretly wants to adopt one of these kids, but doesn't know how to ask Carol and her husband. Wants to ask for ten year old Roxanne but afraid the couple will say "no" because she too has to stay to help her mother with the little ones. After all, Leslyn is getting older and has given up on getting a child of her own, so is eager in wanting to give this child a better life other than in this tenement yard.

She is not smiling now because she is now remembering how Carol once called her ah 'country boo-boo.'[200] That's not nice!!! Not nice at all, like if I never said the words too. Me and dem other town people; Georgetown people, who used to boast and still boast, that we ain't country folks. Thinking that we better while these rural folks planting they food and we dotish [201] buying it from them in the marketplace. Like the people in the South in America that they call "country bumpkins." To heck was dat!!! They got good man in the country too; good fuh a nice husband, not worthless like Ernest and Wendell dem who come from town. [202] Marriage in the country last longer than in town tuh. Ask Fred. He and he wife married now for over fifty years and still going strong. Solid as a rock with a foundation that cannot be uprooted, and they married for all the right reasons unlike the town folks. So

---

[200] A 'person from the rural area'
[201] Acting senseless
[202] Urban area or Georgetown (the capital of Guyana)

72

you see why we shudn't call the rural people all sorts of names like "country boo-boo" and "country bumpkin." Yep, sure rite.

But while I running mih mouth, Gavin ...... y'all remember he, eh? ..... Carol husband. Well he eyeing up the two bottles of rum that is supposed to soak the black cake after they come out of the box oven outside and done cool. That's why Carol did tell sheh cousin not to mek de cake so early, and that they should do it last-minute like some people on the 24th since they don't have to bake theirs at the baker shop. Thank God because that is a trip itself with plenty, plenty people standing in a line to bake theirs, and having to wait hours to stick they batter in.

Is seven big cakes they mekkin and two medium-sized ones that they will give to the two next door neighbors. That's their gifts on December 25th. That's the only thing that this couple could give to Bridget and her kids, and Dookram and he wife cause dem is Carol favorite neighbors. Then two of the big ones going to share out in slices to the other people in the yard.

However, back to the rum on the table ...... allyuh think that Gavin   tekkin dem on?[203] No, he want some liquor to wet he palate. He want a cup of rum on the rocks. He love that drink you see. Want a night cap to relax tonight so that he could be ready to unload that Greek ship tomorrow morning after bullying he wife fuh sex as usual with he drunken

---

[203] *You all think that Gavin taking them on or listening to them*

self.[204] Remember I did tell y'all that he is a stevedore, Well, he does work hard. Unloading them ships all day, while thiefing tuh.

Shooo!!! Don't let him know ah tell y'all suh.[205] He gets upset. Admits he does that, but don't want nobody telling he business. He got a problem, eh? Damn thiefing "rum head."

Cousin Leslyn observing he. She squinting sheh eyes now. Staring boldy at him as she is remembering his wife's complains the last time she went to Hopetown that Gavin was turning an alcoholic and hanging out almost every day by the rum shop on Sussex Street. Then he comes home and argues with her. Oh Gawd!!! .... Oh God!!! Carol noticing now how he hanging around for a sip. See sheh man lurking around the two rum bottles on the table in their tiny dwelling place they call "home."

"Is whuh yuh waan Gavin? De rum is fuh de cakes. Yuh know duh? Yuh mean yuh cyaan see no liquah. Yuh ain gettin none. Aan ah mean it tuh," in a voice that wreaks of distaste for the man she regrets not only having started a family with, but also wasting her youthful years with.

He then heads to their so-called bedroom separated by just a single curtain from the rest of the large room, and not a bedroom door. He looking disappointed and cursing to he self. See why de man got to drink? This ain't no way to live in just a big open room

---

[204] *Drunken or intoxicated*

[205] *Don't let him know that I told you all so*

74

with all of them, but this is all he could afford. Then he doesn't like when Carol embarrasses him in front of relatives or other individuals. By now the children has gotten accustomed to the arguments, but not Leslyn. She is a very "proper" woman and dislikes these kinds of behavior. But guess whuh?[206] That's how a virgin behaves when it comes to men. Puh ting!!! ... Poor thing ... an exclamation of sympathy!!! Yes, she lacks experience with the other sex.

We better let Doris and sheh daughter Sharon teach sheh. Hahaha!!! Oh Lawd, those two is trouble. They will turn that nice, decent Christian woman out. Ah mean that they will turn her into a bad ooman like dey self.[207] Doing all kinda dishonest things and scamping people like what Doris used to do and hand it down to sheh daughter .... conning men, lying to people, wearing nuff, nuff powder in they bosom while they gold bangles jingling like the bells on a Christmas tree, and plenty, plenty other unscrupulous behaviors like a bunch of outlaws.

But why ah leaving out Denise; de "carry off gurl?" Sheh ain ezee tuh ..... she is not easy too. She sneaky because is not always she does bring the men to her house. She goes to theirs. Then does come home like if she a Saint. Partying all weekend and yuh don't even see sheh four chirren .... children. Always at they grandmother house while they mother having ah ball[208] in

---

[206] *But guess what?*
[207] *Turn into a bad charactered woman with criminal intensions sometimes like themselves*
[208] *Partying hard*

75

sheh mini skirts and go-go boots[209] and them halter tops. Trying to seduce de men. So-called slick and hardly mekkin a dollar. Could barely pay sheh rent and de rent man hunting sheh down and the others who din pay dey rent in time. Sharon did want to take her on the ships, but she refused. In man bed and broke. De people in de yard say she is a nymphomaniac too, and Patsy dis avoid her. Yep, you think ah kidding? So let's hope that de seaman sheh meet the other day get serious with sheh and change sheh life. Like if sheh is a 'spring chicken'[210] and not getting any younger.

But why I gossiping? I is only to write this book, not to talk bout people. Look yeh, ai ain perfect.[211]

All this 'hustle and bustle' and all Stanley thinking about is Patsy. He not even shopping, not buying anything at all. No gifts or cards, no pork to make baked ham or garlic pork, no fairy lights or tree to put them on, nor decorations. Ain't soak no fruits all year to make black cake either. It's as if he is in 'la la land' because all he thinking about is Patsy, and neglecting he self. He so in love that he ain't realize that the tattered curtain on he window needs to be changed, but he must be thinking it's not necessary. Ah guess is because he dis sympathize with some of the other tenants who not lucky like he to get a room with a window due to how de owner spilt up de place. Big deal bout a new curtain!!! That not necessary to he. I wonder if he heart more tattered than the curtain? But how

---

[209] *Short skirt with long heeled boots that fit a little below the knee*
[210] *'Young person'*
[211] *Look okay, I ain't perfect*

he expect to impress Patsy who got a man in America? He need to tidy up he place; need to fix up he place and he self.

Don't look like he cut he hair in a long time too, but I not digging nothing. I not criticizing because I don't touch mine but wrap it in a turban. Almost thirty-nine years now. Yep, Phillip would hear this and say, "Yes I." Ah hear he lil roots[212] you know. He partner next door is a rastaman; Ras Ilect. Funny thing too is that the Ras is Bertie good friend. Been he spar[213] long, long time now. Went to Saint Sidwell's school together as little boys.

Anyhow, y'all think Stanley digging anything? He studying if Bertie coming home to Patsy. Like ah said in de beginning of this book, he madly in love with sheh and is now secretly praying that that man in "Straufuss" does not return, cause Stanley waan de binnie fuh he self.[214] Sometimes he wishes he didn't come and live in Punchin Yard. He been here almost three years now. Moved in a year before Patsy. Got a little chokey [215] room in the second house on the left side of the yard. More and more he is beginning to hate it here, but like many others, this is all he could afford by working four days a week as a watchman at a store on Regent Street. His boss so cheap you see. Only paying this loyal worker a stipend. All because Stanley ain't got a security license and plus he been failing the exam some

---

[212] *A little down-to-earth, cultural, conscious*
[213] *Good friend*
[214] *And want the woman for himself*
[215] *A little jam packed*

seven times now. If Patsy hear that is so much times she going to say she ain't want no dunce man …. no duncee,[216] cause he ain't making the grade. No, this fella not passing these basic exams at all. Y'all want to hear he secret? He tell she he only fail de exam three times.

Eh heh, aan waan ooman. He crazy or what?[217]

There I go again …. talking name. Gossiping. Look, leff mih alone. Ai is ah Guyanese.[218] We don't mean no harm when we talk bout people. We are good people that just constructively criticize each other for the good.

Mih daughter Safiyah just come into the room glancing at my computer, saw what I just wrote, and said, *"yeah rite."*

Dhoan worry wid duh girl yeah *[219]*……. don't worry with that girl okay. She loves sarcasm, but you should see how she writes!!! My wish is for her to put out a few bestsellers in the near future. But she can't copy this style of writing because only ah Guyanese could do this. I am grinning now. Oh, how I love my Guyanese creolese!!! Yuh waan [220] confuse somebody? Talk broken English.

---

[216] *Ill-learned and ill-knowledged, not bright at all, not intelligent*

[217] *Yes, and want woman. He crazy or what?*

[218] *Look. leave me alone. I am a Guyanese.*

[219] *Don't worry with that girl okay*

[220] *You want to confuse somebody?*

Some say, "I don't understand you. What did you just say?" Darn!!! Get with it. I didn't mean for you to comprehend in the first place.

Dat's jus ah joke mih friend. Jus ah joke. Ah was jus 'pulling yuh legs.'[221]

All this time, Patsy thinking about Bertie while Stanley thinking about she. You see the confusion? Plenty, plenty confusion. Is like a big, big bag of problems; a big triangle. All ah dem got 'typee.'[222] Both of them longing for love while Bertie mus be pun ah date rite now in America. Patsy missing a man far away and Stanley missing she because he don't see this woman every day, and he falling in love with sheh more and more. Then she only hear from Bertie one time since she call he aunt at Cousin Hazel house. I don't know about she, but something is not right. See, a man going overseas without his woman is not a good thing. They does get caught up with all them different women from all over the world like a famous reggae singer said ..... "girls, girls everywhere." He then went on to naming several countries.

Remember Oslyn man who went to Brixton and get wild? The day he fix he teeth in that England, he turn "sweetbai." Never even voompse [223] on sheh ...... never looked back at her. Ungrateful bastard!!! Mek de girl save up sheh money and buy he

---

[221] *That's just a joke my friend. Just a joke. I was just 'teasing you.'*
[222] *All of them 'missing their lover badly.'*
[223] *Never even thinking about or caring for her*

clothes, shoes, suitcase fuh travel with, then turn back and give he money to walk with. Was so much Guyana money she had to change up to mek English pounds. Bastard!!! Yes, ah said it again. He and he rotten teeth self. I really don't know what she did see in he anyway. Should of saved sheh money to mind sheh son. Oh Gawd, ah hope Bertie don't do Patsy duh ……. break her heart.

Eh, eh, the postman coming just when I beginning to get paranoid about Patsy relationship. Oops! I seeing Doris now…. "Miss Mouth ah Preh Preh." She looking outside sheh front door. Looking to see if the postman going to knock on Patsy door. Yes, yes, I too want to know. I am not going to lie because I feel bad for the girl, but that Doris, you don't know what she thinking. She so evil and bad-minded. Never wish nobody good. Never!!! Like people to feel her own misery.

Aaaah ha!!! That's what I'm talking about!!!

Noel going to Patsy door. He knocking real hard now. Noel is the best postman the yard ever had. He does make sure people get they mail. Not like the other lazy one they had before. He would just knock one time and leave. No patience at all, but you see Noel know that some of them envelopes during the holidays does have raw currency inside; cash money, and he want the right person to get their mail. Nice guy, eh? He knocking harder now and a beaming Patsy has just opened the door with her smile dominating her chubby cheeks. She looks excited and is looking at the handwriting at the back to see who it is from because she has a few relatives in the United States. The smile is disappearing from her face and with a grimace that now appears to want to cry.

"Ah know dis haanwriting. Ah know is who," [224] she mumbles to herself, then glances at Sam's chile motha at the standpipe who is no longer grinning as if she has absorbed some of Patsy's sadness.

"A tough job," the postman yells back at the sympathetic woman who is washing a few dishes, as she agrees by just nodding her head.

Doris lingering by her doorstep then laughs as she is left to ponder about Patsy's predicament; a job that she enjoys doing.

"Why God, Why?" I ask myself. "Why such a nice young woman has to suffer so much for her lover?" But again I say, she is a victim of unrequited love like many other women whose man migrated abroad. But we shudn't come to this conclusion yet because we don't know if Bertie coming home for the supposedly soon-to-be auspicious occasion. Cause you know the tides may turn and this young woman might get the chance again to love up sheh man.

Granny Tinsy got some stories to tell about a certain man she used to date as she also was forgotten by a lover who went overseas, and had to settle locally for someone else. He was sheh

---

[224] *"I know this handwriting. I know is who"*

'sweet man'[225] and did have a wife on the the other side of town; the big shot side. He is Bridget daddy and was the Chinee[226] man that did own the grocery store on the corner of Durban Street and Cemetery Road. She was a "sweetie" [227] back in de day brownskinned with a pretty face, short and thick with full lips, a curvaceous body and a big battom.[228] So the first time de Chinese man set eyes on sheh, he went wild as he did never see sheh before since she was not only his new customer, but was also a new resident to the neighborhood. Started to run behind sheh[229] like how Stanley after Patsy, and whenever she went to buy some goods; food items from he store, he didn't want sheh to pay. He whoan tek[230] money, but she would leave it right there on the counter. She always would buy pigtail and other pieces of meat, and he started to put some nice pieces aside for her, and since a few times sheh asked for delivery, he get to find out sheh address and would send her some free pieces of these meats and other items with his delivery man.

Then one day, he asked her for a date and she refused. But then eventually she gave in and stopped 'cuttin styles' pun[231] he...... and accepted his invitation. Took de advice from one of

---

[225] *Her lovey, dovey boyfriend*
[226] *Chinese*
[227] *A good looking woman*
[228] *Big buttocks*
[229] *Go after her romantically*
[230] *He would not take*
[231] *Giving him a hard time*

sheh friends who said she could get in he pocket and fix sheh life. Get some financial security for sheh children and sheh self.

"Was ah nice, nice date. He treat mih good. Treat mih like ah lady till ah fuhget he did married. Try fuh kiss mih aan ask mih fuh some 'patacake'[232] aan ah bax he. Ah din waan no disrespek pun de fuss date. He tink ah did stuphid, but otha man did waan mih tuh, so ah wonta miss out if he din ask mih out no more. But anyway, he ask mih how tings was with mih financially aan he gih mih five hundred dollas when he dropped mih home. Dat time it was nuff, nuff money aan ah did like he fuh duh. He show dat he did care fuh mih. At least ah did tink suh aan ah go out with he plenty moe times aan suh dat is how we did get togetha. Ah did deh wid he until he dead. Had an affair wid he until de day he pass."

Then she would go on to describe the day she found out she was pregnant with Bridget and the day she gave birth to her. Then how jealous Mr. Ming's wife was when she found out because she didn't have any kids with he……but with some conscience about her wrongdoings and as an accomplice with his acts of committing adultery. She would always bow her head when mentioning this one, and then would add ……….

"Ah did beg Gawd fuh fuhgiveness cauz ah did feel bad. Ah din mean fuh hurt de lady. Ah din really waan ah love ting. Ah

---

[232] *Vagina*

only did hustlin he. But …….. ah did end up fallin in love wid he. Oh Gawd, ah mess up."

"Yuh know how it is. 'When yuh go tuh crab dance, yuh dis get mud.'[233] Yuh know whuh ah mean? When yuh lay up wid ah man, yuh cud get pregnant aan duh is whuh did happen tuh mih," Granny Tinsy declared, and would often times admit why she should not be living in Punchin Yard, and how she was robbed by another lover who knew sheh chile fadda was a prominent businessman and did leff sheh with ah 'few shillings' well.[234]

"Aan ah did pay fuh it when Otis did rip mih off. Ah learn mih lesson. Neva do bad aan tink yuh nah gon pay fuh it. Cauz Gawd dhoan sleep, yuh hear mih? Ah *did brace mihself afta he rip mih off. We was gon start ah lil bizness aan he run off to Barbados wid mih money dat was suppose tuh buy some tings ova dere fuh de bizness. From dat time ah neva ketch mihself aan ah 'bruk.'[235] Ah neva did get de type ah money like mih Chinee man did gih mih, aan ah ain get ah good man like duh eva since. But is mih fault. He did put mih in ah house aan ah sell it as ah laas resort afta being 'bruk.' Now look at mih, Ah had to move in dis yard."*

So that was the demise of this very lovely lady who once had a taste of the good life, not riddled by the everyday struggle

---

[233] *"When you meddle in things, you will get a terrible effect."*
[234] *Left her with quite a sum of money*
[235] *"From that time I never caught myself financially and I am broke."*

that some people call "haan tuh mouth."[236] She would then go inside and to whoever was her audience, would bring outside an old, tattered, picture album for them to get a visual idea of who this once-lover was along with the younger pictures of the product of their relationship. That mixed-race child who unfortunately did not reap the benefits of her father's financial efforts which should have been residual enough to sustain herself and mother until today. Although a different story from Doris, they both repeat the events of their life when perturbed; whether 'sweet' or 'bitter' nostalgia.

---

[236] *'Living day-to-day and barely surviving struggling to put food in one's mouth daily'*

The Goings-On

Christmas lights all over Main Street. The trees looking like they jumping for joy. Even the flowers on them seem to be giggling. Once more it is December and they are being noticed again. In Guyana we call them "fairy lights" and they are the reminders that the holidays are around the corner. These are also the lights that make not only Main Street, High Street and Regent Street look brighter, but also other streets where people go shopping, as business people are awarded this privilege of early lighting, but also appear as if they are in competition with each other. Lights galore!!!

But what pivots the excitement is the facial expressions of the little children who become very excited at the colors that these lights exude. Remember Little Orson who did visit Ulrick when he was washing down his mother; Miss Millie house? That little boy who was not only singing the Christmas carol along with Ulrick, but wanted to plunge into what he thought were small swimming pools in the sunken in concrete? Well, when his mommy would take him to town, he would get so excited, that one time he almost died. He is asthmatic and all that excitement was just too much for him. He looked like he was about to faint, fell down on the street, panting fuh breath, could hardly breathe, and when he did, it was hard, hard, hard, then he looked like he was

86

not breathing anymore while grabbing he chest. He puh mother[237] hysterical as he also started wheezing on Main Street by Tower Hotel.

Then suddenly, a man emerged with an inhaler from he car and took care of him and his lungs no longer constricted. Said is he lil daughta own so we aint got to worry about if he did overdosing de little boy. That is what prevented Little Orson from 'kickin de bucket.'[238] Lawd!!! Don't even let us go there. That would have been a sad, sad day in Meadow Brook Gardens and for the people in Punchin Yard that did know he through Patsy.

Miss Cheryl got she fruit cakes in the line up and thinking what else she got to make. She sitting on she poof[239] scratching sheh head, but is not dandruff she have. That is what she does do when she thinking, and what makes matters worse is that sheh fan just stopped working, so sheh hot. Hot, sweaty and trying to think is not an easy thing. She thinking about making some souse and pepperpot now. Then she says openly to Sharon who just walk in sheh house.

"Ah waan mek some pepperpat aan souse aan bake ah ham. Ah nice ham wid plenty cloves all ova it. Ah thinking fuh mek some mauby tuh.

---

[237] *He poor (as in an exclamation in 'feeling sorry for') mother*
[238] *Die*
[239] *A foot rest*

Sharon then intervenes, *"whuh bout some gingerbeer aan de fresh bread fuh eat with de pepperpat?" Mih motha set some fruits fuh mek wine months now aan yuh cud get some. Plus we gon get otha drinks from one ah dem ships. Ah got ah few more days fuh get some prags. Ah gon do like some of mih 'mattee' dem.*[240] *'Cop dem,' get them from offa dem Scottish ships.*

Cheryl grins, as she knows how skillful Sharon is at acquiring things from off the ships. Also, that the girl knows how to work her sticky fingers wid sheh scampish ways. She laughs again as she remembers how Doris, her mother, had made a mark for herself of carrying away the Englishman's briefcase with all his money. She better do well again this time because Phillip always depends on her for a little help. Last year she bring nuff clothes she steal from a seaman who sheh did seduce. Foreign cigarettes, foreign foods, and liquor was mainly what she took. He even did get some Clark shoes, belts, and a stingy-brim hat.[241] You should see how he dressed up for he birthday with he kerchief in he back pocket like a 'saga bai'[242] for she and other women to admire he. Handsome and looking nice with he douglah[243] self and muscular physique that spelled "Mr. Sensuous." But y'all ever wonder why she de Sharon so nice to Phillip?

---

[240] *'My people them'*
[241] *A hat with a small brim on the edge*
[242] *A man who dresses stylishly and has a reputation of having multiple women*
[243] *A person mixed with East Indian and black*

Well, y'all know 'Mouth ah Preh Preh' Doris ain gon run shih mouth pun sheh own daughta. Y'all wait deh. Sheh know who fuh talk bout. So anyway, Ethel did say that Sharon and Phillip has a 'lil ting' pun de sly'[244] but they been keeping it a secret cause he lil wutless aan 'he haan fass.' [245] He thirty-eight years old and ain gat no job and they cannot get steady because he ain got no money to give Sharon and she six children. No wonder Ethel did seh a day that she did see Phillip and Sharon coming out a 'short time' place[246] on North Road.

But wait ah minute here!!! Sheh betta be careful sheh ain get anotha 'belly' or pregnant because 'goat aan bite sheh' [247] and that sheh could do better than Phillip being sheh chile fadda. Although however, sheh gihing he lil piece[248] rite now. So that's why he does do anything that Sharon ask he to do and does even paint up sheh living room, and put up sheh fairy lights on Christmas Eve. The yard this only need some snow and de place would look like a Winter Wonderland on the side of sheh house because she occupy   the end of the building. Call he sheh 'flunkie,'[249] he don't care. Sheh little 'pwah pwah' or no quality friend who could barely paddle he own canoe[250], but he does make the place look nice for sheh children, and y'all want a joke? He

---

[244] *A secret relationship*

[245] *A little worthless and 'he likes to pick up/steal things'*

[246] *A hotel where couples visit to have sex for a short amount of time*

[247] *An old adage that means ''she is not doomed to get another male partner, as she is very attractive*

[248] *Giving him some sex*

[249] *A 'do boy''*

[250] *Who could barely co-exist economically by himself; could barely take care of himself*

even did dress up as Santa Claus one year and share out gifts to sheh children. Then when he done he went down the street it is said, and shoplift in Bookers Store. All this time people think he was the store Santa Claus, but didn't realize that he big bag had stolen items from other stores too.

You see, people dis be so confused with all de 'goings-on' and all de bright lights, that they doesn't even think bout no Santa stealing. Didn't even pick deh teeth [251] on who appeared to be the usual big belly man in the red suit that gratifies de little children all holiday long to profit de stores with dem cheap toys that they give them. No wonda some of dem chirren dis cry. Y'all think dem little ones ain't got no instincts to know that the stores be robbing they parents. Cheap toys!!! Would be better off if they parents did take their money and buy them gifts off the store shelves instead of taking them to see he. Yep, the little children know they parents getting ripped off year after year especially when they sitting in Santa lap and he being especially nice to them.

Eh, eh. I forgetting about how dem people not realizing what really "Thief man Phillip" doing in the stores ...... that's because they be too busy thinking about which relative might be flying in by surprise and what gifts they going to get. Not realizing that the man was abusing a Santa privilege; a privilege that he didn't have in the first place, since he was a canta Santa.[252] But

---

[251] *Didn't even worry about or was concerned about*
[252] *A make-believe Santa*

90

Phillip, the ole thief man as we know he to be, he did only concern about thiefing …… walking into Bookers and thiefing, walking into Fogarty's and thiefing, walking into Bettencourts and thiefing, walking into J.P. Santos and thiefing, walking into D.M. Fernandes and thiefing …… all in he Santa suit, while people hailing he up as this thief man ringing he bell and hollering *"ho, ho, ho, merry Christmas"* with a packed bag of stolen things. Things that he was longing for all year round and couldn't buy. But could y'all believe what more he cudda get if he had a reindeer and a sleigh? If only Guyana had snow, and he cudda mek moe turnins!!![253] Make that quick getaway without being caught, and making second and third trips.

Phillip ….. only Phillip could pull this off on a Christmas eve night in Guyana. Not even the seasoned thief man Brentnol on Bent Street have he ratings or Lennox and he girlfriend Wendy that dis shoplift too. What did I say earlier? Those individuals excited with the holidays and with the bright lights on Main Street, couldn't 'peep he cards.'[254] But he is a good man fuh Sharon in he own way. He carry back he big, big, heavy, heavy bag that cudda mek he get ah 'goadie'[255] to Punchin Yard, and give away the toys he did thief to de chirren.

---

[253] *Could of visited more places/made movements*
[254] *See through him/or detect his agenda*
[255] *Could of made him get a 'hernia' where his testicles are very enlarged*

91

That was last year and ah think that is why Sharon got a 'soft spot' fuh he.[256] Even Bridget mother, Grandma Tinsy did need a pressing comb and some curlers fuh sheh hair and he happened to have had that in he bag, and he give it to she. Did need dem plastic curlers instead of using newspaper ones that gon suck up de grease when she press sheh hair. Press it with the iron comb long and straight then put grease. See, he does thief anything in he sight cause he know somebody gon need it. She asked him if he had any bedroom slippers and sure enough, when he check he bag, he found three pairs and one was sheh size. Then asked if he got some judebox panties[257] and he had them too. Big and nice for she big bamsee[258] and in some nice fluorescent and sexy colors ..... pink, red and yellow with some blue and white flowers on them that she could hang out on the line in the yard and show off on Doris. She love he you see!!! Cause he is one of them thief men that mannerly and nice, and does tell people what they want to hear, especially de women. Whether young or old. Know how to smooth talk people so they could trust he while he masterminding how to get dey tings by putting them in ah swing up.[259] Hence, due to these so-called crafty ways he had some run-ins with the law.

---

[256] *She favors him a lot and care about him*
[257] *Huge female underwear*
[258] *Big buttocks*
[259] *Lying to someone*

"Ai is ah fuckin ole convict skunt.[260] Ai been tuh jail nuff, nuff times ahready. Everbady know me as ah fuckin outlaw. Been thiefin since ah was fourteen. Leh dey carry deh skunt," he would say when some of the tenants and others critique him.

"Dey talkin, but dey dis still waan mih thiefin tings," while adjusting his stingy brim hat on a head full of hair that he fixes in a ponytail.

But while we laughing bout Phillip, we need to check in at Miss Millie and see whuh going on[261] at she house in Meadow Brook. Wonder if she get sheh linoleum fuh sheh floor, cause last time we know she two sons was going to get the linoleum for she kitchen and and she hallway, and that Patsy was going to go back to help with the floor polishing; the first coat.

Y'all think we should take Doris on this trip? Hell no!!!! We don't want no drama at nice Miss Millie house. But yuh know whuh, leh we knock on Patsy door aan see if she home.

A good person to send is Daphne. She enjoys knocking on the neighbors doors to their rooms. I don't know why. Especially at this seasonal time and then she likes to see if they decorating they house. Fuh some reason, she dis know even though she 'ain all dere.'[262] Then she obsessed with candy canes and like to beg

---

[260] *I am a fucking old convict skunt (a profanity)*
[261] *And see what is going on*
[262] *Not always mentally aware*

for some, and dis try to see if they bake black cake early and does ask for a slice. Now remember Daphne is developmentally disabled and is a 'haan full'[263] most times. She jumps up and down on Main Street like Little Orson when she sees the lights and all the decorations, and dis be calling out to strangers all excited, and the worst thing "Motha Beulah" could do is give her granddaughter Daphne a whistle to blow, because all that noise does be in her ears and de poor ole lady can't even hear when the cars coming to cross the street. Now y'all know how it is when old people hearing going bad with that noise that could burst sheh eardrums. So Beulah learn from last year that she got to carry Daphne downtown just as it getting dark. So they going to walk around for about an hour and leave, or better yet, go with a friend she got with a car. That better cause she could get help in controlling this young lady that still like a chile. Not an ezee job, but sheh trying!!!

"Ello, ello, inside. Is me Daphne, Daphne, Daphne, Daphne." She gets a little repetitive now, as her cognition is impaired and should have said "hello" instead of "ello." She begins to knock louder and louder at Patsy's door while Stanley and Bridget's son Orin looks impatiently at her. In fact, they are becoming fed up of her ranting and raving every other day, and wish that she could become institutionalized. Actually, all the neighbors are beginning to think that she is a nuisance except her

---

[263] *Handful*

grandmother   Miss Beulah who is in denial but complains about headaches all day.

Now ahwe dis [264] know that sheh heachaches is because that girl giving de old lady de 'licks of Lisbon.'[265] This could be the reason why Patsy might be hearing her knocks but does not want to answer. Cannot be bothered because all hell dis break loose when that girl start up.[266] After all, ever since Patsy received the wrong letter at the front door the other day, she has been hibernating. That letter was not from Bertie and could have furthered what appeared to be depression in this lovelorn young woman .... a depression that has seemingly escalated. But, Daphne continues to knock with no answer. She then attempts to peep through Patsy's only reachable window. Her one window, and seems not to be seeing anyone. Then she bangs at the door again. Banging as hard as she could .... harder and harder, and harder.

Told y'all sheh neighbors in the yard think she is a nuisance. But where is Patsy? Looks like she either at work or at sheh Aunt Millie. A car now stops in front of the yard, and out of it jumps Anita, Patsy's co-worker. She walks towards her friend's door and is angered by the determined look on Daphne's face as

---

[264] *Now all of us know*
[265] *A hard time or plenty trouble*
[266] *Become problematic*

Anita knows how presumptuous this disabled girl is. She then shoves Daphne aside who just tried to block her, and attempts to knock on Patsy's door, but gets a sudden slap from Daphne. Then just as Anita is about to retaliate, Patsy opens her door. This answers the question as to Patsy's whereabouts as her friend enters her home. She then slams the door in a disappointed looking Daphne's face who yelled that she did not see any *"lites, lites or, or deck-rations."* She meant to say "lights" and "decorations" as she also has language acquisition that is poor.

More than an hour has elapsed and Patsy now emerges from out of her house with her co-worker Anita carrying a bag. This is the same bag that she would take with her when she is going to stay away for a few days, Doris had observed. I think it's true!!! Doesn't take a Rocket Scientist to figure that one out, except that presumptuous stalker who had just assaulted Anita.

Hazel outside now looking out for sheh cousin Patsy, while Ulrick and Miss Millie trying fuh kill one of sheh fowls[267] that she been growing for de big day. The fowl running round and round, and round in de yard. Seems like he know they want to kill he. Trying to run out Miss Millie yard and tassay. [268] This frantic woman with knife in hand want fuh ketch this fowl so badly. Want it as part of they holiday meal, and allyuh should know that it is the only time of the year; Christmas day that this family and most

---

[267] *Trying to kill one of her grown-up chickens*
[268] *Go away or run away*

96

of the other families eat a whole chicken, but the bird still running around until Cousin Lenny, she older son corners the bird and capture him.

Oh rass!!! If you see Millie how she eager to cut off the chicken head; wielding sheh knife in anticipation!!! Now she jumping up with sheh bad knees and demonstrating how she gon tek aff he head[269] in a kinda karate motion. She doing it now. My God!!! Y'all ever see a fowl after he head cut off? Gosh, the puh ting jumping. Head off and it bleeding and still jumping like he in a 'fight-or-flight response.' Then Miss Millie got de nerve fuh tek[270] the pot of hot water that Hazel just give she by the kitchen step and dash it on de fowl.

Oh Jah, dat ain't rite, not rite!!! But, that is how dem Guyanese and Caribbean people dis do it. Does kill a bird .... all in de holiday "goings-on." Then now Millie giving the bird to Hazel and Ulrick to pick off the residue of de feathers one-by-one and to not have a single feather leff on it. Like if they gon do a good job of it with a million feathers on it. Pure punishment .... fuh sooooo!!! [271] To get all those feathers off. Then after their tedious job of almost an hour on that overweight chicken she going to take the fowl upstairs, pass it over the fire to burn off the tiny feathers that they cudn't pick off, open it up, clean inside thoroughly, wash with limes, and most

---

269 *Going to chop off his head*
270 *To take the pot of hot water*
271 *Plenty punishment, tremendous, a lot*

definitely some thyme. Also, season it with black pepper, salt, garlic, shallots, onions inside and out, and let it marinate in sheh fridge for tomorrow to cook.

Sheh done do that and is smiling triumphantly because she is glad that the mongoose did not kill and eat that particular chicken which is now fat and juicy. Is true, she been having problems with mongoose attacking her fowl pen[272] at night, and had lost over ten chickens. Have seen them coming out of the coconut tree in sheh backyard. For this reason, she has her boys moving her chickens out of the pen and place them in a large box inside the house at night, then take them outside in the daytime. Indeed, this is a hectic job for her two sons with the 'double whammy' of cleaning up all of the odors inside of the house that is left behind in the mornings. Hazel does do it too, but the last two weeks she been helping her mother in planning and running around with her shopping. In other words, they had been making outings together to Bourda and Stabroek or what we call the latter "Big Market" which they rarely do together.

Hazel loves this because it eases her boredom in the house and last time she been out Miss Annie who son did like her, gave her plenty fruits from her stall and some sugarcake and fudge.[273] Then the lady would tell her how nice she growing up and how much she wants Lawrence to marry her. She would also be

---

[272] *A pen for grown chickens*

[273] *Sugarcake is made out of grated/cut up coconut and sugar. Fudge is made from boiled milk mosttly condensed and sugar. Then put in trays to harden.*

commenting on how Hazel hair is so long and pretty, and how nice and white her teeth is, her beauty, her shape and flawless skin. Then proudly say that her son had just gotten a promotion at the bauxite industry as if to coerce this young woman to become his girlfriend and subsequently, wife. Like if news din[274] travel from Linden to Georgetown that sheh son turn wild and been with almost every young woman in de town.

Who want he? Not Miss Millie daughter!!! That's because, remember knock-kneed Jacqueline that Lenny in love with? Well, she know he and bring de news bout he. Sheh from Linden. Rememba? Tell y'all how news does fly quickly. Tell allyuh how people dis talk. News dis fly even though de place is 83,000 square miles. Nutten does hide. Nothing. You want news on somebody? Somebody dis know they business; good or bad ……. "mouth open, story jump out."[275]

Meanwhile, Miss Millie 'using sheh brains' [276] and meddling with the other vendors nearby by trying to bargain with them on lowering the prices of their spices. After all, lower the prices "yes," because these are the items and others, that she still needs to prepare her meats and other foods with.

---

[274] *Like if news didn't*

[275] *"Mouth open and people's business or private matters being revealed"*

[276] *Mentally manipulating*

"Eh, eh, me aan like de price fuh dem shallots. Dey dhoan look 'suh catholic.'[277] *If ah buy it, ah cud only pay ten cents fuh de bunch,"* with a coercive attitude.

Then she goes next door to Gladys stall and bargains again ...... *"Is how much fuh yuh thyme Gladys?*

The tired looking Gladys then lethargically answers, *"Is okay Millie, yuh could tek de bunch fuh ten cents. Is ahrite ah seh."* Then nods her head again as she is too tired to debate.

Miss Millie then smiles triumphantly as she knows too well that she has just gotten over on that lady who is about to close shop and go home after sitting at her stall for over ten hours today. Gladys is yawning now as she reaches for the cord to her fairy lights and pulls it out of the socket on the wall. It is almost time to close up and the vendors are all tired; the time when Millie likes to 'prips thru'or pass through Bourda Market. But, today she is late and cannot visit Big Market with her only daughter, and is happy that she was once more able to manipulate some of the vendors into lowering the prices of the items she so badly needs. Also, of course, Hazel's visit here is an initiation or training on how to economically maneuver herself in the marketplace.

Both mother and daughter are heading home now, and from their hire car, what do they see? .... Stanley perched up by he workplace on Regent Street talking to Yvonne who does pick

---

[277] *Not so good*

100

fares.[278] Man if you see he!!! Striking a pose in he security clothes. He pants very short ….. it "floodin" as if in prepaing for a flood and don't want his trousers to get wet. Then he shirt tight on he now-forming pudge belly. Check he out …… acting like a 'star bai' with he hands about an inch from Yvonne bamsee.[279] Then with he six gold teeth at the top of he mouth shining as if they in competition with the lights on the Christmas tree next to them; the lights that mek Miss Millie and sheh daughter see he trying to hustle Yvonne.

You see how if it wasn't fuh dem lights that they wonta see he? Talking bout how he love Patsy. He with he frowsy self. Word is he don't even own a bottle of cologne. Dis just put lime under he armpits which is a natural thing, but that ain't good enough because he still smell like a bush hog.[280] Then Yvonne laugh with sheh friends later that night and said, *"he gat 'stink mouth' tuh. Bad breath. Who waan duh bannuh? Not me,"* she cringes. *"Duh person muss be really 'hard up.' Ah ain so 'desperate' fuh ah man."* Can't even pass the security test and trying fuh 'get in'[281] with another woman.

Both mother and daughter shocked beyond words. Hazel look like she bursting out in a sweat from both disbelief and anger. Then sheh motha 'suckin sheh teeth' …… Steupppppse!!!![282]

---

278   *To prostitute oneself*
279   *Buttocks*
280   *A pig who lives in the bush*
281   *To be with*
282   *Mother pulling her teeth in disgust and anger*

Then vexing up she face. They cannot believe it. Oh God, if only Patsy could see this!!! That yuh cyaan trust men at all …….. all of them.

"Some ah dem only waan yuh fuh get in yuh drawers" as Donna did imply earlier in this book.

Y'all tell me if that ain't good advise? Tell mih nuh? I don't like these 'goings-on.' I just don't like de vibes.

This man is a liar. Ah mad tek he out mih book cauz he 'twassin up mih itation.' This canta security guard with he pwah pwah self[283].

Orin is a very bright boy. He did pass for Queen's College and did tell Stanley once that he had "no logics." That boy is brilliant and that's why he getting good grades and want to move he mother out of Punchin Yard from around people like this fool. Stanley must have "no logics" because he would not stand in the bright lights with Yvonne fuh people to see he.

Phillip would have done that with he Santa Claus suit on, disguise he self, and not in he so-called security uniform. He really pagalee.[284] But whuh mek matters worst is that non-perceptive Stanley ain't realize that when Yvonne come out is fuh 'cop ah bannuh.'[285] Meaning she looking for a man who she could take

---

[283] *This make-believe security guard with he no quality self*
[284] *Awkward and clumsy looking*
[285] *To get a man or potential customer*

advantage of and see if she could run through he pockets. You should see sheh!!! Powder in she bosom like most road ooman, powder on she neck, powder on she back and even under sheh armpits. Only leff for she to disguise sheh face with some of the same white powder; the same way that Carol eleven months old son did look with flour on he face that people didn't recognize he when he followed he mother and Cousin Leslyn in de yard to put the cakes in the box oven. This tells you that sheh be "nice and fresh" like she just had a bath ...... that Yvonne. All in an attractive attempt to get some money.

Waan de man dem know dat sheh jus come out de shower aan headin down by Lombard Street, but is when sheh 'sight up'[286] that ass Stanley that sheh stop to see what sheh could hustle from he after leaving sheh bruk pocket man she got at home on Bent Street.

Oh, oh!!! Somebody just yell out de word *"wutless."* Yes, is truh.[287] I forgetting to mention that bout he .... that sheh man worthless. Thanks fuh reminding mih. Thank yuh, tank yuh!!! Allyuh is a good audience. Mih nice Guyanese people!!! Love y'all.

---

[286] *Noticed*
[287] *Yes, It's true*

Anyway, Yvonne saying something else now about sheh man ...... *"he ain worth ah 'bab,* [288] she would tell sheh fren dem, and *"yuh gon hear when ah get rid ah he."*

Get rid of he? ..... whuh side duh? How yuh mean? Is not true. He gon be right in sheh house.

He up in that house six years now, and they been together seven long years. Now she out there almost every night fuh 'pick fares' fuh mine he. He aan he 'deh bad' self.[289] Thank God she ain got no kids for de "no good man." Word is people see she over six times in de "slip aan fell" ward[290] at de Georgetown Hospital.

Whuh y'all talking bout? Ah ain lying.

Yes, Sam cousin is a nurse there. Yes, truth ah Gawd. Said Yvonne was right in there trying to abort the third one when de girl; the nurse recognized sheh. Playing she hiding, but in Guyana or in the Caribbean somebody will see you.

That one made me laugh so hilariously. Laff till mih tear gland mek mih cry. You know that does happen to some people sometimes. I call it tears of laughter.

Now I am not laughing at the idea of the child she kill, but as ah seh again ...... that in Guyana, people does always see, and

---

[288] *He is not worth twenty-five cents*
[289] *He who is doing bad financially*
[290] *'Abortion floor or ward in the hospital*

that nobody could really keep a secret when they go to de "slip and fell" ward. The excuse is that they slipped and fell and that's why they get a miscarriage. Lie!!! Is kill they kill de baby. Little baby; little God Angel.

"*Be fruitful aan multiply,*" rasta Empress Yeshimabeit or as she is familiarly called ..... "Sista Yeshi" is blackin up.[291]

This sistren has seven cubs herself and deeply defends procreation. Hence abortion is sheh kinna,[292] as she further reasons ...."*Eye aan Eye*" .... meaning everyone collectively, in unity or 'inity'...... "*mus preserve de black race. Is race preservation InI deh pun in dis 'iwah'...... 'hour.' Nuff ahwe suffah in de Middle Passage aan pass on in genocide. Black people come from Royalty .... of Inciency. All ahwe people of color as ah mattuh ah fact. Suh yuh overstand eye reasoning? Seen?!! Eye aan Eye need fuh kulcha up as black wombman; Queens, Empresses, Goddesses, Mama Afrikas, Empress Menen, Sojourner Truths, Empress Zawditu, aan all de otha SoulJahs ..... jus like Eye aan Eye ankhcestors. Mek we warriors fuh deArmageddon aan bun out all dese follies.*" She agains adds .... "*mek yuh yuts ah seh. Preserve yuh lineage.*"

She then adjusts her turban on her dreadlocks or covenant, and adds, "*live accarding to de principles of de Most High aan dhoan worry bout how yuh gon mine yuh "yuts" ..... youths ....*"

---

[291] *Reasoning or stating*
[292] *Something she dislikes badly*

105

cauz Jah will bring yuh thru. He will provide. Clean up yuh heart aan come if yuh erred in dese ways" while Sista Jahkeda and Ras Jaherald Selassie nods in agreement as bredrens Kebra Nagast and Yehudah Haile are giving her the Royal Salute. She then further quotes one of her favorite verses in the Bible ...... *Behold, Children are a heritage from the Lord, the fruit of the womb a reward like arrows in the hand of a warrior are the children of one's youth"*.... Ises I, Yah RastafarEye!!!

Just then, a few miles away, a man just pass de hire car that Hazel aan sheh motha in. They hearing all that loud motorcycle noise and when they look .... is who? Gavin. He speeding up in front of them and they now sure is he because they know de shirt he wearing. That was the same shirt he had on the last time they visited Patsy in Punchin Yard, and is the same color of he motorcycle. Well yuh know that he is a stevedore and done work early, but they are guessing now by their facial expressions, and their guess is right. He is heading to exactly where they thought he was going ...... to the rum shop on Durban Street, he new hangout spot, according to Carol. He stop going on Sussex Street because sheh find out he whereabouts and she did stalking he; even if sheh had to ask someone sheh know with a car or ride de bus.

Yes, they seeing he blue motorcycle in front, and wish that the darn hire car they in would giddy up.[293] They just pass he

---

[293] *Hurry up or rush*

106

because the driver speeding like hell and they 'heart in dey haan'[294] as the driver just failed to stop at a traffic light. That is Gavin bike; that bike that wakes all his neighbors up very early every morning except when that brewing alcoholic get a hangover, and either stay home or go to work late. He wife Carol fed up now and been complaining about his drinking.

"He followin bad company. Gettin drunk allmos every day, den coming home fuh argue wid mih or try fuh gih mih moe pickney.' Is not good fuh me aan dem chirren. Ah gon leff he, aan he shortin up we house money."

This is her contention with the man that she had planned to spend her entire life with. But allyuh notice that he not even marrying to sheh? Now that he is a drunkard and careless, is there ever going to be a wedding? Too long overdue, but leh mih mine mih bizness!!! He need ah good lickin.[295] Need some sense in he head but hardly does be sober anymore and act like he flighty.[296] Sam did want to fight he a time because he did cheating in the dominoes game, and then lying too. All because they were gambling fuh money.

Then Carol picking up fire rage [297] for she so-called 'not want to marry man.' Before she sit sheh rancid self down. Then

---

[294] *Heart is racing as if it came out of their chest cavity*
[295] *A good licking or beating up*
[296] *Not all there in the head*
[297] *Taking sides or being biased*

Doris jumped into the argument and it was nearly ah poshway [298] in de yard ..... all sorts of insults at each other, all sorts of cursing; all sort of profanities, all sorts of ruckshuness[299] and telling one another the secrets they did holding for each other for years. Doris who we know mouth buss was telling Carol about the abortion she had a few months ago because she like to talk too much. See how yuh cyaan tell dis ooman yuh bizness?

They then somehow end up in front of Mother Beulah front door to sheh building and they was about to fight. The old lady ran outside to stop them, and you think Gavin did care? He just sipping he rum on the rocks with some ice cause that more important than Doris squaring up[300] in front of his reputed wife. That was too much confusion for de ole lady and she ran inside fuh sheh bible to pray. After all, she is a Christian and already got to pray for sheh granddaughter Daphne. Now this!!! Two grown women and Mother Beulah trying to "save them." Save them from the temptations of the devil and eventually tek them to the church sheh dis guh tuh.[301] Tek dem to get saved. So now she confusingly turn to a tattered page in her bible and utters ....

"Refrain from anger, and forsake wrath! Fret not yourself; it tends only to evil." "But you, O Lord, are a God merciful and gracious, slow to anger and abounding in steadfast love .... "

---

[298] *A fight or disturbance*
[299] *Rudeness, profanities and all kinds of bad behaviors*
[300] *Getting ready to fight*
[301] *Take them to the church she goes to*

Just then Daphne yells hysterically for her grandmother and she closes her bible, looks sternly at the two warmongers and disappears inside.

Post Office Time

Debbie, remember she? Bridget adopted daughter. Well this time she looking out for de postman. Said she getting some box from Canada from sheh mother brother. Now Little Debbie is just eight years old, but she said some clothes and other things coming for her and the other children in the house. Well nobody never ask the question why she living with Bridget. That's because Debbie mother had so many problems at the people she did renting a room from in East La Penitence Housing Scheme, that she started to guh out sheh head.[302] Then when things got worse about November last year, she just did bring sheh daughter for the holidays since ting was bad.[303] Actually, she did think that Bridget brother Gary did sending a barrel so the little girl who was seven then could then have had good food to eat and nice drinks to wet sheh palate.[304] But, that didn't happen because Bridget brother only send a barrel this year. So this little child who is not no relative to Bridget still staying with them, since she mother run 'helter skelter' to Paramaribo it is said. The people in the yard only guessing that is there sheh deh because nuff, nuff people from Guyana was going to Dutch Guiana for a better life. Then rumour is also that she went to a small island with an island man also. But, all we concerned with is that she never come back for she little

---

302 *To get mentally disturbed or sometimes insane*
303 *Hard times, things were not good for her*
304 *To drink something, to quench one's thirst a little*

offspring. Sheh ain't ezee, eh? But guess what? She and sheh no good self was Denise, the carry-off girl partner. Those two used to walk de road looking fuh what they didn't put down. Always like batty aan poe.[305] What that mean? Ah gon tell yuh jus now. Wait nuh. That's after I tell you how them two did meet.

Well Denise, knowing she, went to somebody party under a bottom house[306] in Kitty, and was dancing with somebody man. De man 'sweet ooman'[307] then went up to the Denise while dem two was dancing, and tell Denise to loose sheh man; stop dancing wid he, and Denise refused. Cuttin up sheh eye on de woman and doing ah fine wine[308] on de man. Next thing you know, the lady throw a punch at that presumptuous Denise trying to seduce she man.

Bap, bap, bap!!!! Licks throwing like madness. Now de man becomes a spectator to the fight that he just cause because he shudda loose off *from* Denise. De woman punching and slapping, and it look like she about to pick up a chair and whack Denise with it. By this time everybody in this little house party gathering around, but by Denise well-known for sheh bad reputation and some other women know sheh tuh, they not stopping de fight. They want the woman to 'gage in sheh ass.'[309] Then because the chair didn't land on Denise, the woman look like she going in she

---

[305] *Well acquainted and always together*
[306] *An open dwelling space under a house*
[307] *Girlfriend, lover*
[308] *Physically gyrating on someone close when dancing*
[309] *To aggressively beat up someone*

purse and in sheh rikatiks [310] now. Rose did seh that sheh hear that de ooman is ah ole "kangahlang."[311] But what she going in sheh purse fuh? Rass!!!

It look like something with a blade ...... is a knife!!! You mean some blood gon shed here tonight? Well, Roxanne now tackle the woman and tek way sheh bag. Thank God, the knife did fall out sheh haan and drop on the floor ...... or else she might have get she face cut or Denise might have been stabbed up. Then Roxanne feel sorry fuh she and grab Denise and flag down a car coming down Public Road, Kitty, and tassay[312] quick, quick. So that is how Debbie mother, Roxanne, and Denise did become spars[313] .... also because she; Denise, did never mess with any man that Roxanne did know .... end of story.

Oh shux!!! Ah did pramise fuh tell y'all whuh 'batty aan poe' means. That is like a rear end sitting on a posey[314] or "poe" to excrete in. In layman terms, a utensil to sit on and defecate or urinate where one cyaan function without each other ...... like those two who did become like best friends and going everywhere together.

So here comes Noel. Smiling as usual and he weighing down with the holiday mail under the Wednesday midday sun.

---

[310] *Madness with a bad temper*
[311] *A woman of rude character from back in de day*
[312] *Left*
[313] *Good friends*
[314] *A circular enamel utensil to urinate or defecate in*

Patsy did disappointed last time, so let us pray now for Little Debbie while Noel reaching in he pocket for a handkerchief to wipe de sweat that pouring down from he hair into he face.

But wait ah minute!!! The anxious little girl not seeing no box, not knowing that yuh dis have to go to the post office with the slip that Noel does give people to pick up the boxes. This is not like overseas where the mailman or lady comes in a truck and delivers letters by placing them in the mailboxes on individual houses or apartments. Boxes are delivered also mostly at people's door front by not only the Post Office, but by United Parcel Service, Fedex or other shipping companies. No, this is a country where the postman mostly walk on foot to the nearby houses to deliver mail. Yes, it kind of slower over here.

Meanwhile, Debbie biting sheh fingernails and looking so anxious that sheh little red face looking redder now. This little girl been looking out days now, and she getting more and more anxious because her uncle told Bridget to expect the box any time. Granny Tinsy noticing the little girl stressing, and says

"Ah dhoan like dis. All yuh doing is worrying. Dis aan no way fuh ah lil chile 'tek ahn'[315] *like dis in yuh yuteful days while yuh 'good fuh nutten'*[316] *motha deh some way enjoyin sheh self. But dhoan worry, yuh gon be ahrite. If de box aan come, ah gon*

---

[315] *Take on or be depressed over*
[316] *Good for nothing, or no good mother*

go by Barclays bank aan get some money, aan ah gon buy de tings yuh waan. Yuh hear mih?"

This newly adopted grandmother then grabs the little girl and squeezes her tightly as if she doesn't want to let go as a sign of comfort and adoration. Meanwhile, Noel is just two doorsteps away, but the little girl breaks loose from Granny Tinsy and runs to the postman. She is waiting patiently as he searches his stack of mail. Then just as the little girl begins to feel that she has no mail, he gives her a letter. She smiles and it appears now as from her gesticulations, one could see that she is enquiring about the box. This postman then further reaches into his pile of mail and hands her something that appears not to be a letter. He is looking apologetic now as Granny Tinsy then gets closer to her as the child is delayed for too long. This adopted grandmother then looks hypnotized by what appears to be a white slip. It look suh. Looks like the ones; the same white one that the mail man used to bring to we house stating that a box from overseas was at the post office for us and from whom.

I remember one time that when my mother did send us a box that did mark "Guyana" from Chicago, some fool in the post office did send that box to "Ghana." Now what the heck was that fool thinking? He or she don't know geography? He is ah ass or whuh? "Guyana" is in South America, not West Africa.

Now all ahwe Guyanese know that there is a far cry from where we come from, and you know what? Up to this day, I still

114

vex with de postman or woman because me and mih sisters were planning to go to a fete in we clothes and the darn things didn't come on time. Y'all know how yuh look when yuh 'laan up' at a party[317] in 'Straufuss' clothes ….. 'American' clothes. Yes, those clothes nice yuh see!!! Yvonne would agree because if she had them clothes with all the powder she put on, she would get more customers.

Ah hah, people call sheh ah 'viyahrago' aan seh all kinda tings bout sheh, but sheh wudda 'come off' at de party. [318]

Yes, again, I still vex that mih clothes din come in time to go to the party in Lamaha Gardens. We 'cudda talk cheese,' dey din sen it.[319]

Damn post office in Chicago!!! But the people in Ghana send it to the right place. Then they say African people ain't got no sense. Ah don't think so!!! That is de same people who build them pyramids, okay. I met nuff ah dem in the university in America and they brite[320] you see. Fela was always studying in the library. Topped our chemistry class and went on to become that pharmacist that he wanted to be, and you know what? He knew his geography. Nothing like that imbecile at the post office on the Westside of Chicago. Fela would have sent that damn box

---

[317] *'Arrive' at a party*
[318] *Yes, people call her a 'very contankerous person' and say all kind of things about her, but she would have 'looked nice' at the party*
[319] *We could have talked all we wanted' or fussed about it but they didn't send it*
[320] *They are very intelligent*

with we clothes to "Guyana." If only Fela was working at de post office ..... a little part-time job while in school. Then multiple boxes would of gone to they right destinations.

Little Debbie is lucky. Her box did not go to "Ghana." It came right where it belongs .... to "Guyana." Y'all think ah playing. I still got 'beef' with that postman or woman in that windy city. Yep, the little girl is holding her white slip. Betta she than we!!! Cause we own did take months to come. The slip that she will take to the post office by Robb Street fuh get sheh box.

Some people does get lucky and get boxes. Boxes from all over the place ...... boxes from England, boxes from America, boxes from Canada, boxes from Holland, boxes from Surinam, boxes from French Guiana, boxes from Panama, boxes from Belize, boxes from Venezuela, boxes from Brazil, boxes from Holland, boxes from Barbados, boxes from Trinidad, boxes from Saint Lucia, boxes from Jamaica, boxes from Antigua, boxes from Montserrat, boxes from Grenada, boxes from Guadeloupe, boxes from Dominica, boxes from Saint Kitts, boxes from Anguilla, boxes from Nevis, boxes from Martinique, boxes from de countryside and from de "bush" or hinterlands in Guyana, and boxes from all over de world, including some boxes from pen pals in Europe and all dem other countries in this universe. Of course, boxes is 'de ting' at this time of the year. But, bewildered Patsy still looking fuh sheh box. De only box she got in sheh house is a box with sheh few belongings.

Ain't Little Debbie luckier that she? This nice little girlie dressing right now to go with Bridget to the post office before they close. Man if yuh see dem!!! Bridget putting on de little girl 'Sunday Bess'[321] to go get the box. Bridget now beaming in smiles while she putting two big bright red ribbons in the little girl hair as it correlates with the colors of the holidays. Meanwhile Orin she very smart son reading the letter from Debbie uncle. He shouting out the things on the list as he other siblings getting excited. He mother face looking happy, happy, and she suddenly drops the comb on the floor beside them.

"*Mih haan get nervous. Ah excited yuh see. Ah cyaan wait tuh get de bax. De tings is fuh all ahwe. Dis gon be ah good Crismus mih chirren,*"[322] his mom says as they huddle closer to Orin to view the letter.

Granny Tinsy then chimes in saying, "*Gawd is good. Dis is ah good year fuh we. We aan gon get no 'white mouth' dis year.' We gon 'pack we belly.'*[323] *Plus we get de barrel laas week. Oh Gawd, we room full ah foodl. Yuh see 'duh man upstairs,' he good. Tell mih if he aan good? Dat's why yuh see people shud go tuh chuch aan pray to de Lord.*"

---

[321] '*The best dress or "Sunday Best" that someone has .... usually could be worn on a Sunday outing like church*

[322] "*My hand has gotten nervous. I am excited you see. I cannot wait to get the box. The things is for all of us. This is going to be a good Christmas my children.*"

[323] '*We are going to pack our belly' or eat a lot*

The children are grinning now, as they anticipate that more overseas items are soon going to be arriving at their house for the holidays. This time it is from Canada; a place that they hear is very cold from the letter that Orin was just reading. The letter also said that Ovid did work overtime to send the things and he crying out that he got arthritis in he right knee now, and that he wears three layers of clothes in Toronto when it gets below the twenties. Ovid working at a factory at night and got a part-time job at a tire shop in the daytime. "Is a good thing," he says, that his grandfather did teach he to change tires at he shop on Louisa Row.

"*It come in good,*"[324] he writes, since he was able to get a job with an Italian man as soon as he arrived. Then was able to save up some money quickly to move out from his cousin who sponsored him to live in Canada. He then got an apartment.

"*At ah cheap price,*" he says, and not far from the train station in a part of Toronto where he could travel to work with quick access on the subway back and forth.

He continues, "*I did take in a roommate and we splitting the rent. Is a Barbadian fellow and we getting along good. The rent is $500.00. Is two bedrooms with a slum lord and it need a little fixing up, but I glad for it.*"

---

[324] "*It paid off well.*"'

118

That time rents were cheap and people 'cudda see dey way.'[325] That's of course after he moved from Sarnia, Ontario, which was too isolated and where he couldn't see as much Caribbean people and moreso, little or no Guyanese like he sees now. He just like Bertie who refused to stay in Poughkeepsie, New York, because he said *"it was too country and was too far from Brooklyn."* Believe me, dem Guyanese like to go to a fete; a party where dey mattee deh. [326] That's a way of acculturating in these countries as they become a part of the cultural fiber with other immigrants. Anyhow, Little Debbie Uncle Ovid, got tired of he wutless sister Roxanne and come thru [327] this time fuh he niece. Last year he was not in a financial position to send a box and a letter with a lovely card for this nice little child, but this year he is showing her that he cares.

Like Miss Cheryl did say, *"dis ain gon be no deh bad Crismus."* This little girl has suffered enough from the 'lick aan promise' [328] from other relatives and friends who were supposed to send her a box also ………….

Sheh mother cousin in Holland did promise, sheh father brother in Trinidad did promise, sheh Godmother in New York did promise, sheh aunty in Canada did promise, sheh Godfather in England did promise, sheh mother other brother in Saint Lucia did

---

[325]   *'Could have managed monetarily'*
[326]   *Where their country folks are*
[327]   *Kept his promise*
[328]   *'A promise not kept'*

119

promise, sheh kindergarten teacher that did migrate to Barbados did promise, sheh once neighbor that now live in Anguilla did promise, sheh cousin in Venezuela did promise, sheh Grandmother landlady that living now in Brazil did promise, sheh father brother friend in England did promise, de lady that played the piano at the church that migrate to Sweden did promise .... all ah dem breaking they promises.

Indeed "promise is a comfort of a fool," making the little girl cry every day towards the holidays when she not hearing from them. Then the house sheh in ain't got no phone. As a matter of fact, is only one phone in Punchin Yard; in Gavin house. He is a stevedore and could afford one. Does charge a dollar for a local call, people say. But that is really he betta half [329] hustle. That's Carol ah talking about. She 'weigh down,' burdened down financially with all dem kids and had to leave sheh job at Forgarty's. She getting desperate now and everybody in the yard does get overseas calls on her fone, and she charging them three dollars to receive a call because she know that sheh neighbors desperate to speak to they relatives abroad and going to have a chance not only to hear they voice, but to beg them for something.

She aan ezee, eh?

Now who does charge for incoming calls, and look de price? Just because those calls from foreign. But I can't blame her

---

[329] *Partner*

120

because Gavin drinking out he money. He hardly giving she anything now and is hard for her to buy tennis rolls and cheese for the children snacks when they come home from school in the afternoon, or even flour for she to make some rock buns or bake. [330]

So ...... she devised a hustle. A good hustle. Ah hustle that is going to make her children eat well. Especially since is holiday time and all dem overseas calls coming in. She praying that everybody call, even though they be coming in sheh so-called living room with they dirty shoes with sand and mud on it and be messing up sheh polish floor. This is especially when the rain fall. Gosh!!! She hate when Sharon run up and down in sheh place getting all them calls from the men off them ships. You see Sharon got plenty money, so Carol charges her a dollar extra for a call. Sharon does not care that sheh being exploited because she makes money off those sailor men .... men from British ships, men from Norwegian ships, men from Greek ships, men from Panamanian ships, and men from Scottish ships. Then she also has customers on the local ships like Bookers. But, she does complain about dem Greek sailors. Said they get vex too much and "if yuh 'get tuh much on dey wrang side," [331] they would throw yuh overboard.

---

[330] *Buns for a snack made of flour and bake also but for mostly breakfast*
[331] *"And if you get too much on their wrong side"*

Eh, eh, but is whuh happen to this box that Little Debbie receiving? Well, ah think she and Bridget now on their way to the post office. Yep, ah told y'all so. Is after lunch and they heading to ketch a hire car to take them downtown. You could see the little girl from miles away in sheh red velvet dress and red ribbon bows. Them bows laughing on sheh head. They big like goat horns and bright to blind yuh eyes.

Oh Gawd, is whuh wrong wid sheh blasted Auntie Bridget?

The ribbon bows more than the little girl hair on sheh head. Weighing down sheh head, only to gih de lil chile a headache. Now does this make sense? Only in Guyana and some other places that these people does get so confused fuh Santa Day.

Don't talk bout Bridget!!!! She in a midrift top that yellow and a purple crimplene bell-bottom pants that covering sheh dilapidated pink kickers with heels that worn down. Y'all know now that that look crazy. She gone mad now in mismatching and wearing pants that don't suit sheh figure. She belly hanging over more than an inch over de trousers. Head not working right all because she so excited to go for a box at the post office, and want to look like she come 'from away.' [332] Then sheh nice curly hair that she get from sheh Chinee father and sheh black mother

---

[332] *"From abroad"*

supposed to look like an American afro like yuh see on Soul Train in America, but it looks like ah 'ants ness.'[333]

Is whuh is duh? Is whuh is duh pun sheh head?

Sheh could style up sheh hair instead of that crazy hairdo. Now she holding de child hand and reminiscing about the day she received her barrel. She thinking and thinking and getting more excited and a car almost lick dem down[334] because she crossing de road bad.

A woman looking at her like she head not good. Looking down at sheh foot side. De woman can't believe what she seeing!!! Pink kickers; those pink high heel shoes with them fat heels that need throwing away. The woman laughing and showing sheh friend Bridget shoes. But you think Bridget cares, cause she going and get the box ...... that very important box her household so desires and very excited about.

Bridget don't give a damn. *"Leh sheh karry sheh skunt,"* [335] Bridget is saying to herself.

She want to say it out aloud, but "Lil Deb" there and sheh don't want to look like a rude and unruly woman. Cannot add to de lil chile anxiety. After all, this was a moment that her now

---

[333] *Her hair that looks like bush; bushy and untidy looking or unkept or disheveled*
[334] *Knocked them up*
[335] *"Let her carry her skunt/backside".. a profanity*

adopted daughter has been waiting for after numerous promises, and hence, disappointments.

Finally, the moment is here, and the two people have arrived at their destination …… the Post Office. Hallelujah!!! At last!!! They are extremely overjoyed as they make their way to join the line ahead of them, while the little girl clutches dearly unto the long awaited white slip. By this time, Bridget has become the center of attraction for all of the onlookers within the confines of this place where letters, small parcels and boxes come and go all day long. Noel, their postman, sees them and hides, as he is imagining what has gone wrong with Bridget's attire today.

"She must not be seeing right," he is saying to himself, as he stares questioningly at her midrift top, her stomach that is ridiculously hanging over her pants, and those pink shoes that needs discarding in the garbage.

He now comforts himself with the idea that she is getting a replacement in the box. But he did see the box and little do they know, it was not as big as these two people might be thinking. Only he, and he alone, have this knowledge and they will soon find out for themselves. Yuh know this is how my country folks and them other immigrants does think at this time of the year …… all of them expecting big boxes from overseas and letters with money inside. Is as if money giving away abroad. That's why

Ernest din gih ah shit [336] and "chilling." Puffing on he joint or tobacco leaf filled with ganja and not thinking about he mother and all them who think he sending them a barrel. Lying every time he call them on the telephone with he empty promises with he spliff and Heineken in he hand, and talking in the slangs he pick up in New Jersey and from he Caucasian girlfriend and he so-called friends on the street.

"What's crackin? Say man, Imma send you a barrel. You dig it? Just mail me a letter with all dat you want, yuh feel me. Hurry up and holla at a cat if you trynna cop some dead presidents too cuz I'm all about bizness and helping a brotha out," as he gives out a very boisterous obnoxious laughter when hanging up the phone.

Then to his mother ……. *"Ma, Imma get you some bread, don't trip. I ain't jivin you ma, the barrel gon be there."*

Then he rambles on about what shipping companies he knows and that the barrels would not cost too much to send, knowing very well that he was not going to help anyone in the family whom he had promised. That "Wutless Ernest" ……. another visa wasted by the American Embassy!!! Not worth the while for that son-of-a-bitch. Living on the puh ooman and not 'tunnin ah straw.' Get "sweet skin*"[337]* when he come to America. Is a good thing that Miss Ethel niece didn't send fuh he in England.

---

[336] *Did not care*

[337] *Living on the poor woman and not 'getting mobilized to do anything in life. 'Get lazy.'*

Why? Because he is a disgrace to all dem hardworking Guyanese men. Bertie know he, went and visit he one time and left never to return.[338] Did not want to be associated with that lazy, good for nothing man. Then he ask Bertie to borrow some money from he hardworking security job in the Bronx. Complaining bout how New Jersey colder than Brooklyn and the Bronx.

But what about Manhattan? That darn idiot!!! Who be galavanting all up in colder places like Buffalo and Boston in the dead winter. Even went to Alaska a time running after a woman. See how man is? Would travel to de end of the world fuh run down skirt tail[339]. Doing duh while always promising he family barrels at the end of the year and he stuphid girlfriend that he be cheating on lying fuh he tuh. 'Hard up' girl.[340] Like if she cyaan get another man. She want a lying confidence-trickster so bad? He and worthless Roxanne should hook up together and be the lying couple in this book.

"Yuh feel me," as he would say. But he think he slick and it going to turn round on he. I mean karma going to be his reward one day. The only thing I really feel bad about is that he mother caught up in he lies bout he going to send a barrel with a fridge in it. Year after year…….. and the same lies. Darn fool. Wearing a suit and a briefcase every time he go out to impress people, especially when he go to Brooklyn and playing a big shot on he

---

[338] *Went and looked for him once and left*

[339] *To run after women*

[340] *Lying for him too 'Desperate' girl*

ex-classmates from Christ Church Secondary School. Like if they don't know he is a 'pressah foot,' "ain fit ah shit" aan 'lyin thru he teeth.'[341] That's why they don't invite he to they class reunion parties.

"Ain't nobody got time fuh dat." No, they don't want to see that fool. No, not at all, okay!!! Them colored girls don't want he either. They could do well without he and he bogus self with he throw off clothes[342] from he cousin who it is said works on Wall Street, and whose clothes Ernest dis only wear, but don't take to the cleaners. Always with a ring around he collar. Nasty, but always 'pompazetin'[343] he self, and ah know he tuh. Who aan know he!!!

Laas time ah did 'buck up' pun he on Flatbush, he tellin mih stupitness aan ah mek he feel like 'ah cent ice in ah glass ah mauby.' Yes, ah did. He 'meet he meter'[344] with me. Steupppppppse!!! Vexation to we spirit and we "kinna."[345] But that's all for that fool, cause we have to check in back with Bridget and Little Debbie who been standing in the post office line for sometime now.

Ahrite, ah seeing now!!! Look like they moving up slowly but surely, as the woman anticipating this "big box" remains the

---

[341] *Is an 'imposter.' "No good" and "always lying."*
[342] *Pretensive self with his second-hand clothes*
[343] *Showing off*
[344] *And I made him feel like a nobody. Yes, I did. He met the right one with me.*
[345] *Our dislike*

center of attraction. She just see sheh next door neighbor over the fence next to Punchin Yard and calling out to her. Want Beryl to see that she in the line to receive boxes. Showing all she teeth with one missing on the side that downplaying sheh high cheek bones and nice sexy slanted eyes. Talking above the normal tone of her voice while the anxious little girl grabs onto her midrift shirt.

Miss Beryl then comes over to her and shares her excitement. They are both engaging in a discourse that is only focusing on how lucky Bridget's family is this year, and what they will be cooking for December 25th. The lady is also skillfully pleading for help as she is indicating that she will have little or no local, much less foreign food to include in her menu. But yuh think Bridget listening to her? Sheh mind is on 'what and what' is in the box, as Little Debbie is now nervously clinging to the string on her bell-bottomed pants. Beryl seems now to be understanding that all she is saying is coming out one ear, and going through the other of her so-called friend and next yard neighbor. This lady then rather disappointingly bids her farewell.

"Ah gon do fuh sheh, sheh showin off sheh self,"[346] she grumbles to herself while walking away. *"Is only time wid me aan Bridget. Ah gon ketch sheh ah day. Dis life aan done yet."* She then quickens her footsteps ….. increases her steps faster in vexation as she walks away.

---

[346] *"I am going to do for her, " or retaliate since she is showing off and acting better than me*

128

The two women had often times leaned over the fence talking not only about each other's neighbors in both Punchin Yard and the alley way, but also about the current events in Guyana, including how much prices were rising in food items and other matters. Also, about how hard it is for Beryl to take care of three small children since their dad had been locked up in jail over a year for pick-pocketing a tourist on Main Street. But, Bridget pretended in the post office like she hardly had known this "very nice lady," as she had often described her, aan din 'bat an eye' [347] on Beryl's lamentations all because she was about to receive a box from Canada. See how people stay? Thinking now like she better than this woman and don't want to hear anything about her struggles, and acting like a 'neva see come fuh see.'[348]

"Next" ..... a burly and rather handsome man shouts at the counter. Then impatiently, he yells the word out aloud again ..... *"NEXT."*

By this time, the little girl and adopted mother moves up to the counter and the former hands the slip now almost drenched with perspiration to the postal clerk. He looks at the little hands and comes to the conclusion that it is because of her nervousness that the palm of her right hand is sweating profusely.

"Have you ever received a box before from overseas little one?" that is grammatically correct and not in the typical

---

[347] *And didn't 'listen to or pay attention to'*
[348] *Not accustomed to anything*

Guyanese creolese spoken by the natives. This is a variable that tells us that he had been well-schooled and refuses to speak in broken English at all times. He then smiles in anticipation that this child will say "yes."

By this time Bridget is explaining to her what the word "overseas" means and reconstructs the sentence very quickly...... *"He mean if yuh eva did get ah bax 'from away'..... before?"* [349]

Little Debbie then shakes her head from side to side as if to say "no." This is how most kids in this country and even adults would respond physically when saying other than "yes." Immediately after, the man leaves the counter and has gone to the back to retrieve the box. Of course, also after Bridget has shown him her passport as an ID card since the child's uncle had also addressed the slip to her.

Ah hearing somebody trying to ask me what Bridget doing with a passport ...... mine ..... mind yuh damn business!!! Leh we concentrate on this box.

Well, de story behind she passport is that sheh brother did say he going to send for her and she scraped up all she fine change; all she few jills[350] to go get it. Even she mommy Grandma Tinsy did withdraw she few shillings; money out of Bank of Guyana to help sheh daughter go to America, but de boy never did send de

---

[349] *"He means if you ever got a box 'from abroad' before?"*
[350] *Her few coins/pennies*

letter of invitation. Six years now and he still ain't do it. Only got he sister on a false promise. Not far from you know who? But, we ain gon call name. So, all "B" does do is walk round de place with de passport in sheh handbag. Only a picture in a book, but no stamp from the American Embassy. No visa inside. Puh ting!!!!

But anyway, let's get back to business ...... is de box we did talking about. A box that de little girl did never receive in sheh life and she excited. Excited now that she two hair ribbons sticking out like she just got electrocuted from the excitement, while she companion striking a pose in she throw off American clothes with sheh protuberant abdomen like she five months pregnant in pants that don't suit sheh.

Oh, if you see Bridget!!! Man she looking and looking and like the clerk can't come quick enough. Stretching sheh neck and looking like a gaulin; that white bird that be grazing by the water all over the place with the long neck.

"Whapnin? Is how he tekkin suh long wid de dam bax?"
351

She is looking impatient now, and finally sheh see he coming while the little girl peeping from under sheh armpit.

---

351 *"What is happening? Is how he taking so long with the damn box?"*

131

But, wait a minute!!!! He don't look like he 'straining.' [352] He face ain't got that grimace. He looking comfortable. He don't look like he fetching anything heavy. Bridget 'stupsing up sheh mouth' [353] like she vex now and de little girl suspecting that something ain't rite. The clerk is almost to the counter. Ooops!!! Ah don't like de look of this. He resting the box on the counter.

"It look suh small," the annoyed woman saying to herself, while the disappointed little girl looking like she want to cry.

Oh Gawd!!! Why Uncle Ovid kunta send[354] a bigger box than that? Now he got them wondering if all he promise in the letter is in the box. Look like it measure 20 inches across and 15 inches tall. Don't run fuh y'all rulers or tape measures .... allyuh Guyanese people not ezee!!! Tek time and mek a good guess in yuh heads. Tek time and visualize how this box look. Raphi, I know you done figure it out ...... genius!!!

Well, de box aan suh big as we all did expect, and de lil gurl look like she waan cry[355] again since she know how a big box look like. She been standing in de line too long fuh not know how a big box look because a lady in front of them just collect one ..... a big, big, big one from England which sheh son had to help sheh fetch pun a dolley. Yes, or he wudda strain, was gone be too heavy to fetch. Y'all laughing? Yes, it did too heavy and it look like it

---

[352] *A facial expression denoting that something you are lifting is heavy*
[353] *Sucking on her teeth in vexation*
[354] *"Why he couldn't (as in asking a question) have sent/'*
[355] *The little girl looks like she wants to cry*

got all kinds ah nice things in it. Now that's what I call a box from foreign.

Oh shux!!! Now somebody coming in the post office with a wheelbarrow. Yes, a wheelbarrow!!! Is I seeing rite? Now who does go to pick up a box with something like duh? Only Lenny …. with he mother taggling behind he, and he talking loud, loud, loud as if nobody else in de place. Talking and yelling at he mama who people seh deaf and pun top uh duh[356], he look like he waan put sheh fuh sid down pun it while they in de line. One wonders if he bring sheh pun it as they live further up Robb Street; de same street as de Post Office since sheh cyaan walk too far or fast. Sheh is eighty-seven years old and with sheh little mileage running out, and he ain't got no patience with sheh. Yes, you see why a man nodding he head in confirmation that duh is how he bring sheh. On the wheelbarrow. Somebody just ask he why he didn't leave her at home and he seh that de slip to collect the box is addressed to her, and that he just come to help out. Then he used a few profanities cussing he sista in de Bronx as if sheh dhoan trust he. Lenny who like Carol man, that cyaan *see* a rum bottle.

Now, now, now!!! Debbie with sheh little red [357] self looking pink and maybe, furious, since even though she may not understand what it is to be furious, the facial expressions of her make-belief mom has triggered her emotions to the point where it

---

[356] *And on top of that*
[357] *Light complexioned self*

has affected her epidermis. She just scratched sheh skin since it appears now that the nervousness giving sheh a rash like an anaphylactic reaction. Puh chile!!!

Bridget is now muttering to herself, *"ah mess up. Ah shudda walk wid de letter in mih haanbag aan open dis bax rite heh, aan check fuh see if everyting inside dat he seh he sen is truh."* [358]

She then turns and cuts up her eyes [359] at the clerk who just gave her the box, as if he is responsible for it's size.

"All de way from Canada aan dis is whuh Ovid sen? Dis blasted small ass bax?"

She is so angry now that she just stomped her feet and one of her shoe heel falls off. She is limping now and feels embarrassed as she is receiving even more attention from onlookers because of her gait or manner of walking.

"Ah need fuh fine ah place aan open dis bax," she grumbles to herself, then yells, '*Oh Gawd, mih shoe bruk up now."*

Meanwhile, Little Debbie begins to look confused and yawns. After all, this little girl has seen enough for the day including her adopted mother who is now walking 'hopety-

---

[358] *I messed up. I should of walked with the letter in my handbag and open this box right here, and check to see if everything inside that he said he sent is true*
[359] *Looked at him in anger with her eyelids blinking*

134

drop'[360] with only one side shoe on. This scenario becomes so frustrating for this puh lil God Angel that she asks Bridget to use the bathroom.

"Ah haffa open de bax Deb. Ah waan see if ah shoe inside as Ovid did pramise. Yuh aan see mih one side shoe ain good no moe, aan ah had to throw it away?"

The child then nods her head, as Bridget adds, *"ah gon tek yuh inside Brown Betty fuh pee, ahrite. Ah pramise yuh."*[361] Then she beckons for them to sit on the sidewalk around the corner from the post office.

"It nice aan clean heh. We cud sit heh."

Little Debbie then looks down at her dress. That red velvet dress that looks immaculately clean and hesitates to sit, as if saying that it will get ripped from the edge of the concrete that is protruding from the grass.

"Is ahrite, yuh dress gon be ahrite. De place clean." Eager to open the box, "B" then attempts to cut the tape with the sharpest of her fingernails, but to no avail, it refuses to cut.

---

[360] *'Lopsided'*
[361] *"I am going to take you inside Brown Betty to urinate, okay. I promise you."*

"Is whuh kinda tape is dis? It suh strang. Ah cyaan get dis ting open."[362]

Meanwhile she forgets that the little girl has to urinate. She is tugging the tape and trying now to bite it with her teeth, but again, to no avail.

"It ain 'comin tuh come. It suh hard fuh cut,"[363] she fidgets again. Then she gets up and searches around for a sharp object on the ground and does not find any.

"Even ah nail wud wuk," she grumbles. *"Ah shudda bring mih scissors if ah did know dat mih shoe wudda bruk. Well is whuh kinda shit ah put mihself in heh tuhday?"*

Then gets worked up again and complains ….. *"aan I ain even bring enuf money fuh buy ah scissors. Oh, ah got ah idea!!! Ah gon go in duh store ova deh aan ask them fuh cut it fuh mih."*

She then smiles and with box in one hand, and with the little girl's right hand in the other, she walks briskly in her one shoe to the store. She is looking off balance now but does not care since her agenda is to satisfy her curiosity. Has she lost her mind? This is total nonsense, as walking with one side shoes is not only uncomfortable, but could affect her physically. We ain gon tell sheh dat cause sheh might 'buse'[364] we out as we done see that

---

[362] *"Is what kind of tape is this? It is so strong. I cannot get this thing open."*
[363] *"It is 'not making progress.' It is so hard to cut"*
[364] *To abuse verbally or curse someone out*

sheh in a bad mood .... a very, very bad mood with sheh black, black foot bottom. Germs galore!!!

"He suppose tuh send mih ah nice pair ah sneakers aan some dress shoes," she reminisces.

"Excuse mih Miss Lady, ah cud borrow y'all scissors?"

It is a fabric store, and of course, there are many scissors in here. A young woman then hands her one. Bridget snatches it so quickly that she could have damaged a customer beside her or Little Debbie. It is as if time is running out; as if this box is going to disappear in thin air, and as if its contents would disappear also. She is now managing to get the tape off.

"Is whuh wid Ovid? All dis dam tape. Is whuh wrong wid he? He put tuh much on. He mus be use ah whole roll pun dis lil bax,'" as she is viciously trying to cut through the very resilient tape.

Then finally, the box opens up and the little child is curiously peeping in while Bridget looks harder. Perusing its contents as if she is checking the things mentally against the letter that her son Orin had read to her before she left her house. She is now outside the store. Debbie is looking drained and frustrated from an obvious adrenalin rush as her companion is beginning to swear louder and louder.

"Is whuh de hell is dis? Is whah kinda skunt is dis? Ai ain seein no shoes nor de doll fuh yuh Debbie. Whuh kineah[365] small ass bax is dis? Dese tings look like some clothes people done wear. . Is wheh he get dese tings from? Then it look like people perspiration pun dem. Must be whuh yuh call it? Ah hear dem people away does go to 'triff'.... she means 'thrift' stores.... *"aan den dis lie aan seh is new tings, "* while the confused looking child stares at her.

She is digging deeper now as some of the items are almost about to fall on the filthy pavement.

"Aan is wheh yuh toys deh? Oh Gawd, all ah see is one pair ah shoes fuh yuh Debbie aan it dhoan look like it cud fit yuh. Leh mih see something .... Oh Gawd, de bottom look like it wear. Like is some chile done wear it in Canada. It second haan. Look it gat some black tings pun it. Look nuh Debbie. Cheap skate!!! Now he aan send mih de shoes he pramise mih nor fuh dem boys fuh go tuh 'chuch.' Ah did always know he was ah blasted lier. Gawd, is whuh aan gon do?"

She then digs more to the bottom of the box and sees a pair of brown rainboots that Ovid had mentioned was for Granny Tinsy.

"Ah gon gaffuh wear dis home even dough it lil big."[366]

---

[365] *"What kind of small ass box is this?"*
[366] *"I am going to have to wear this home even though it is a little big."*

She then slips them on and discards the last survivor of her pink kickers onto the roadway with a delirious anger, as if she was pelting Ovid. This is after tossing the broken one earlier on by the post office and it did almost hit a man. She is swearing louder now but calms herself down as she and the little girl enters the door of Brown Betty restaurant. Its patrons are appalled at her appearance since her attire seems as bizarre as her boisterous behavior that was loud enough for them to hear her before she entered the door. Little Debbie then rushes to the toilet. This is the kind of thing that they say in Guyana that causes chirren to get 'weak bladduh.'[367] They suppose to go when they have to go!!! When they have to urinate. Selfish Bridget ….. all caught up with the box. That box from Canada that was supposed to be bigger than that.

"*Wait till dem chirren see. Oh Gawd, is whuh is dis heh, eh Deb? People suh full ah shit. When yuh grow up yuh mus tell de truth. Yuh promise mih*"?

The little child then nods her head in compliance which is still burdened down by those heavy ribbon bows. They are about to take another hire car now by Stabroek Market to head home. What an experience for such a young person? Bridget has truly added so much drama to the entire event of going to the post office that this day is appearing to be a catastrophe.

---

[367] *Damage to their bladder to the extent that she will not be able to hold in her urine*

"Inside, inside. We reach. If allyuh only know."[368]

By now, Bridget's children are at the front door. Orin, as detailed as he is, meets her with Ovid's letter in hand to double-check the box's contents. He could safely presume from the size, that it could not hold the forty-one items that the sender had declared was inside. The boys are looking disappointed with her other son Trevor looking like he want to cry.

"Eh, eh, is whuh ah seeing? Duh is de bax? Duh is whuh he sen? Is whuh wrong wid Ovid? Ah did tell yuh dat he is ah lier. Ah blasted lier. Talkin bout he sennen ah big bax. Look ah fed up yeh."

That's Granny Tinsy's remarks after scrutinizing the box as Bridget struggles to take off the now tangled tape. Little Debbie is now fast asleep on the bedding on the left side of the floor in the room, and curled up in fetal position as she is extremely tired from her gruelling experience. One of her ribbon bows has abandoned it's post like a sentry at a military base and is now on the floor by her left ear. What a relief indeed. "Yes, I repeat ...... "like a sentry in a military base" that tired of standing at de gate and just run and leff it. Yes, that thing which is bigger that the plait on the left side of her head has caused her a headache during the entire trip. What a burden!!! The other bow looks like it wants to jump off also, but is hesitant since it is enjoying its place as the

---

[368] *"Inside, inside. We reach. If you all only know."*

140

only one left, and appears to look now like a red dog ear like Clifford on the children cartoon. Indeed, it has gotten a whole lot of attention today. Nevertheless, its victim is getting the much needed sleep that she has been yearning for hours now, and is totally unaware of the outbursts from the other household members.

"*He aan 'fit ah shit.*'[369] *Dat Ovid. He rass yuh see. Mek mih rush down deh aan de bax aan got nutten much. We waste we time yeh. Puh Debbie. Owh, ah sorry fuh sheh. Sheh no good motha yuh see, aan de lass person was Ovid. Aan he let sheh down. He cudda send sheh 'dollie.*'[370] *Jesus Christ, ah hate he!!! Dem dis get opportunity fuh go away aan dis mess up. Ai waan go away tuh, but ah ain gat nobody fuh sponsuh mih. Yuh see if ai went away, ai wudda neva do duh. Pramise people ..... aan den dis disappaint dem.*"

The bewildered Bridget then yawns as Orin and his other siblings is checking everything that came.

"Mom, I have scrutinized the entire content of the box," Orin yells.

"*Repeat whuh yuh just seh, ai ain understaan whuh yuh jus seh?*" his mommy replies.

---

[369] "*He is not worth it.*"
[370] *Her 'doll'*

The young man smiles and repeats in layman terms ....
"Mommy I mean I have looked over the box and checked out all
that is inside. The items that Mr. Ovid sent, that is."

His mother squints her eyes as if she is now
comprehending what her son is saying. Remember, he is known
as the "English Duck" [371] in the yard, and had passed the Common
Entrance Exam to go to Queen's College. Despite the fact that
they tease him sometimes, they are proud of this very brilliant
young man.

He then further adds, *"mom, one bag of white socks, a little
girl Cinderella sheet set in the bottom for Debbie, I guess. Three
jerseys[372] of all sizes and three rolls of toilet paper wrapped up in
them, a bag of sweety or candies, one can of kidney beans, two
hard pants,[373] a nightgown for Debbie, one pack of pencils, a pack
of pens, and a pack of college-ruled paper"* ....all not
wrapped up and some tied up in the sheet that was at the top of the
box. Plus de rubberboots that Bridget got on.

*"No wonda ah kunta[374] guh down moe in de bax. All ah
cudda get was tuh de jerseys, aan de nite gown aan de rainboots.
Blasted lier!!! Yuh sure Orin, yuh sure duh is all? Aan who tell he
we waan tailet paper. We is shit he think? He full ah shit."* Bridget
then adds, *"aan who seh we waan skool tings. Skool done open*

---

[371] *A term originating from a British education and someone who speaks perfect English*
[372] *Three t-shirts*
[373] *Denim Pants*
[374] *No wonder I couldn't have*

142

aan mih cousin Lorraine in Barbados done sen pencils aan suh fuh y'all." Then is more agitated and adds, "*aan we waan any kidney beans? We ain got bad kidneys like dem fuckin people ova deh. Sorry mih chirren fuh cussin.*"

Uh, uh!!! Look like Uncle Ovid collect those school things at a back-to-school event in Canada. Y'all overseas Guyanese know what I talking bout. Think he slick and don't want to spend money. Pacifying he little niece by padding up de box with dem tings so that it could look big. I don't like he. Damn scamp!!! De Canadian government should send he back home fuh he lyingness. Take away he visa.

Meanwhile, Granny Tinsy has taken Debbie to the other pretense room, changed and spunge sheh off.[375] Then tucked her into bed.

"*Oh Gawd!!! Ah fuhget we ain eat. Gawd, we did too busy wid de bax. Duh fuck up box,*" [376] yells a very frustrated and deranged looking Bridget.

The old woman then responds, "*mine de lil gurl get gas.[377] Owh, yuh cudda get shih two cheese rolls aan ah glass ah 'swank'*

---

[375] *To tidy up with a rag or wash cloth with water in a receptacle, and not a shower*
[376] *"Oh God!!! I forget we didn't eat. God, we were too busy with the box. That fucked up box."*
[377] *Mind/be careful the little girl get gas*

143

³⁷⁸ or a sweet drink from Bernard stand. Yuh know sheh like cheese. Owh, puh chile, owh!!!"

The old woman then shakes her head from side to side and looks at her daughter in disgust. If she was younger she would have ring her ears³⁷⁹ or pick up the wire cane and 'gaghe in sheh ass.' I mean give her a flogging for not adhering to her advice before she left the house. As we could all see, she neglected to feed the child when they were on the road. Moreso, since Granny Tinsy had given her some money to buy "Lil Deb" a snack.

The old woman then complains again, *"den yuh pass by Brown Betty, yuh kunta buy sheh ah cone aan someting fuh eat; ah nice big cone wudda full sheh up lil bit caus sheh belly small."* She then sucks her teeth.

Bridget apologizes as she senses her mother's anger and they both are discussing the box again, then decide not to announce to the yard about their profuse disappointment with its content, as this was the opposite to how they had felt when they had received their barrel a few days ago. This one is a letdown, and surely confirms that not every relative in America or Canada or England, or elsewhere keeps a promise in its entirety. Then even if some do, they are not quite truthful as to the content of whatever they send you; whether barrel or box. Now who dis sen³⁸⁰ a box

---

³⁷⁸ *Ah glass of lime water sweetened with sugar*
³⁷⁹ *Turn one of her ears with one hand in a circular and painful way*
³⁸⁰ *Who sends*

144

like that 'from away?' Dat was ah real 'shockatock'[381] fuh Bridget aan dem, and now she screaming to the top of sheh voice before going to bed ……..

"Ah feel 'like ah cent ice in ah glass ah mauby.'[382] Y'all hear mih? Ah waste mih time today. Ah sarry, but is not mih fault chirren. All ah want is fuh Lil Debbie aan all ahwe enjoy de halidays."

She then yawns, as Grandma Tinsy watches her daughter abuse her pillow from her day's pent up anger. More than ten minutes has elapsed and she is now slowly falling asleep. What a day!!!

---

[381] *A huge shock. An unexpected one*
[382] *"I feel so terrible. I feel so small and embarrassed "*

Last Dash

Patsy at work thinking, thinking, thinking. Thinking what she should do. She can't make up sheh mind. She is not feeling so well today and all week long she lock up in the house hiding from sheh neighbors in Punchin Yard. She stop chiming in when Gavin waking up the whole yard with that noisy motorcycle, and as a matter of fact, another fight did break out with he and Carol earlier this morning. Looks like he did want his betta half[383] to make him some tea cause you know now that he getting up late from staying out all night drinking. But, Patsy just went back to sleep after Miss Doris and the others had intervened and stopped the fight. Even Sam did throw a few punches at Gavin and reminded him that he is a coward that must be afraid to fight a man.

"Yuh fight ooman, den fight mih. Yuh is ah coward or whuh? Ah wud whip yuh ass yuh see. Always beatin up de ooman when yuh drunk, aan yuh pickney dem seein. Fight mih now ah seh, becauz yuh know dat we dhoan beat ooman up suh. Yuh motha wudda neva like duh yuh know. Ah sure sheh teach yuh fuh respek wimen." He then pauses again with a balled up fist, looks at Gavin, and continues ……… *"skunt hole."*[384]

---

[383] *Partner*
[384] *A profanity*

By this time 'Mouth ah Preh Preh' Doris is almost in Gavin and Carol house. Seems like she does not sleep at all because whenever an incident occurs in the yard, she is the first to appear on the scene like a police detective.

"Yes, yuh motha din teach yuh dat, ah sure Gavin. Yuh jus dhoan kaye. Yuh come in drunk aan *allways beatin up Carol. Owh, ah feel suh sorry fuh sheh. Owh, sheh is ah good ooman. Den yuh come in aan waan fuh put yuhselj in sheh in de nite when yuh horney. Den next morning yuh beat sheh. We ain gon staan fuh dat no moe. All ahwe fed up wid yuh beatin up pun Carol with yuh drunken self. Dem chirren sufferin tuh seeing dey motha like dis,"* Miss Doris reiterates after a very angry Sam.

Carol then emerges to her front door with tears in her eyes. She is now pleading to her neighbors to help her get to her mother's house.

"Ah cyaan tek dis no moe. Ah fed up yuh see. Plus dis is Crismus time aan he aan even buy nutten fuh dem chirren, but beatin mih up. Drinkin out he money aan gamblin tuh. Hardly anyting fuh eat in heh. Is only leff fuh me aan mih chirren get white mouth. [385] *We properly punishin. Ah waan go to motha house in Wortmanville. At least me aan dem chirren cud get ah nice Crismus."*

---

[385] *When the corners of the mouth is white and one looks malnourished*

147

Many of the neighbors are agreeing that they could help her to get there later in the day. Gavin then emerges through the doorway as if nothing had happened earlier and walks to his bike, revs it up, and proceeds to work. Of course he is going to work late, and does not look embarrassed as he has little equilibrium which suggests that he is stale drunk. Usually, like most alcoholics, when he gets completely sober after sleeping, he will not remember today's events unless if someone relates to him what had exactly happened.

"Ah dhoan know whuh yuh talkin bout Dookram. Yuh lyin,"[386] with most times an innocent look.

That is Gavin's usual response over and over, and over again, unless the evidence is a buss head[387] or bruised up face that he had obtained from falling down and hurting himself from being overly intoxicated. When there is no proof, he would usually smile and reach for a cigarette in his pocket. This appears to be his coping mechanism and an alternative to answering. One wonders if there is any guilt or a conscience since he sometimes exhibits the characteristics of a sociopath which could be induced by his alcoholism.

---

[386] *"I don't know what you're talking about Dookram. You are lying"*
[387] *A burst head that has a wound/cut open*

"Is ah shame," Sharon yells after him. *"Yuh is ah stevedoe aan ain gat no money. Yuh shud gat money. Yuh 'pickin fares'*[388] *wid it tuh? Maylene did tell mih dat yuh sooring sheh."*

The neighbors are silent now......is as if one could hear a pin drop.

"Oh shit," Miss Cheryl exclaims, while Carol becomes tight-lipped from shock.

This is news for the residents of the yard for gossip today. Miss Doris looks excited and glances over to Ethel; her gossiping partner. Now allyuh know what to expect .... 'nuff, nuf' talking about this drunken man and his "betta half" [389] as on the other hand, we may want to call him; her "worst half."

But like we forgetting Patsy, and getting absorbed in the domestic problems between Gavin and Carol. Remember we in the "last dash" before the holidays and Patsy got so much typee ..... meaning she lovelorn and ain't even prepared for the auspicious day. Is Christmas Eve day after tomorrow, and she still in a trance over Bertie while Stanley still going after her. He in love with she, and she in love with Bertie. Now ain't this something?!!! Anyhow, sheh head on sheh boyfriend in New York and she cyaan function. She is a mess you see. She forgetting that she got to get up at a certain time to go to work, and she arriving

---

[388] *'Soliciting prostitutes for pleasure'*
[389] *Partner or girlfriend*

to work late. She not cleaning her little place, she not washing her clothes, she bathing only six times a week when she used to bathe about thirteen times, she not visiting sheh family in Meadow Brook thrice a week like sheh used to, she not coming outside in the yard like before to even empty sheh potty in de latrine, she not eating and drinking like before, and most of all, she not answering the door when Daphne banging away at it. We blame sheh?

She doesn't answer because she knows the girl crazy about candy canes and she ain't got none. All she doing is coming home from work and jumping de fence from over on the alleyway side near sheh door so that sheh neighbors don't see sheh, and sitting in she little chair or on sheh little cot crying. Crying fuh Bertie because sheh not hearing from he and is now Thursday afternoon when everybody on they "last dash." She thinking now that he auntie keeping secret fuh he, and maybe the secret is that he got a woman up there in New York. The reason she getting more worried now is because the Auntie Avril always telling sheh when sheh call is that *"he nat home."*

"But how come he neva home no moe?" Patsy is asking herself. *"Nat at lease one time wen ah call?"*[390] while laying in supine position.

Her imagination is running wild now and she is starting to sob; trying not to cry too hard for Carol to hear her because the

---

[390] *"But how come he is never home anymore?" Patsy is asking herself. "Not at least one time when I call?"*

walls thin. See, they living in a cottage that the landlord rent them that break up into two small rooms, put front doors on them with no separate rooms like a kitchen and bedrooms, and have them sharing the same makeshift zinc sheet bathroom and 'latrine' outside. Some of them even lucky if they get a window. So the walls thin, thin and everybody could hear one another business cause is as if they in the same house. Even they does hear when each other getting intimate with their partners.

This does make Patsy jealous because intercourse with Bertie brings back sweet memories and pleasant nostalgia. She dis dream of him caressing her nipples and entire breasts, caressing her neck, caressing the lobes of her ears with his fingers and nibbling at her ears with his tongue, caressing her back, caressing her thighs, caressing her buttocks, caressing her all over. Then she does remember his juicy tongue enticing her mouth, and his anatomy teasing her clitoris, then entering her body to an explosive climax. This is what my American friend Lee would say, "exploding like cherry bombs and fireworks on the 4th of July." Allyuh see what ah talking about?

Y'all now know why Patsy head tie up in sheh man. Allyuh now see why she not preparing for the holidays. All de neighbors getting they groove on at nite, and she nostalgic. Nostalgic and longing fuh sheh man; longing fuh de lovemaking too .... not one, but almost three years now. Entertaining pleasant memories of she and Bertie in bed and craving for his chocolate colored body.

151

Cyril, the little boy that used to play hide-and-seek with the little girls in the yard and molesting them after telling them that they going to be mommy and daddy, talking loud outside Patsy window about how he going down Regent Street, Water Street and by the Vendor's Arcade with he mommy to shop. The little "force ripe"[391] boy so excited you see. He yelling at the top of he voice, and just wake up Patsy. After she did start reminiscing, she fell in a doze. I mean she was sleeping lightly before that boisterous boy started to raise he voice hard, hard. He talking to Saheed, Dookram son, about what he mother buying he for Christmas.

"Ah going tuh see Santa Claus at Bookers," Saheed replies, *"ah excited man. Ah waan tuh get ah good gift. Meh lil sista did cry laas year. She afraid of Santa and sheh cry all de way home. Sheh jump outta Santa lap wen he put sheh pun he lap, and mih fatha had tuh run afta sheh. Sheh get bigga dis year, suh ah dhoan tink sheh gon do dat."*

Cyril eyes starts to light up and he is yelling again, *"what yuh waan from Santa dis year Saheed? Ah gon ask mih motha fuh carry mih tuh."*

Then he mumbles on and on about all of the toys that he wants and how he wished his father was around. You see this boy's father had long abandoned them after he had gone to visit his

---

[391] *"Maturing prematurely, mannish"*

cousin in England, and he never returned. Those were in the '50s and 60s" when many Guyanese and all people living in Commonwealth countries took advantage of the 1948 British Nationality Act and began making their way to England. After all, they were given full rights for settlement and entry into that country. Others that arrived immediately after the passing of this Act were called the "Windrush Generation." Those sailed in on the SS Empire Windrush as the first Caribbean immigrants to Tilbury Dock in Essex, England in 1948 also. These were also the days when some fathers, and not the mothers, upon putting their feet on the British soil had long forgotten that they had left their offsprings, a wife or girlfriend behind.

This boy's father had left in 1960 when he was just a mere four months old. That's why Maxine, Cyril mother, does look for mail from Cyril grandmother on he fadda side [392] in England mostly around this time because the old lady is devastated at her son's irresponsibility and tries her utmost to support her ex-daughter-in-law and grandson financially. But anyhow, the boy and his mother struggles, but gets by. As a matter of fact, just yesterday, they received mail and in it was one hundred pounds. That's a 'brite small piece'..... plenty money, and that is why he mother taking him shopping today.

In remembering what it is to have a "hungrie belly" in de past, Maxine turns to her son and says, *"pig ask he moomah,*

---

[392] *On his paternal side*

moomah whuh mek yuh mouth suh laang suh. Moomah seh wait
bai yuh guh come, yuh guh see." [393]

Although she has to clarify this statement, she uses it as a learning tool for her son to grasp the idea of how much she has suffered. Hence, to emphasize too that she has the wisdom and understanding of life's struggles, and coerces her son to be compliant to her advice about her traumatic experiences through her as he must learn from her past experiences.

Yes, the mail comes safe because the postman is seasoned and knows from the feel of the envelope that it got money inside, even moreso when is the holidays. Noel brings it safe, and he does mek sure that he only gives the mail to who it is addressed to, especially in this case where this mother and son's survival depends on the safe delivery of its content. He is a good postman and nobody complains on him like the postman they had before who used to dump they mail on the Seawall this time of the year. This is after he went through all of the mail looking for money. They cudda talk cheese[394] because he didn't care. That son-of-a-bitch who also worked in Lodge and did the same thing, worked in Linden and did the same thing, worked in Plaisance and did the same thing, worked in Agricola and did the same thing, worked in

---

[393] *"Pig ask his mother, mother what make your mouth so long so? Mother say wait boy you going to come,   you going to see." (Mother warns her young one as to why she acts like that due to her own traumatic experiences,   and that one day her son will learn too).*

[394] *They could talk all they want*

Vreed-en-Hoop and did the same thing until he worked in Buxton and dey 'peep he cards,'[395] Beat he up and then get he fired. He 'meet he meetah'[396] cause dem Buxton people dhoan play. They are 'rebels with a cause' who don't like stupitness and injustices. Remember it is said 'Buxton people stop train' in their adamance in rebelling years ago.

That's why tuh Noel does watch he mail cart 'like ah hawk'[397] and mek sure that "thiefing Phillip" who did know that 'thiefin ass, faas haan' postman don't get to it. People even seh dat dem two were partners in crime with them same mail that was found on the seashore by Luckhoo Pool. He dis watch that bastard with three eyes. Y'all think ah joking!!! He knows that man ain't up to no good and that if yuh only turn yuh back he thief from yuh. He might even thief you too if he ketch yuh off guard.

"Noel dis bring mih mail strait cauz we dhoan have otha dan de post office fuh get we money,"[398] Maxine declares.

In thinking back, she might be right because there was no Western Union or any other money transfer companies back then. Times has changed now though and everybody happy.

---

[395] *They could foresee what he is about, his agenda*
[396] *'Meet his match' with no-nonsense people.*
[397] *Very diligent in guarding something, watching carefully*
[398] *"Noel brings my mail straight because we don't have other than the post office to get our money"*

But we ain talk yet about how Cyril dress. Cause dressing up around this time is a big deal in this "land of many waters." Yes, y'all waan hear? Gladstone who upholstering Miss Beulah little dilapidated armchair saying "yes."

Well, now I have to tell de story about de little boy outfit……he got on a red and black flannel plaid pants, a black shirt and some fancy shoes. He looking like ah Englishman and smiling and looking down at he self. He looking at he shoes that is black and white. He feeling good you see. Dressed in that black shirt in the hot midday sun and he perspiring. Hot and fanning he self with a newspaper that he just run inside he mother house and get. Now this is something else because he did wear them same clothes from year before the last and he pants; looking just like Stanley security clothes that be 'floodin.' Pants short as if preparing for a flood. Then he shirt tight and he wiping the sweat that running down he face from the black wool beret on he head.

Now who does dress up in so much black and in this kind of weather when black is a conductor of heat? Now this mekkin Guyanese people look like fools; looking like if we never did do a Science class. I did know about this in Mr. Ramsundar class since I was about twelve years old at St. Joseph's High School. Did know about heat and the type of clothes to wear and that how white clothes is better when it hot outside, and believe me, that teacher was a genius who did 'drum it' in we head'[399] that we

---

[399] *Emphasize over and over' when teaching us*

could never forget ……. that "black is a conductor of heat.' What kind of stupidness that Cyril and he mother indulging in? Black clothes is for when it cold. Does keep yuh body nice and warm. Like right now in Arizona it cold and the clothes that Cyril wearing is good for this kind of weather. Don't talk about New York, Boston, Washington, Seattle, Philadelphia, Buffalo and other parts of America, and elsewhere. Them places so cold right now that all 'GT massive'[400] wish we were home.

Maxine; he mother dressing now. She inside. Let's see what sheh going to wear cause she so think she could dress and dis be sehing dat people dis 'bad eye' sheh caus sheh dis look good.[401] That's why last week Sunday sheh went to church in all red; a red long-sleeved wool dress "fuh tek off de 'bad eye' from dem bad mind people,"[402] she insisted. Hope she don't make herself a damn blasted fool again today because she not living in the cold. Anybody want to bet on what she gon wear? Cause we done see what she put on sheh boy. Lawd!!! This is funny. Ah love how this story going!!! Life is good when we could laugh ….. laugh till we belly buss.

Eh, eh. I see the door opening. Look like somebody coming outside. Leh we hope is Maxine. I did see Rosie from the other yard run in sheh house and in there for over half an hour now. Wonder if is she coming out or is Cyril mother? Okay, I see. Is the

---

[400] *A term used to describe Guyanese people, especially abroad*
[401] *Be saying that people usually 'give her the evil eye' because she looks good*
[402] *"To take off 'the evil eye' from those badminded people"*

two of them coming out together, but Rosie with she plump-self blocking me from seeing Maxine. They coming closer now and I seeing clearer now. Ah wish ah had some binoculars cause they live in one of the back houses.

Hold on here. Let me check she out ...... well not bad at all. I seeing a white skirt, yes. But, wait a minute!!! What? A red turtle neck long-sleeved sweater? Oh Gawdo!!! ...... Oh God!!! What? Black stockings? Then what? Red stiletto-heeled shoes and they high, high, high, and about four inches tall. Oh my!!! Now I know why Rosie was in there. Was to help fix Maxine hair. You see Rosie does do hair and kinda good at it, but I don't like this hairdo on sheh customer. That hair looks like it was in a hundred curlers and full ah grease. Greasy and shining like a bottle of vaseline in she head. Now we all know that the hairdresser does give she customers whatever they want, and that it must be that Maxine must have insisted that she want sheh hair like that.

After all, Rosie towing de line;[403] getting she little hustle on and since Maxine got some English pounds. Y'all know de deal. She want supposedly a sophisticated hairstyle while I feeling sorry for dem paper curlers that just suffocated in all that grease. Yes, paper curlers that the women used to use at that time. Eh, eh, they didn't have them plastic ones so much. Anyhow, now she get de

---

[403] *Going along with someone for profit or to gain things*

hairstyle she wanted, and now like sheh son, she 'sweatin like ah horse.'[404] Even "Stupitey Bill" would laugh at she.

Y'all remember them two brothers? "Stupitey Bill" and "Sensee Bill" or "Sensible" Bill? Those were the good ole days!!! But, is true. She put de stuphid[405] brother to shame. He would laugh at her you see, since everybody does laugh at he. He been longing for donkey years[406] for somebody to laugh at and he would get a pre-holiday laugh with this one. The vaseline now turning to oil and it running down she face. Cyril handing she he handkerchief to wipe sheh face from de oil that mixing up in the pink powder and running down to the top of sheh mouth. Now powder, oil, foundation and red lipstick mingling together. God, is whuh is this? This takes the cake!!!

Bright midday and this woman and sheh son looking like two comics in front of the gate that if a clown from the circus passed by, he would get a good laff too. But is who they waiting for? Cause that four inch heel she wearing can't take sheh too far cause sheh walking funny in them. Almost tumbled down just now with sheh two fine foot that got bony calves that cannot help sheh if sheh step on a brick? No way!!! That woman would tumble down as she looking shaking ahready and Cyril holding sheh up. Then to go shopping at that? But, oh yes, she got English pounds and Carol just yelled out to sheh that Mr. Lowe with the taxi

---

[404] *Sweating profusely*
[405] *Stupid*
[406] *For countless years*

159

business sending one of he cars to pick she and sheh son up. Yes, she moving on wheels too because of the stacks of money she get from England in the mail yesterday and about to change it up at the bank.

I wish she would go inside and take off that turtle neck; that red piece of garment that so hot. Imitating Santa Claus and he colors and can't make sure that sheh clothes suit de climate. The only thing is that she wearing the colors wrong in dem kinda clothes and she footside[407] is uncomfortable. I not wearing de clothes, but ah feeling the heat fuh sheh. Now since de hair press, it look like it turnin back.[408] Hair corners looking grumsee[409] from de heat and the top looking straight and hard at the same time. Then the small curls looking smaller now and the grease starting to look white in sheh hair cause it mixing with sheh sweat and shrinking.

This is a disaster …… a blatant disaster!!! But all in the fun of "the last dash" on December 23rd. Let's see how this goes. The day that Maxine is having a 'bad hair day' as the folks abroad would say, but is adamant about taking her boy holiday shopping. But let we leave these two people alone and check in by Miss Millie and sheh chirren. Oh, ah fuhget. Remember Jason who head didn't suh Catholic[410] and was laughing at Patsy with she winter

---

[407] *Her feet; her shoes*
[408] *The straightness of her hair is disappearing*
[409] *Her hair corners is looking nappy, nappy*
[410] *Head isn't so normal. He has mental challenges.*

clothes on last year? Well, he seem to be smart enough to know when somebody ain't dress too well, and he laughing now at this mother and son. He leaning up by the hibiscus shrubs in front of the yard and getting a belly full of laughs. He laughing till he crying while he pointing at the two idiots. He get kept back in Third Standard, but he know when somebody ain't looking good. I think he got a knack fuh fashion. That might be his strong point and maybe one day, he might be a fashion designer. Y'all know that could happen cause everybody don't do so well in school, but have other potentials.

Always a nice 'ice breaker' to get away from Punchin Yard and check on their friends whom they got to know through Patsy if this mother and son is able to stop by before or after shopping. Well, talking bout Patsy, looks like she over there now. Hazel and she brothers sitting downstairs and I seeing another girl. Yep, that's Patsy. They doing something. Lenny putting a second coat of lacquer on they chairs and they laughing and joking about how much Lenny is in love with Brenda, the young lady from Linden that just moved into the neighborhood. The thing is that he asking their advice as to what to buy sheh for Christmas. They tantalizing[411] he and he looking shy, much to the disgust of Jacqueline who I must remind y'all, is on vacation from Cayenne and just joined them under de bottom house. She and he 'coo coo

---

[411] *Teasing*

161

dhoan boil' [412] when they attended the same school because he had a bad reputation of telling on the kids in his class.

"Miss Callender, Aubrey jus knack Caroline," "Miss Callender, Joey jus put ah mirror pun de ground fuh look up unda dem gurls clothes," "Miss Callender, Linda puttin gum under de desk dat sheh jus tek out sheh mouth," "Miss Callender, Petal capying from Ruby." "Miss Callender, Sophie jus pass ah note tuh Dolly."

Miss Callender would then give those students a very stern look while stamping her feet with her notorious black laced-up granny boots. Then if matters got worse with that Lenny running his mouth with the words flowing out like he had a laxative ..... diarrhea, this teacher would grab her wire cane and beat a student if he once more complained on them. This is why this young lady dislikes Lenny.

"He dis run he mouth tuh much," according to Jacqueline, which resulted in her cousin Linda and other students being beaten several times by Miss Callender because of his excessive babbling.

Fuh 'Thy Kingdom Come' he whoan shut he stink mouth." [413]

Yep, ah said it; "stink mouth" because he is de biggest wagonness[414] in de whole school.

She utterly despises him because the cane that this teacher used had left marks for months on her cousin's hands that was not only very painful, but took long to disappear. Then what made matters worse is that when Linda arrived home and her parents saw that the teacher had beaten her, they gave her a second beating. This was how things were in Guyana at that time with parents looking upon teachers as figures of authority who gave your children a flogging because their child deserved it, and thought that people like Miss Callender were always right. This like I said, warranted a second punishment.

I still could remember a certain teacher of mine at Smith's Church Congregational School who was quite an abuser with his red tie and white shirt sitting on the top of his pot belly standing at the front door. With wire cane in hand, and almost always in a bad mood, he would look to see who was arriving late. He had forewarned us that whenever he wore a red tie, that he was in his 'royal madness' or very bad mood. Those were the days that his flogging was beyond child abuse. I often wished that that bastard would drop dead or resign because of his attitude towards those who were coming sometimes just one minute after 8:00 a.m. because we had stopped a corner away at the "lump lady" stand to

---

[414] *Complainer who intrudes mostly by telling on people*

either buy some lump [415]or pickled mango with salt. Some arrived even later as they walked slower trying to digest the rumour that she often times scratched her leg with the very same knife she used to cut that hardened sugar candy.

I am going to be honest that when most of us heard that he had passed away, we were not very sad with our pent up anger and residual dislikes of him. Nevertheless, with our small mercies, we prayed that he would rest in peace. After all, we were always his potential victims at that front door or if we were summoned to his office, we received stripes in the palms of our hands with his floggings. Jacqueline's distaste for Lenny had increased also after she had heard the complains from her best friend Hazel as to how annoying he was with regards to criticizing guys who were trying to tackle her. No, that fool don't like no man trying to court Hazel.

"Now he gat de nerve fuh give advice," [416] Jacqueline is whispering to herself.

She then cuts up her eyes*[417]* at the now very bashful young man and he realizes it. Dat snitch!!! ….. as people would call him in America.

Little Orson enters the yard and climbs unto Ulrick's lap. Last time Jacqueline was here she was teaching him the French

---

[415] *A candy made with sugar and water, then left to harden and cut up into pieces*

[416] *"Now he has the nerve to give advice"*

[417] *Moving one's eyelids up and down depicting anger*

that she had learnt from her boyfriend, and wants to know if he remembers by asking ……..

"*Quel age avez-vous?*" …… "How old are you?"

She is asking him his age and he ponders for a moment and responds, "*quatre ans*." He means that he is "four years old."

Everyone is both shocked and elated that the little boy has remembered what he has been taught and they are ecstatic. But this should not be a surprise as after all, language acquisition is easier at an early age as proven by most scholars. Jacqueline then mentions the word *"un cadeau"* and the Little Orson giggles. Hazel is asking what does the two words mean and learns that they mean "a gift."

Ulrick then gets up and puts the boy on his shoulders and is now running around the yard as if to say that he is also very proud of him. The child is chuckling now as this little boy likes the new phrase he has learnt and whispers the words *"un cadeau"* again. See how this child is smart and remembers that Jacqueline had promised him a gift. This is the time of the year that individuals get very excited, moreso children. Gifts are expected by everyone and as we speak, Grandma Tinsy has just left to purchase a doll for Little Debbie. Uncle Ovid's box was a disappointment and for days now the little girl has been feeling down from her appearance.

"Dat Ovid lie tuh we!!!"[418] Bridget exclaimed as her mother was leaving, while Phillip declared that he could steal one out of the store.

"Ah tell allyuh ah cud get anyting allyuh waan. Me aan know why allyuh buying aan buying suh fuh. Allyuh know ah is ah ole tiefman. Ah got stripes fuh thiefin round heh aan all ova de place," he says with confidence.

He then takes out ah wad of money[419] to show off how much he has made from selling his stolen items in the last few days. He is digging deeper into his pocket with a triumphant look on his very slim face that has a mouthstache and sideburns.

"Dis is de bess time of de year fuh mih. Ah dis 'move thru' dem stores. Ah gat tatics. Ah dis get orders tuh. Allyuh cud still put in orders aan yuh know ah gon gih y'all ah discount."

He then smiles revealing a mouth full of gold teeth which is a façade of wealth, and says, *"ah gone. Going aan do mih job."*[420]

I am smiling now because I know too well that the huge gift box in his big shopping bag has a hole in the bottom that is

---

[418] *"That Ovid lie to us!!!"*
[419] *A stack of money*
[420] *"I gone. Going and do my job."*

connected to another smaller box which collects all of Phillip's stolen items. Y'all think ah lying? Ask he.

He then yells back, *"whuh kinda doll yuh waan?"*

Bridget then responds, *"ah white one. We ain waan no black face doll in heh"* ....

Typical of a colonial mentality that just absolutely erks me to the point of profanities, but ah gon hold mih tongue pun dis one. Don't cuss aan go on bad and mek mihself look like a viharago or a common place woman. Den ah gon waan to teach some history. "Puh ting, sheh cyaan think no betta." [421]

Doris by the standpipe washing clothes and she shaking sheh head. Little do allyuh know, she is a rebel and done tell sheh daughter to only buy black dolls. She remembers the stories from her elders of the unkind treatment they received from the colonizers and even expatriates which is much to the disagreement of Miss Bruckner; Miss Millie boss from England.

Hole … Hold up deh!!! Look like Dookram, he wife Parbattie, son Saheed, and they daughter Sattie going out now. Well we could guess where they going because the little boy did tell Cyril earlier that he wanted to go see Santa Claus. Then we

---

[421] *But I am going to hold my tongue on this one. Don't curse and go on bad and make myself look like 'a woman who misbehaves like fighting or cursing.' Then I am going to want to teach some history. "Poor thing, she can't think no better."*

know too that it got to be at Bookers. Should I continue? Cause I hearing somebody shouting ………

"Is whuh dey wearing, tell we whuh dey wearing?"

Y'all so spoiled. Why every time ah have to tell y'all de people business?

Okay, okay!!! Looking good, looking good!!! Saheed in he green and white stripe shirt and blue pants. Then on his feet are some white yatching boots. Those shoes are what we call sneakers in America, whilst Parbattie as usual is wearing a sari that is red and beige in color with silver sandals. Their two children are almost dressed alike in dungaree bottoms; the girl in a skirt and the boy in a long pants. Little Sattie is also decked out in a red and white chemise looking top. They are Muslims and live by humble means ever since Dookram had lost his job as a head cook at one of the local hotels. Bring a man from Trinidad and replace he, and left de puh man 'high aan dry.' [422]

Demoted financially, they moved into Punchin Yard. Parbattie on the other hand has been a homemaker all her life, but is now selling curry chicken and roti on Saturdays and ice all week. Life has been tougher for them, but de little ice hustle from de fridge that she sister in Canada help sheh buy has helped this family to get a daily income. Why? Because they are the only ones in the yard with a fridge. Yes, a little penny here and there does

---

[422] *Left the poor man 'in a dilemma'*

add up to buy a meal and pay rent along with the weekend cooking that I mentioned earlier while their faith remains intact by constantly praying to Allah daily.

Hand in hand, the couple and their children are making their way down the street to catch a hire car to downtown. Dookram looks into the far distance for it, while his little boy tosses a brick into the roadside trench at what appears to be a pool of small fishes. Who could remember cacabelly?[423] Well, they look like duh ….. but how ah could leff duh out? Cyaan rite dis book aan ain put tings like duh inside. Dis is raw kulcha…… ah gihing[424] y'all raw Guyanese culture ……. One of my aims in penning this book.

Anyway, back to de lil bai[425] and he family ….. he then joins his father in looking for the mustard colored vehicle that will enable him to visit Santa. Little Sattie grins up at her mother who has a grimace on her face from the afternoon sun. They are a happy bunch and it is evident this afternoon that they hardly ever go on family outings other than to the local mosque down the street. Although rare and priceless an occasion in spending family time, I must emphasize that this couple is merely trying to please their son who has succumbed to peer pressure in celebrating this holiday as it is against their religion.

---

[423] *Fish who usually swims in the small trenches outside people's houses known also a coco belly or mud fish*
[424] *I am giving you all*
[425] *Back to the little boy*

169

Looks like before we know it, everyone in the yard will be making their "last dash" today to do some real shopping after window-shopping for many months.

"Ah did look at some tings ah waan ah long time now," yelled Ms. Cheryl. *"Ah did see some blinds fuh mih windows at ah vendor in de Aracade aan ah went aan snatch dem up yestaday. Den ah went to Bettencourt aan get ah table cloth fuh mih dining table. Ah early dis year. Y'all hear mih? Ah ain able wid de runnin up aan down. Mih barrel come early aan ah organize mihself ahready. De last ting ah got fuh mek is mih souse early pun dat special day. Ah waan it fuh be fresh aan nice. Eh, eh is who ah seein?*

"Well ah tell yuh. Allyuh look like y'all bringing home de whole store," she grins.

That's Cyril and his mother arriving home with some bags and a big box. Seems like another box has arrived in the yard, and this time it's from England. Well, what a surprise!!! No wonder those two people were so excited when leaving earlier. That Maxine could keep a secret, eh? She know too how to school sheh boy to keep he mouth shut, and he be quiet you see. Fraid ...... afraid he mother going to beat he if he tell people sheh business. One day sheh did canx[426] he up and beat he up for announcing that he step-sister coming from Liverpool. Now he heart dis be in he

---

[426] *Knuckled up his temporal lobe with her right or left hand*

haan[427] everytime he mother pick up sheh belt. But nevertheless, he is she only chile......he "mammy nice chile"[428] and sure enough, he lives up to it. That is what we call loyalty, but word is, according to the few so-called psychoanalysts in de yard ..... that *"sheh arrested he maturity."* That might be true you know because I know some cases like that and the children never did really grow up when they became adults. Anyway, that's that!!!

Just mek sure y'all don't arrest yuh chirren maturity. He matured though ... Lil scamp ..... to brace up on the little girls when playing hide-and-seek and lying to them that they going to be mommy and daddy. Ain't that a shame?!!! Then he and he mother hiding they box like if anybody want something. Like a secret. But what I saying? Because we already know that somebody gon waan[429] something.

Gwen did just mumbling that she don't have any money to buy sheh children gifts and enough food to last sheh through the new year.

Gawd, ah feel fuh sheh. Ah shud gih sheh some money. Y'all see I not stingy. I writing and feeling bad fuh sheh at de same time.

---

[427] *He gets very nervous*

[428] *A term used in Guyana and some Caribbean countries to describe a good child.*

[429] *Going to want*

"Ah only cudda tek mih pickney dem fuh window shap cauz money shortin. Dey see plenty tings dey waan, but ah jus dhoan have it. Life hard yuh see. Ah now see why Sharon dis go pun dem ships. Ah cyaan blame sheh," Miss Gwen has been saying lately.

This is typical of the socio-economic dilemma of the underprivileged in this country; tainted by the absence of some fathers. Although, as I could remember growing up, there were just a handful of women in my neighborhood without a husband or partner. This is because the British influence of marriage was very rampant as I want to reiterate Queen's College and some students not being able to gain admission because they were born out of wedlock, especially since that school and Bishop's High was introduced for expatriate children. So even though the plight of Gwen needs not to be overlooked, instead she and many of the other single-parent mothers need to be applauded for their ongoing strengths. In this era also, many mothers did not work as the custom were for them to stay at home and take care of their children along with chores such as cooking and housecleaning. Most times, it was the single mothers who worked out of the home or very educated women who pertinently thought that their position was to be in the workforce.

This box!!!! Maxine and Cyril inside now with the box. When Denise ask sheh if it come from England, she said *"eh, heh."*[430]

Daphne got excited and was following them as they entered the yard. She is not that developmentally delayed to not recognize that it was a box from overseas. She kept walking faster and faster after them as they quickened up their pace…..them selfish two!!!

She kept yelling *"candy canes, candy canes, candy canes. Ah waan some. Gih mih, gih mih…… candy canes."*

Then as her obsession grew, she tried to snatch the box out of Maxine's hand, but without success while her son acted as her bodyguard. Duh ….. that conniving, selfish little boy. Ah tell ahyuh how he stay. Ahyuh din believe mih.[431]

As for the content of their seven shopping bags, no one knows. This mother and child may never reveal what they bought other than the sound of a whistle blowing inside the house. That Little Cyril also did not answer when asked what he got from Santa. I see them peeping as if they have defeated all the onlookers. Yes, that is the way some of the people behave as the holidays approach. It is like if there is a race to see 'who has what' and 'who has more' and 'where it's from.' I guess that's why some

---

[430] *"Yes"*

[431] *I tell all of you how he stay. All of you didn't believe me.*

religions call it a Pagan holiday and do not celebrate it because of how commercialized it has become. Also, the greed and envy that brews from it.

Oh, I see Grandma Tinsy in a distance. She is not a spring chicken[432] anymore, but she coming along gingerly[433] with a bag in sheh hand. This old woman like   Miss Millie and many of the other elders has worked beyond physical endurance as domestic servants with foreigners and bourgeoisie locals throughout their lifetime.

*"Mih mileage run out. Ah tyad…..*she means she is tired. *"Ah wuk hard yuh see aan ah try hard. Ah is seventy-three years ole aan ah cyaan give up. Ah love mih grands aan mih daughta. We dis brace one anotha up."*

Then she smiles and adds, *"ah love dat lil gurl yuh see."*

She then points to Little Debbie and adds, *"sheh like mih own blood. Ah dhoan know how ah motha cud walk away suh aan dhoan look back at sheh lil chile."*

She then takes her arthritic ridden right hand and wipes the tears flowing from her eyes. Hers is a display of real adoration. So, here she comes with what might be the doll she went to purchase for her adopted grandchild.

---

[432] *A young person*
[433] *Slowly, but surely*

"Is whuh is duh?" [434] nosey Doris asks, while trying to look into Miss Tinsy's bag which seems to be guarded.

The old woman nods her head and doesn't answer as she appears to be exhausted from her five hour outing. She then answers saying that it is a doll.

"It nice yuh see. Is fuh Debbie. Ah gaffuh hide it till Crismus day. Bridget gon be disapointed becauz ah buy ah black one. Ah din fine ah white one, aan ah din able fuh search more. Ah think dis one betta dough."

You think is true? Y'all know that what de ole woman just said bout dat [435] white doll ain't true. She got just what she had intended to look for, okay. How Bridget expect that woman who celebrates Ghana Day and Emancipation Day to be compliant to her requests? She…Bridget, stupitey or what? Sheh is ah lamatha? [436] She mother does pay attention to history and been another survivor of colonialism and neo-colonialism. She darn right not to provide Little Debbie with an object that would promote feelings of inferiority or social mobility complexes. For sure she will teach the little girl about her history and culture. I could see her dragging the little child to the Ghana Day celebration to pay homage to our ancestors since most of our foreparents came from Ghana, West Africa, which was

---

[434] *"Is what is that?"*

[435] *About that*

[436] *She … Bridget, stupid or what? She is a slow person?*

175

discontinued in 1964 but made a comeback after 47 years in 2011. But nevertheless, the elders still remain passionate about this holiday and hold their little drumming sessions every year like seven years later here in 1971. Now today in 2022 this Ghana National Day celebration on March 6th featured the Sankofa bird which means "go fetch come" or "you look backwards to gain wisdom to go forward." It also was to honor most of Guyana's revolutionaries who came from Ghana and also to recognize that this country was the first to gain Independence on the African continent. This celebration is also important to Guyanese because of the synonymous cultures.

That's the day when Granny Tinsy and the elders congregate in their traditional African attires and celebrate that day "Ghanian style." You should see rastaman Omowale on the drums!!! Dressed in he dashiki and beating the goat skinned harps to the sounds of his own heartbeats while Kofi shakes the shekere. Meanwhile some of the sistas like Niyah are dancing to the music with the brothas who are also decked out in their most flamboyant African garb while Tinsy and an older gentleman is now in the center of the circle that has now been formed as Little Debbie giggles. The little girl has just found some new friends her own age group and they are the spectators to the two people who are the nuclei of this circle. They are both whining to the beats of the drums as if they are youngsters with both hands on their hips and are gyrating in unison.

Oh, how sweet it is to prolong our cultural customs and culture!!! Oh, how Mama Africa still lingers on in our souls; the descendants of the slaves who were brought through that perilous Middle Passage to our shores and many others!!! Oh, how resilience and persistence has encouraged our survival .... just like our Chinese,[437] Portuguese[438] and East Indian[439] brothers and sisters who were brought here as indentured laborers to till the soil on the sugarcane and rice fields. They too have endured through the loogies and the small stipends after working the land beyond physical endurance. So, why not dance. Dance away the sorrows that was once so alive. Dance to those drumbeats that keep hope alive. Dance through the political turmoil and bedlam that once was. Dance that pleases the ancestors. Dance like if there is no tomorrow.

So, as they are dancing and singing, what about checking in again with our friends in Meadbrook Gardens…….. Patsy is fast asleep on Cousin Hazel's bed, whilst Aunt Millie is titivating in the kitchen. She is seasoning what appears to be meat and Hazel

---

[437] *The Chinese; the last group of laborers, arrived in Guyana on January 12, 1853, called the "The Chinese Arrival Day." Many were all Christians fleeing prosecution in their motherland. This is called The Boxer Rebellion from November 2, 1899 - 1901. This uprising was infused by the* Yihequan Movement *which was a violent anti-foreign and anti-Christian occurrence towards the end of the Qing Dynasty.*

[438] *Some 39,645 Portuguese indigent peasants arrived as laborers in Guyana between 1834 and 1882 from Madeira and the Azores Island in a boat called the "Louisa Barille" to work on a sugar plantation in Demerara .*

[439] *On May 5, 1838, the first British ship that sailed from Kolkata, India, to Guyana, South America brought East Indians there called "Indian Arrival Day" and is celebrated each year, it signifies the arrival of the East Indians here. Traumatically so, the Rosehall killing of 15 sugar workers on March 15, 1913, on Plantation Rosehall in Berbice remains unforgettable.*

177

is washing something in the sink. Meanwhile, Ulrick is making his way upstairs with Little Orson trailing behind him.

Eh, someting smellin nice," Ulrick says. *"Oh, okay. Ah see."* He then walks to the stove and curiously looks into the pot.

"Careful yuh get bun, dhoan come too near," Cousin Hazel yells to Little Orson, as Miss Millie stretches over from the sink and dumps a few more pieces of meat into the pot. She putting in some pieces of pork, beef, tripe and cow heel now.

"Ah did jus letting de pigtail, pigfoot, de pig ears aan cow ears boil fuss since dey lil tuff."[440]

She then reaches again to the other side of the counter and picks up a bottle with a black liquid inside called cassareep,[441] and calmly says ......

"Is de peppahpat ah mekkin. Ah mekkin plenty fuh sen with Patsy tuh de yard. Rememba ah dis always sen fuh dem every year. Dem who ain got nuff food. Gwen aan sheh chirren aan who else waan. Beryl pun de next yard aan dem kids, yuh know. Ah get dis bigga pot. Miss Cheryl sen it wid Patsy. It nice aan big aan enuf fuh everybady."

---

[440] *"I did just letting the pigtail, pigfoot, the pig ears and cow ears boil first since they are a little tough"*

[441] *Cassareep is made of grated bitter cassava, then by squeezing the juice and let it rest for a day. Next day throw off the liquid and boil for half an hour. The product is now cassareep and the sediments. remaining becomes starch used to put on clothing before ironing.*

She then smiles as her daughter throws some more meat into the pot along with some spices including cloves, fine leaf thyme, ginger, orange peel, a little sugar and two big red peppers to make de pepperpot hot and nice.

She then adds, "*it haffa full tuh de brim cauz is nuff, nuff ahwe eatin,*" [442]while the little onlooker yawns, indicating that Ulrick must accompany him home next door.

"*When ah come back mammy, yuh think ah cud get ah lil taste?*" Ulrick begs.

But we Guyanese know that de pot ain't done yet. All that meat in that big pot is going to take long, long to cook. Then Millie does make sure that sheh meat cook right. Then by the pepperpot is a dish that special for Santa Day, they dis make it look like if that fat man in that red suit coming to dinner. They usually let that pot stay on the fire for hours to the big day.

My mommy dis say that "*pepperpot dis only taste nice when it stale, aan yuh have to eat it with nice fresh bread or white rice or provisions like eddo, cassava, yams, potatoes and tania. Yuh dhoan always haffa put it in de fridge afta it cook. Yuh jus heat it up every day aan eat it until all done, aan always use ah clean spoon in it.*"

---

[442] "*It has to be full to the brim because it is plenty, plenty of us eating.*"

That's the mistake that Bertie auntie friend did make and Miss Avril pepperpot did spoil two days after Christmas. Mekkin joke with a Guyanese and this dish!!! She was so sad and made some more for the New Year's.

So y'all hear mih …….. *"Ah clean spoon yuh hear, especially when yuh leff it out."* That's Mammy Parris!!!

Always heat it up morning and afternoon, and remember, always eat it the next day after it done cook …. when it stale. She says that it better this way when the casareep hold onto the meat; colors the meat……. or allyuh is not no Guyanese. Y'all know de deal. Now this indigenous Amerindian dish was created from that casareep; that dark liquid that Miss Millie had in that bottle. It mek from cassava juice and since those indigenous people ain't had no fridge, they figure out a way to make that delicious meal.

My ex-classmate Wendella Mohabir Britton just interjected and said that ….. *"some people with no fridge use to put dey pot of pepperpot on de roof top so it cud ketch de nite dew. That was to make it dhoan spoil."* Then she reiterated ground provisions as part of the meal also.

Now even though I don't eat meat no more, I cannot bash a person's dietary choices. Well yuh know some people still eat it, enjoy it, but still picks on the Amerindian people and think they backward because they live in the places like Lethem, Matthews

Ridge Port Kaituma Area where Jim Jones had he Jonestown settlement, and some other places in and around de jungle.

Now what de heck?!!! Because it tek genius to think up a dish like this ..... that same pepperpot from cassareep ..... that don't need no refrigeration and the more you heat it up, is the more tastier it gets, and don't spoil. So what kind of nonsense to be calling them names too because they live in the interior and all them jungle areas and ain't got to pay no light bill, rent, mortgage or water bill to live in they benabs.[443] Chilling half-naked with no lust and throwing every living thing they find around them in the pepperpot in the huge container that sitting on the fire in the middle of the village. Oh yes!!! Food galore with de pot bubbling non-stop so everybody could eat. Living nice and natural and getting into they boats and not cars, with the water as they roads.... nice and simple and cultural. Self-sufficiency at it's best!!!

Then I did hear of a term de town people use calling de Amerindians that mix with black "buck aan people" or "bufianda." Now what is that, eh? They not responsible if they mothers get them with porknockers or somebody else. A black man ah mean or in the latter, other races too. Them girls nice though. My cousin did like one of them. He say she fluffy like Patsy and thick with nice curly hair down she back. Get sheh from Lethem. Well, he

---

[443] *A small hut with a thatched roof where indigenous people live*

181

just lusting. But please, no name calling, okay. Everybody is people. God's people.

Now Lenny come home now and he got an electric polisher. Saying he borrow it from he friend up the street because he don't want Hazel fuh get black knees and whoever else helping. The floors polishing over tomorrow and Jacqueline who did dozing off in the chair by the front door chimes in.

"Is how much times yuh dis polish de floor? It look good to me. Hazel yuh mek de souse yet? Ah waan piece. Yuh waan mih cut up some cucumbers in case? Oh Gawd, mih mouth waterin wid duh smell in de kitchen."

She then gets up and walks toward the kitchen.

"Gawd, ah hungrie. Allyuh cud cook, eh!!! Ah wish mih motha did still alive. Dis time of de year ah dis miss sheh suh much. But de good Lord knows best."

She then lifts up the pot cover and admires the meat sizzling in the cassareep; the nice black and tasty looking sauce inherited from our native people that we was jus talkin bout[444] ……. de Amerindians. She then nods her head from side to side as if in affirmation that it's the food that makes a Guyanese Christmas. After all, this dish especially has to be present on a countryman's table on that day; both at home and abroad. Then

---

[444] *We were just talking about*

they got to get that fresh white bread to eat with it. Some even lining up in long lines on a Brooklyn street on Christmas eve to get that nice freshly baked white bread at a known woman who makes it. Also, they stopping traffic how de place so pack up with dem "GT" people standing all over and they cars parked all over the street without discretion. Then they don't even care while they gossiping too if police pass by and gih them tickets, ah hear. All for that bread ….. just out the oven; soft and warm to dip in that sauce while devouring the meats that have been disguised by the dark color.

"Auntie Baby, is whuh is duh?" [445] one of my cousins would say, while trying to distinguish 'what meat is what.' Then relying on his taste buds to satisfy his curiosities.

"Boy eat it nuh, aan den yuh gon see. Ah got all kinda meat in deh. Ah throw everyting inside dat ah cud get at de butcher shop like de buck people in de bush," [446] my mommy would reply.

Millie pot like that too. She dumps everything inside and still turns around and mek garlic 'poke' …. pork. Plenty comic-relief, eh? I still live and survive in that nostalgia. All like "wutless" Ernest, he cyaan get none. No pepperpot fuh he in New Jersey,

---

[445] *"Auntie Baby, is what is that?"*
[446] *"Boy eat it okay}and then you are going to see. I got all kinds of meat in there. I throw everything   inside that I could get at the butcher shop like de buck/Amerindian people in the bush."*

Manhattan, Staten Island, Bronx or worst yet, Brooklyn. None!!!
He too "wutless."

Miss Beulah shaking she head in agreement. Lawd!!! She
going fuh she bible to pray fuh he. No, let we leff dat lady alone.
She got a lot on sheh hand. Patsy say Daphne been tormenting
sheh all week to go see Santa and the fairy lights on Main Street,
and they supposed to go tomorrow of all de days; Christmas eve.
Let's pray!!! Cause that ole lady don't have de strength for that
kind of 'ruff down shuff down'[447]....... all de crowd with the last
minute shoppers bulldozing they way down Main Street into
Water Street.

"Better she than me," Lenny is thinking, as he sits in
solace on the stairway of the house and wishes that the girl he has
that secret crush on passes by. He longs for her and questions
himself as to if this is the first girl that he has really been so
attracted to. He then realizes that he just has less than two days to
buy Brenda that special gift. Then he stops daydreaming and
comes to the reality that his financial resources is limited, and that
he really cannot afford to buy her the gold necklace that he saw
with the heart on it at a goldsmith around the corner from he. He
must brainstorm on another gift that he could purchase with the
thirty dollars he has in his pocket.

---

[447] *'Confusion' like social order*

184

"Yuh look suh sad. Is whuh yuh thinkin bout? Tink ah cud guess,"[448] Hazel looking out the living room window shouts.

Lenny smiles and then continues to 'prop sorrow.' Y'all know what I mean. His right hand is holding up his jaw.

"Ah tink ah know. Is duh knock knee gurl yuh studyin. Gimme ah break. Yuh cud do betta dan duh. Aan duh gurl ain studyin yuh,"[449] as his sister continues to tease him.

This sister then gives that sarcastic grin as Jacqueline follows her and laughs even louder saying, *"Son of ah bitch!!! He used tuh run he mouth in skool. It good fuh he. Dotish."*[450]

She then childishly blows a bubble from her bubble gum and pops it just as Lenny glances at both her and Hazel. He hates when she does that. He is angry now and walks out of the yard.

"Yuh goin aan look fuh sheh?" his sister asks, but he refuses to answer.

"Is smellin he smellin he self. Barely mek couple dollas cuttin grass aan waan fuh spen it on dat gurl," his mother declares.

---

[448] *"You look so sad. Is what you thinking about? Think I could guess"*
[449] *"You could do better than that. And that girl ain't studying you"*
[450] *"So of a bitch!!! He used to run his mouth in school. It is good for him. Doltish (stupid/idiotic)."*

"He shud go look a part-time job in the masquerade band as 'Mother Sally.'[451]

Well Phillip arrive. He come back. Got he big gift in de bag. Rememba I did tell allyuh that is a 'canta' or 'false'gift. I mean is not a real gift cause it got a smaller box under de cut out hole that does house all the stolen items. Then the way that the gift look and how it wrap, people would believe it real. Well, leh we see what he thief. Clear de way!!! ……… Sharon running to he. Eh, eh, like they got something going on in truth. The so-called gift look heavy and she just kiss he. Well, is whuh ah seeing? Other people watching tuh. Doris washing she grandchildren clothes by the pipe loosing sheh concentration and almost make the basin with de clean clothes fall over in de dirty water accumulating in the sunken in ground below. See how sheh fass.[452] She looking shock cause she does not want her nice daughter with no nutten pocket thief man. But wait a minute!!! He just had a wad of money before he left. He does prosper this time of year. So Sharon playing sheh cards rite.[453]

It getting dark and is hard to tell from where some people standing up as to if she mother vex or pleased because it sounds like she grunting now cause Phillip hands deh by sheh daughter bubby.[454] Doris grunting again. She mad, she angry, but she

---

[451] *"Is smelling he is smelling himself. Barely make couple dollars cutting grass and want to spend it on that girl."*
[452] *She is fast or inquisitive*
[453] *Acting good or behaving well in order to gain material things or love*
[454] *Phillip hands there by her daughter breasts*

186

staying quiet, although sheh did just answer Miss Cheryl who outside sitting on sheh front stoop when she asked her a question.

I know what she saying …... *"dis good fuh nutten son-of-ah- bitch!!! Ah dhoan like he*!!!" [455]Yep, that's her favorite verse with regards to Phillip.

But who cares? It's the holidays and de man got money to give sheh daughter today. Then who knows what inside the gift box? We know he good tuh. He got prags. Plenty items in that supposedly gift box. Sharon is very slick. Taught well by her mama. She don't play she games wrong, okay. She 'hangs sheh mouth where de soup falling,'[456] and surely the soup falling right about now in Phillip pocket, and no doubt he got gifts for sheh youths.

Then Sharon know how to tempt de ole thief man too …... she dress up in sheh pink halter top mini skirt dress with a plunging v-neck. See why de man hand was in sheh bosom that look like two oversized mangoes? Then like Maxine, it look like a silver shoes day today, cause Sharon wearing silver slippers with one-inch high heels that elevated enough to kick out the back of her dress. Meanwhile, her perfume lingers around the yard. Respect!!! She ah playah!!![457] Phillip loves this kind of seduction and looking lil confused. She slowing he up now because all he

---

[455] *"This no good son-of-a-bitch!!! I don't like him!!!"*
[456] *She embraces opportunities in her financial favor*
[457] *A hustler*

doing is looking at sheh. He tekkin too long to let we know what inside of the damn box. He distracted now.

"*Ouce,*" Sam yells. "*Yuh tekkin too laang bannuh. Leh we see whuh yuh bring. Cauz den ah gon know whuh fuh buy fuh mih chile motha aan mih dawta. Hurry up. Shit.*" [458]

Sam is known for this kind of aggression acquired from when he used to be a boxer, and Phillip complies immediately.

"*Ahrite, ahrite,*" ….. "Alright, alright," he replies to his frustrated looking neighbor, while still being distracted by the seducing Sharon.

"Police coming, police coming," Carol shouts.

This outburst was intended for Phillip to hear and he hands the gift box to Sharon, quickly jumps the concrete wall at the back of the yard , and heads into the next door alley. It appears like some informer has told the police about Phillip's whereabouts and they have come to recover the stolen items. But, this man who is seasoned at what he does has a modus operandi; a ways and means of dealing with this situation and always has a getaway plan in place if need be. He is very cunning and street-smart and since this is not the first time that the police has tried to raid him, he is always very alert and prepared to escape through pathways that

---

[458] "*Ouce,*" (an exclamation used to draw attention to oneself or something) Sam yells. "You are taking too long boy. Let we see what you bring. Cause then I am going to know what to buy for my child's mother and my daughter. Hurry up. Shit."

188

they are unfamiliar with. Word is that when some of his neighbors help him out, he dis palm dey haans, [459] and although these military men know the alley, Phillip even has houses in that very same alley in which he could hide for a few stolen items as payment. He could be in one right now. Meanwhile, one of the cops is trying to pursue Sharon.

That fool is saying, *"who bought you that big gift, beautiful? He is a very lucky man,"* as he quickly peruses her sexy body.

She then flirts back while handing her mother the "presumed gift" to take inside, *"yuh cud outdo he yuh know. Ah always deh single aan disengaged. Plus ah like men in unifarms tuh."*

Lie!!!!! She hates them, hates them, hates the dirt they walk on, cause the police always hassling de 'rootsman dem,' the 'down to earth' or grassroots man dem in the ghetto.

"Deh like tek bribe tuh. Especially from de man dem wid money,"[460] she had said only last week when she saw a police van passing.

---

[459] *Give them bribes*

[460] *"They like take bribe too. Especially from the man them with money"*

189

"You want to go out tomorrow nite beautiful? I really like you," asks the tall 'lampy pampy'[461] looking cop as in trying to impress her, he disguises his creolese-way of sometimes talking.

Meanwhile, his partner keeps knocking on Phillip's room door. That persistent and loud knocking is getting to Sharon now.

"Only if yuh padnah stap giving mih ah headache cauz dat man gone 'ova de river' tuh spend time wid he family fuh de halidays. He leff three days now,"[462] Sharon persuades this officer as he continues to be intrigued by her.

He then calls out to his partner and tells him what he just heard about Phillip's whereabouts in the country with his relatives.

"He leff laas week Sarge fuh Berbice. Dis beautiful lady now tellin mih," as he has now abandoned the perfect English that he was uttering before. But she didn't say "Berbice." He ears right?

Maybe it's an attempt to show Sharon that he could be down-to-earth too linguistically. Sarge; the Sargeant, nods his head as if in disappointment, takes his dingy police hat off and scratches the middle of his head on what appears to be a balding spot. He is now adjusting his shirt which has a ring around the collar in his very soiled pants.

---

[461] *Overly tall and awkward looking*

[462] *"Only if your partner stop giving me a headache because that man gone over the river to spend time with his family for the holidays. He left three days now."*

"Duh is mih 'kinna' aan is duttiness,"[463] Miss Cheryl did say when a man from next door was trying to get with her. *"Ah dhoan like dutty man like duh. Look like he dhoan wash he clothes, much less he skin. He collah black aan dutty. Dem kinda man sweatey tuh."*

This had caused much laughter under the tamarind tree on the far side of the yard whenever Stanley's friend hollered at her from over the fence. The sergeant who carried himself like this man, has a reputation of only leaving the station to round up certain so-called criminals for contraband, stolen items and drugs. He lives by his wits and not only a salary; a characteristic that defines him as a "crooked cop." He also could be seen lounging on a chair in the police station which he only leaves when he has an agenda. He also drinks a lot Yvonne had said, because she has been his client over and over again, as his marriage has failed years now. "Sarge" who has not been able to acquire anything from Phillip today seems frustrated, and is now beckoning to his cop buddy for them to leave, who is now handing Sharon a piece of paper with his number for her to call him. He then winks at her and heads towards the police van parked in front of the yard, as she giggles not with him, but at his naiveness of telling his counterpart that Phillip is not in Georgetown.

---

[463] *That is against me and is dirtiness*

"Ah mine 'play he,' she is thinking, *"like if ah like he? Me aan like he."*[464] Then longs for Phillip to come out of hiding to keep her company tonite.

"He think yuh dotish or whuh?" Doris says to her daughter as she enters the house. *"Yuh ain stuphid. Look de bag heh."*

The young woman then takes it to carefully scrutinize the content of the supposed "gift box." She is removing item by item out of the box and smiles as if approving Phillip's dishonesty. She loves what she is seeing and pounces upon a doll that must be intended for Little Debbie. It is almond color like her with kinky hair, and she smiles again. There are now about thirty items on her bed, until she digs deeper into the bag and goes into the smaller box at the bottom. She now discovers some gold jewelry. It is a gold bracelet which she assumes is for her.

"Dat Phillip ain ezee," she says to herself. *"Ah shud neva give up pun he. He know how fuh hussle. He dis thief yes, but ah like he. He young aan dis grind mih rite."*[465]

She is now reminiscing upon a rendezvous that they had two weeks ago ….. he kisses her softly and engages in long foreplay unlike the fellows that she does business with on the

---

[464] *"I mind 'use he,' she is thinking "like if I like him? Me/I ain't like him."*
[465] *"That Phillip ain't easy," she says to herself. "I should never give up on he. He know how to hustle. He usually thief yes, but I like him. He young and grind/screw me right."*

192

ships. Then when he kisses the nape of her neck and fondles her breasts she goes wild with excitement.

"Yuh is mih 'sweetie'. Deh wid mih nuh,"[466] he would whisper softly into her ears as he enters her craving body.

Then she would surrender herself to his moaning and climax. Theirs is becoming more of many irresistible encounters recently and she is now questioning herself as to if she is falling in love with him, plus recently, he has been telling her that he wants her to stop parading on the ships. He has also been convincing her that he is trying hard to do better in finding a job as a stevedore.

"Ah gon tek care ah yuh aan dem chirren baby. Ah waan do better fuh we. Ah love yuh bad bad," [467] as he would embrace her warm and tender body.

She is believing him now, as she sees him striving to do better daily, even though tonight he took some risks to get her and the neighbors what they want. Her thought processing is now interrupted by one of her crying kids who is throwing tantrums about wanting some ice-cream from the passing vehicle outside. She then scrambles up from off her bed and goes outside to purchase delicacies not only for her kids, but also to comply to the wishes of their playmates who are outside in the yard as to

---

[466] *"You are my 'sweetheart.' Be with me please,"*
[467] *"I am going to take care of you and those children baby. I want to do better for us. I love you bad bad"*

whatever they want from the van. Sharon is very kind and knows what it is like to be deprived. She also understands that not too many women would choose the profession that she has, and that also like her mother, some has aged-out of the physical attributes to continue that profession.

"Yuh haffa be lookin sharp," Doris would say, *"aan yuh gat fuh be young tuh. Ah ole now. Ah cyaan do dat no moe. Ah tell yuh whuh dough, ah dis teach mih daughta some ole tricks."*[468]

She would then burst out in laughter as if she deserves to earn a trophy for her craftiness at ripping off the Englishman many, many years ago. She also seldomly boasts about how she deserves stripes for pulling off the biggest robbery against a visitor from abroad. Ah mean, that she was the only person amongst all de ghettos to rob an individual of so much money, as hers was the most in pounds. Even "Sarge" doesn't get the respect that this lady gets on the streets when she steps out. Then knowing her, she collects a little freck[469] here and there from the young hustlers who of course, salutes her for her reputation. Moreso, when she comes decked out in she gold jingles[470] and chains at de "gangsta dance" on Boxing night.

---

[468] *"You have to be looking sharp," Doris would say, "and you have to be young too. I old now. I can't do that   no more. I tell you what though, I usually teach my daughter some old tricks."*
[469] *Some dollars*
[470] *Gold bracelets*

Man, you should see sheh!!! …. sheh hair press and she dis put on sheh notorious black kongol with she black and red armless dress …. a ting of the 'ole heads' cause she 'carryin ranks. *[471]* Gold bangles from she wrists up to midway sheh elbows on both hands with gold rings on four fingers, except she thumbs. Then complemented by two big, big gold earrings which she porknocker boyfriend did give she back in de day. Charlie did love sheh you see and he always did 'nice sheh up'[472] by bearing gifts. See how man foolish fuh little loving? Some of the gold bangles he give she too, and did even take her to the dentist to get the 'open face' [473] gold tooth she got on the upper front of she mouth. He never did give sheh up and did make sure that she was ahrite; a thing of men like him who went to the hinterland to dig for gold and diamonds. Theirs was an agenda of fixing up[474] they wives or sweet ooman with nice dresses, jewelry, and what ever else they wanted. All in all, they indulged in splurging money or what we might call; spendthrifts.

"Ah did only foolin he," she would say when boasting under the tamarind tree. *"Ah did only like he fuh whuh he cud gih mih. Ah din studyin he,"* she would heartlessly say. *"Ah 'ketch ah pakoo aan buss he back' cauz duh is how ah stay."*[475]

---

[471] *Has a very high reputation*

[472] *Did 'make her pleased or happy'*

[473] *Gold around the teeth with a space in between*

[474] *Making or adorning their wives or girlfriends on the side with items that would make them look beautiful*

[475] *"Catch a stupid person and brutally use them because that is how I am."*

This old woman was 'ah playah' back in de day,[476] and as a result, have numerous stories of her countless encounters with men; not only of all ages, but colors. She still has her residual good looks which tells you that she was a 'knock out' in those days and does not wear any make-up because she still little pretty. Dressed up as she is at the dance, she would sit there all night and gamble with sheh black purse in she bossom that would start to change color from de powder melting on she chest from sheh perspiration that now tangled up with sheh perfume. Then being careful enough to secure her gold jewelry because "no, no" not at all would she loose them because those are her only assets from "back in de day." She would also assure Sharon that if at any time they were in need of money, that she would pawn her jewels. Lie!!! That is lie!!! Doris ain't gto do that. She love dem things too much. No way, Jose!!!! Do or die ..... she ain't pawning sheh gold jingles,[477] earrings nor chains!!! Lawd, sheh picking up de vibes that ah talking bout sheh and vexxin up sheh face. Who cares!!! Is de truth ah telling.

Eh, eh. I hearing some footsteps. Yes, just like I suspect. I talking to Rosie from the other yard. We brace up by the fence and it getting late, but still little bright that we could see Dookram and he wife and kids coming in. They look both exhausted and happy. All I seeing is the son teeth. He smiling so much like he really had a good time, while he sister is being carried by the daddy because

---

[476] *A woman who really didn't love men but played with them. Lied also to them.*
[477] *Gold bracelets*

196

she fall asleep. They got three miserly bags, but is alright. The fact is that they went out; something that they rarely do, and you know what, we ain't going to bother them to see what they buy. It too late for one, plus minding people business is not a good thing at all. Y'all hear me......minding people business is not a good thing!!! It does cause too much confusion and too much mix-up.... and too much "seh seh."[478]

The couple and they kids now inside and I just hear Little Saheed blowing a whistle he padnah Cyril did do earlier, and he just yelled out, *"Santa, Santa."* Well is true. They did take he to see that man with a silver beard and red suit. He lucky, he thinking, cause the little rasta yutman .... youthman in the alley way next door not going to see Santa cause he is "Satan Clause" and that he daddy and mammy tell he that they not carrying he. Said they does only celebrate ...... "ilabrate" Ethiopian Christmas on January 7th. Well, to each his own and we ain't going to judge, although I does only ilabrate that day tuh. But, is just "niceness" fuh everybody who like that December 25th.

The lights off now in the Dookram's house because is after eight. They gone to bed early tonight and we could guess why because they kind of was looking tyad .... tired. Oh mih Gawd ...... Oh my God, but we ain't know what was in dem bags!!! They muslims. Allyuh rememba? So it must not be Christmas things, cause they don't put up fairy lights and doesn't

---

[478] *Gossiping*

197

cook garlic pork and pepperpot. Only strictly Indian dishes, but because dey little chirren force them to take them to see that bearded man, they try to please them. Ah bet y'all they ain't spend too much. They thrifty you see!!! Parbattie did say a day that they saving for tickets to go to Canada when they papers come through; the papers that sheh brother file over two years now. So, any day now they going to be leaving Punchin Yard for a better life abroad. Yep, they going to be saying "good bye" one of these days.

"Dey is some nice neighbas aan we gon miss dem," Ethel of all persons did say while Mother Beulah chimed in, *"really nice yuh see. Ah like dem cauz dey understand Daphne when sheh start sheh stupitness. Dat Parbattie does mek roti aan curry aan gih all ahwe tuh when we aan gat money. Nice East Indian people. Ah like dem. Gawd bless dem. We gon miss dem."*

Meanwhile, at Miss Millie house, she just turn off she stove cause sheh pepperpot done. Hazel and she cleaning up de kitchen and they laughing at how Lenny basidee[479] over Brenda. They done now while Jacqueline curled up in they living room sofa and Patsy just left to go home. She has to go to work tomorrow, she said, but we all done know that is Noel she going to "clock"[480] early in the morning to see if he bring mail from Bertie. After all, tomorrow is the day before the big day and she getting worried now, but Lenny and Ulrick who sitting outside just

---

[479] *Confused or deliriously in love*
[480] *To "diligently look for"*

assured her that she is going to be fine. Said they got the feeling that Bertie might be coming home. She looks relieved and waves goodbye to her two cousins, and as if their dog is detecting her feelings, he licks Patsy on the leg and wags his tail as she passes him by the front gate.

Christmas Eve

Bridget outside with a bucket and a scraper[481] scrubbing the front steps of her building as it is her turn today and she calling out to Patsy who as usual, is trying to sneak inside sheh house.

"Patsy is wheh yuh went? Ah was callin fuh yuh aan ai ain hear nutten," in a more than enquiring voice.

The woman continues to scrape away at the board on her stairway with a piece of metal with what appears to be a wooden handle attached to it, but gets no response from Patsy who seems to be extremely tongue-tied today.

"Is ahrite, go aan get some ress. Ah understaan," Bridget succumbs.

She then rinses what appears to be an old rag or "floor cloth" in the bucket of now filthy water and continues to the fourth step on the dilapidated stairway. She has two more to do as one could also smell the Jeyes Fluid [482] in the water, then smiles at her efforts of making the others that has been completed their original color. In this country, it is customary to not only mop in one's house, but also to scrub the wooden steps one by one. It is only when this is done that one's home is regarded as entirely clean.

---

481 *A piece of metal with wood attached at the top as a handle*

482 *A dark disinfecting fluid made for cleaning of a black color that is manufactured*

Almost all of the women have mopped their rooms already, leaving just Ethel to do hers. Sometimes it's the older children in the family that does this task, and mostly girls. That little selfish Cyril does do he mother steps after she begs him more than a million times because she gets back pain. Like if he dis do it good? That's why Gwen daughter finishes up the job, and yuh think that Maxine gives her a few coppers[483] for helping out? No, because sheh haan tight [484] and only gives the little girl a plate of food after the task.

Dis aan dat, aan dis aan dat [485]......... then the whole yard does take on a new appearance with everything nice and clean, and smelling good. A few dogs in the yard and they also sprinkle the Jeyes Fluid to keep the yard from smelling putrid and rancid. It's a good thing cause it keeps down the smells of animal urine and fecal matter. Dookram keeps his little puppy inside, so we don't have to worry about that one defecating or urinating on the grass or concrete.

Bridget inside now and it seems like everybody busy as the yard looking empty now. Then some other people went to do their last minute shopping today like Carol whose Cousin Leslyn didn't leave as yet. Changed she mind and decided not to return to Hopetown today. Never had a town[486] Christmas and she excited.

---

[483] *A few pennies/coins*
[484] *She is stingy and does not want to get rid of money or a pay up*
[485] *All in all, and all in all*
[486] *The city; Georgetown*

Remember she been helping out a lot around the house trying to make the kids happy? Now she babysitting so that Carol could go downtown and get somethings for the kids. Sheh even empty out sheh purse and give she cousin more that three hundred dollars. Y'all calling sheh an "ole maid?"[487] Them does have money to burn. Ain't got no kids and dis save. Went to the bank this morning and happy to help buy gifts and other things for she cousin children. But, she mind not at ease because not only that she feeling guilty that she just tell she mother that she not in no good shape to travel, but also that Gavin might come in drunk later and cause trouble.

"Oh God, I hope he is not coming home to argue and beat up Carol tonite," she whispers to herself quietly in grammar that denotes a very good education.

She is now remembering the last incident where the neighbors had to intervene, and how Sam was challenging the drunken Gavin to fight. What angers her is how it affects the children and how Carol is constantly depressed. She is even thinking that for the new year she should encourage her cousin to relocate to Berbice with her. This would enable them to get a better living; free of domestic violence and the peace of mind that any battered woman deserves. The children also, she is thinking, would benefit from this solitude. Besides, Cousin Leslyn owns a

---

[487] *Or "spinster" and a British term with regards to a single woman considered too old for marriage*

202

three bedroom home and is willing to give Carol and the kids access to two bedrooms and of course, the rest of her house to dwell in. Her specific concern also is that the police does not recognize the impact of domestic violence and treats it as a patriarchal privilege, unlike other places in the world.

"Me aan know why dey dhoan lack up de men dem. Ah cud even rememba how one ah dem did tell de husbaan tuh beat de woman up some moe becauz she din done cooking he food. Dem police dhoan protect we. Dey dis encourage de men, aan me ain like duh," [488] said Anita, Patsy's co-worker, who is a strong advocate against Intimate Partner and Domestic Violence.

She then went on to describe her past relationship to the ladies in the yard as she sat in Patsy's doorway a few months ago. She seems to have been very affected by its events, and hence, has suffered severe Post Traumatic Stress Disorder. To me, she needs counseling, but where are the counselors? Pertinent indeed for PTSD as it is a condition that replays itself over and over again.

Patsy inside now and looks outside to see if it's Noel voice she is hearing. Yes, it's him, and since today is December 24th, she will ask if he has a letter for her. She becomes nervous now, and decides not to enquire, but will loiter outside to see if he will hand her an envelope. The postman is two doors away, and will

---

[488] *"I don't know why they don't lock up the men. I could even remember how one of them did tell the   husband to beat the woman up some more because she didn't done/finish cooking his food. Those police don't protect we. They usually encourage the men and I don't like that."*

be here soon. He just smiled at her and she is becoming hopeful that she is getting something in the mail. Noel is coming closer and closer with the stack of mail in his hand with some appearing to be cards from their sizes.

"How are you Patsy? You're alright? Are you ready for the holidays? Haven't been seeing you," the man who delivers letters questions her.

He then hands her a small blue envelope; the ones that we all know are from England. Patsy fighting the tears from her eyes, takes the letter from the very well-spoken Noel and goes inside. She then tears it open and reads ....

Dear Patsy,

Hope all is well. How are you and the rest of the family in Hopetown? I know that you all are blessed with good weather but not us. Brixton is very cold today and as a matter of fact, all of England at this time of year. I know Bertie must be home by now and I want to wish you both a Merry Christmas. I know that you must be so happy and excited that he is there. You two lovebirds must miss each other so much when apart, reminding me of when Dennis had left me behind for all those years in Guyana before returning to marry me ....

Patsy cannot read the letter anymore and pelts it on the floor. Although her cousin Bernadette in England means well in the letter, it's as if she is taunting her and that is the last thing that Patsy wants to hear .... about if Bertie has arrived, and truthfully, he is not there. She wants to continue reading the two-page letter, but refuses to. It is saddening her especially since the big holiday is less than twenty-fours away and she has barely nothing and has not even thought of decorating her home.

But what we talking bout? That darn cousin didn't even send her a little 'small piece'........ couple English pounds to spend and have a nice time. Not even a greeting card too, but a letter!!! Only showing off and exalting herself about sheh Dennis going back to marry her. Big deal, and so what?!!! Patsy remembers how that Bernadette used to cry every day and beg Dennis to come back and marry sheh. Lost weight also and turned a Christian when she think he wasn't returning. She and sheh mother every Sunday walking up Brickdam going to church with they bibles to pray for a wedding. Then to bible lessons every Wednesday. Marcia did say that they used to arrive so early, sitting outside before de church doors open as they wanted to pray so much. Almost did "leff pun haan"[489] and now showing off. But she got the nerves!!! Trying to send Patsy to de mad house.

"Look leh sheh carry sheh self duh side." Is I saying so. I hope the cold bite sheh rass!!! Yes, sheh backside!!![490]

Patsy in bed now, and not going to work. Just did get little strength and went by Carol to use sheh fone, but she wasn't home. So, Cousin Leslyn let she use it and didn't charge sheh. Felt so sorry for the teary eyed, lovelorn girl that she just pass the phone to.

"May the God Lord give you the faith, health and strength to deal with your situation, I pray for you."

Cousin Leslyn is a school teacher, so she speaks as perfect as she wants, and when she wants to. She then closes the door behind her as Patsy has just left and says, *"Jesus, no weapons formed against her shall prosper."*

---

[489] *Almost did "not marry"*

[490] *"Look let her carry herself that side." Is I saying so. I hope the cold bite her rass!!! Yes, her backside/ass!!!*

It is then that Carol's eldest daughter brings the bible and asks her mother's cousin to engage in some bible lessons. The God-fearing woman smiles and then turns to where they had left off from yesterday afternoon.

"Dis place need dis in heh. Gavin is like ah devil now drinkin dat devil soup aan bringin nuff confusion in heh. It need prayers like duh in dis house,"[491] Carol would repetitively say everytime there were bible lessons within the confines of her walls.

Well is who ah seeing now? Phillip who did hiding out next door crawling in he domain. Stanley following he and they look like they up to something, but I ain't going to focus on they affairs. Them two does usually go and smoke they little weed especially when Phillip call out to he and say that he got a "lil draw." [492] Is de holidays so they 'nicing it up.' Tekkin a little pressure off they head, you know. Sharon not home, but Phillip happy cause he got sheh 'in check'….. under control as he ooman now and they gon have a nice day tomorrow. He gave her some more money two hours ago apart from what she hustled and she took the kids out.

Doris inside doing the little 'odds and ends' and saving she strength for another 'ole head' dance night after tomorrow where all the experienced older hustlers or ex-ones go to. She does dance

---

[491] *"This place need this in here. Gavin is like a devil now drinking that devil soup and bringing plenty confusion in here. It needs prayers like that in this house"*
[492] *"Little smoke; a spliff (as like of marijuana)*

you see. Dis get up while she gambling and do a little "two step" when she hear one of sheh favorite songs. Yes, she does. Ain't too old to dance. Is good exercise and good therapy too, and when you sweat, yuh could sweat out the toxins that could shorten yuh lifespan. Guyanese big people not ezee!!! They does dance and have a great time. Drink they rum and Banks beer, and eat they cook-up rice, black pudding, pepperpot, souse, chow-mein, cheese rolls, boiled channa, dholl phouri and curry chicken, and all the dishes they cook and enjoy deyselves.[493] Some that turn vegans and vegetarians dis got dey ital food[494] tuh. So Miss Doris know what she doing by going out.

Oh skites!!! Is whuh going on? Like we forgetting once more to check in by Hazel and sheh mother dem. Ah wonder if Patsy over there again? She not only frustrated now, but she sneaky like hell. She leffin sheh house; sneaking out and nobody not seeing her. Then she friend Anita telling sheh soldier man to park he car far so that nobody don't see when she come to Patsy or pick she up. Dem two real close and they does hold heads together even on the job when the manager want to overwork them. They "dis do fuh he"[495] and sometimes be calling in sick the same time. They stick together and don't give a damn if he vex. But, that's all fuh dat. We want to know what dem folks doing ..... Hazel, sheh mother and two brothers. Then we gon see if anybody else over there cause is the day before the big day and things going

---

493 *Themselves*

494 *Meatless food mostly ate by Rastafarians*

495 *Plan for him (in a spiteful way)*

on. Plenty, plenty things like more cooking, fixing up house ......
and so on this bright Friday afternoon.

This is what does go on pun this day in Guyana. Then de
relatives from abroad be all bout de place[496] talking in they fancy
accents that they get from abroad and overdressing so that people
could tell that they only on vacation and not living in this country
anymore. Dem that call themselves "overseas-based Guyanese."
Hahaha!!!

I remember a time we did go to the airport to meet a
relative. Ah trying to remember is which relative cause we did
have so many of them coming and going. But anyway, back to mih
story .... so I see this fancy accent East Indian man and he two
daughters with two white dolls coming through Timehri airport
and saying to he drooling relatives ....

*"Hey guys, I left my baggages in New York. Yeh, I didn't
get them. Those guys will call me when they arrive. So many
baggages that they couldn't hold on the plane,"* while trying to
keep he cock teeth [497]in he mouth. Gosh, in New York suh laang[498]
and couldn't even buy some bracers!!!

Ah wonda if is true cause now I thinking back, he could
have been lying knowing very well that he didn't bring a darn

---

[496] *All about or all over the place*
[497] *Protruding teeth that need braces*
[498] *So long*

thing fuh he relatives. Then it was Christmas eve at that and some of them started to look disappointed with they heads bowing in despair. But look at he!!! Not a blasted thing for de ones he supposed to love. That fool didn't come bearing gifts. He and he cock teeth lying self; no example to his two girl children. Should be ashamed of he self. See if was me, I wudda leff he rite deh stranded. Went to America and come back with 'he too laang haans.' Catch ..... ketch ah taxi yuh wretch from de damn airport tuh whuheva yuh going.[499]

You see when he chose to travel? So he could make an excuse that there were too many baggages at this busy time of the year and his were left back, and later lost. But is who he fooling? Cause me and mih twin sister see he with three pieces of luggage that he seh was he own and that the balance gon come later.

"Bloody disappointing," my daddy would say. *"That lad is bloody disappointing."*

You know my daddy always used them British terms ..... "bloody" and "lad" and then some Latin sometimes cause he was the first one to teach me at the dining table the word "modus operandi" when I was about ten. Teach me nuff, nuff big vocabulary words to mek mih bright by comprehending what

---

[499] *Went to America and come back with empty hands. Catch ...... catch a taxi you wretch from the damn airport to wherever you are going.*

people saying. A good Papa he was with the last name like the capital of France, and 'double RR…ed.'

Ah getting carried away now and want to cry like Patsy…. I crying fuh mih father that I miss and he dead, and she crying fuh sheh man that alive and she think not coming back. What a "catch 22"!!! Well, ah know mine cyaan come again so we wishing Patsy well. She is a nice girl and don't deserve to be treated like that, and that "Auntie Avril" of Bertie beating around de bush when de girl call and can't tell sheh something other than *"he out."* Out where, and with who??? Sheh is a big woman and ah going to respect her, but ah got to say it …… "sheh playing de ass of sheh self. Tell Patsy de truth if she suspecting that Bertie cheating. Come on ole fowl.*"* [500] Yes, I just called sheh an "ole fowl" because she hiding fuh sheh nephew. Tek lil stress off de gurl!!! [501]

That Jacqueline; Hazel friend from Cayenne she ruff you see. Rough and heartless like hell. She looking at we thinking we fools sympathizing with Patsy, and shudn't do that. I do not like her. She is very unsympathetic. Change since she went to Cayenne. They should chase sheh ……. Hazel and Miss Millie. Warming up they living room seat three days now. Come to eat, belch, and you know what else. Ah mean use the bathroom and leave. Then she ain't even buying back de toilet paper that sheh use up. Ain't

---

[500] *An old woman whom is not looked upon with adoration*
[501] *Take a little stress off the girl*

211

dat a shame!!! Fuh me, when it done, for she rudeness, she wudda have to use newspaper. Yes, newspaper. Wet it and use it.

"Hide de toilet paypuh mammy," [502] Ulrick did say yesterday, but nobody didn't listen to he, now they down to one roll.

Maybe she using it to wipe off sheh make-up too. But that's not an excuse.   She too uncaring and never did buy "un cadeau" for Little Orson next door. Lied to   de lil boy bout buying he *"a gift."* Only wanted to show off the French she know….. not nice at all. "Neva see come fuh see" …….. not use to anything in life, excited and shows off.

So don't let we get no indigestion talking bout that mean girl and the paper she been using up cause according to my Jamaican friends, seems like "big tings agwaan"[503] by Miss Millie and sheh chirren house. The back door open and we smelling food that they dog Jeff hanging around and looking like he drooling. Who say a dog don't drool allyuh? Y'all got a lot more to learn about these animals, and they got sense tuh. Jacqueline again ….. she just chase de dog and Hazel said, *"leff he."* Then she called de dog back upstairs. They had he for years and he is an obedient pet and a good watch dog. That girl cruel too yuh know. That Jacqueline!!!

---

[502] *"Hide the toilet paper mommy."*
[503] *Big things are happening*

Now somebody else coming to de door. De person running back inside. Cyaan miss sheh. Is Patsy. Puh gurl,[504] is she. Must be aan got de energy to go to Berbice or visit she other relatives over de river in Den Amstel. Prefer to come right back to Meadow Brook with sheh nice auntie and cousins. They nice yuh see and dis do they best to make her happy. They dis feed sheh up tuh. She don't get no 'hungrie belly' there. Lenny just offered her a piece of cake that he mother took out the oven and it cooling off.

"Cousin Patsy, yuh waan some black cake? It warm. Not too hot aan sheh aan soak it wid rum yet, so yuh ain gat tuh worry bout gettin drunk aff it. Plus mammy dhoan put plenty rum pun sheh cake unless yuh ask sheh fuh put some more pun yuh slice."

The young bewildered woman then beckons as if to say "no" and walks into Hazel's room. She is retiring to bed early; very early and is exempting herself from the day-before-the holiday happenings. She sleeps a lot now which is one of the indications of misery and unhappiness, and could lead to many more mental health issues if this condition prolongs. Her relatives in the countryside are sensing this and have asked her to go home and celebrate with them tomorrow, but she seems to no longer have zest for life. She hardly writes to them nor even calls, as they have a telephone that sheh Cousin Pam boyfriend that work on a trawler boat did get installed in they house fuh dem. That Aubrey want to keep track of he fiancée, so that's the reason why he put

---

[504] *Cannot miss her, Is Patsy, Poor (as in sympathy) girl.*

that fone in, while Patsy……. all she thinks about is Bertie, and if or when he is returning home. She is giving up now because most of the people she knows with relatives and partners abroad has arrived already. Her life is now a "hell hole" because she is being tormented by her man's absence and time is running out.

"We cudda guh downtown tonite aan 'lime'[505] *by Bookers aan den walk ova to Tower, but Patsy gone in sheh bed,"* Hazel whines. *"Ah did guh laas year aan it did nice. Ah did see plenty of dem chirren ah did guh tuh skool wid from away."* By saying *"away,"* she means "from abroad." The children who are all grown up now that she attended school with and return home from time to time for the holidays.

Jacqueline and her brothers seem eager to go, and Miss Millie chimes in, *"allyuh cud guh. Spend lil time aan den come back aan help mih do de last minute tings in de wee hours of de morning. Ah ahrite."*

But Lenny says he will not go anymore, but instead that he will stay back and assist his mother. Not only that, y'all know is Brenda he want to see. That's why he staying back. But ah wonder if he buy sheh gift yet? Christmas time and want girlfriend and ain't got no gift? Stanley laughing at he. He know de ole tricks. He not been going after Patsy about three weeks now cause he know he ain't got no extra money fuh buy sheh a gift. Cheap

---

[505] *We could of gone downtown tonight and 'hang out'*

skate!!! Joining them other fools who does break up with they woman or stop hustling them during the holidays and then want to mek up back[506] after the New Year.

"Trutha Gawd, ah ain lyin or Jah gon smite mih."[507]

Well is only a hard up woman[508] would tek dem back like Roxanne; Little Debbie mother, but she did deserve it fuh de way she never did look back at de little girl. She did really desperate for a man!!!

"Leh Stanley guh duh side yeh."[509]

Patsy not studying he, and was thinking that earlier. She in "snoresie land" now. She fast asleep and trying to block out sheh worries.

The others are dressing to head downtown to go hang out by Bookers. How Hazel know this? Sheh Cosmopolitan friend and the niece of her grandmother boss did carry she two years in a row and she like it cause she could eye up or scrutinize some of dem nice mixed-race boys. Some of them from Queen's College, Saint Stanislaus, St. John's, Central and them other schools. She hoping that she see Tony whom she met at Claire birthday party on Hadfield Street a few months ago. They danced and danced,

---

[506] *Or stop hustling them during the holidays and then went to make up back or reconcile after the New Year*

[507] *True to God, I am not lying or Jehovah is going to smite me*

[508] *A desperate woman for a man*

[509] *"Let Stanley go that side okay."*

and danced all night long after he had stood staring at her for almost an hour. She knew he had liked her and would eventually stretch his hands toward her for them to dance.

Like Little Debbie in the post office, his palms were sweaty and trembling. He couldn't resist the song *"Cover Me"* by Percy Sledge. Hazel quickly got up as she felt an instant attraction for this handsome young man. Also, it was her favorite song and before that she had refused some other young men, hoping that Tony would eventually ask her. Now y'all see she wasn't baking pone.[510] Ah mean that she wasn't like Denise long time ago who no man asked for a dance because she was little too much on the heavy side. That's why eventually when she was asked to dance after she had lost weight, and then, was asked to accompany the young men home, she readily said "yes." That's why she is now known as the *"carry off gurl"* and not only dancing with her partners, but providing sexual favors after.

See what poor self-esteem dis do, then excitement? But Cousin Hazel had earned her reputation of being a nice girl and a virgin. That's what Tony knew about her from the gossip amongst the boys who were standing to the side sizing up the girls. Watching them carefully. They knew exactly who was a "slacka"

---

[510] *An action of a young woman sitting all night on a chair or sofa with no man asking her to dance at a party*

216

[511]and who wasn't. But who cares!!! Tony didn't care about the other girls because his eyes were on Hazel ...... only Hazel.

Then the music keeps belting out.

"Girl, my love for you gets stronger everyday

Oh, darling I don't want to lose you

Oh, cover me, cover me"

Is Nigel on de turntable. Well yuh done know he. This party cudn't get a better DJ than that, and he is much sought after since he dis full a party up. Everybody follows "Big Nigel" Sound System cause he is the best in town. Man if yuh see!!! De couples on de dance floor cause this is a top tune by Earth, Wind and Fire. Can't stop de oldies ..... party "tun up"[512] with this one and Hazel smiling with sheh white teeth the color of the toothpaste she brushes them with. She loves to dance as Tony embraces her in sweet synchrony. They waltzing and filling de corners while some couples "renting ah tile."[513]

Could you imagine two people so close together that they could fit in a make-believe tile? They dancing close, close, close and some of them look like they can't breathe in de little space that they have designated for themselves. Two "regulahs" ......

---

[511] *A slack or loose woman*

[512] *Turn up or really, really nice*

[513] *Dancing in the small space as if in the space of a tile. The two people are close, close to each other*

regulars, that I know too well; two young men that used to pope ^{514} every party know what ah talking bout with they tight shut, drain pipe pants and clark shoes.^{515} Some in de dark and yuh cyaan even see 'who is who' and they kissing in the corners too, even though some of them just met. How I know some of them kissing? How yuh mean? Whuh wrong with y'all? I did see it over and over at de parties in mih own house in Eve-Leary. All in de fun!!!..... some ah dem boys dong a lil fine wine^{516} on de girls and de girls liking it. Cousin Hazel little shy and she hoping that Tony don't try that on sheh.

"Hazel, ah tellin yuh mih chile. Dhoan leh dem boys dance too close wid yuh cauz de next ting dey gon waan is sex,"^{517} Miss Millie would say to her bashful daughter.

Someone is calling her name, and Hazel stops daydreaming. That was a night to remember, as she continues to scope out the crowd for the young man that she hopes to see again.

Noel of all persons just went into Tower Hotel with ah binnie who look like she 'come from away.'^{518} He all arms and arms with her and he dressed up. Then he clothes look foreign too. If only Cousin Hazel and Jacqueline could smell he clothes

---

^{514} *To intrude in without an invitaton; an uninvited guest*
^{515} *Tight shirts, tight tight pants fitting close to the bottom and British. clark shoes*
^{516} *Physically gyrating on the girls*
^{517} *"Hazel, I am telling you my child. Don't let those boys dance too close with you. because the next thing they are going to want is sex"*
^{518} *With a young woman who looks like she 'came from overseas'*

because them clothes got a scent that different from the clothes at home. A nice smell that tells you that they not from there. Y'all remember de smell before yuh did migrate? …… that nice sweet smell when yuh friends or relatives did open they suitcases and when they wear dem clothes. Ah ha!!! Could never forget. Clothes that were really fancy and fashionable, setting the trend for what was 'in style' in whatever country they travelled from.

That Hazel and Jacqueline ….. they thinking now to cross de street and follow Noel and de binnie, and talking bout how it is rumoured that some of the people at the post office steals some customers things in they boxes and then be all dressed up. Maybe they should suggest to Ulrick to run across de street and ask Noel about a letter Patsy expecting. Then they could go up to he and also scrutinize he lady. They fast, eh? Noel is a good postman and he do not need to be harassed on a night like this. They thinking, they studying!!!

"Eh, eh Hazel. Allyuh cyaan do duh. Leff de man alone. He mus be 'ketch ah ting.' Is de halidays. Leff he."[519] That was Ulrick. He non-complies and is telling them to stop the nonsense.

They laugh and turn their attention to another couple who is kissing passionately on the sidewalk in front of Bookers. For Hazel this is uncommon because she hardly leaves the house and finds it indecent. On the other hand, Jacqueline finds this amusing

---

[519] *"No, no Hazel. You all cannot do that. Leave the man alone. He must be find a new woman. Is the holidays. Leave him.'*

as she begins to tell her friend about herself and Jean-Pierre, her lover. Ulrick then interrupts and says that it is time for them to go home. A disappointed Hazel then nods in agreement as their mother had stipulated that they should only stay out for three hours. She had not seen Tony and begins to feel sad. But, she has chores at home to do before tomorrow morning.

By the time the three people arrived home, Patsy has shone the floor with the much needed floor polisher that Lenny had borrowed from his friend. In the far corner of her bedroom, Miss Millie is sewing what seems like curtains, while Lenny is measuring the kitchen floor. Ulrick joins in and fetches the linoleum that was leaned up against the living room wall as he begins to tell his brother about the "goings on" earlier tonite downtown.

"Yuh cudda tek ah lil stepout tonite Lenny. Whuh, yuh was lookin out fuh Brenda? Yuh cudda come aan get some fun. Plenty people was out deh aan was laughin aan talkin aan havin ah good time. Ai even see Patrick who went tuh school wid we. He come fuh spend de halidays from England. He look 'fair, fair.' He complexion lighten up, aan he talkin fancy dat ai cud barely understaan he. He send fuh seh "hello."

Lenny smiles with tape measure in hand and resorts back to deep concentration as this family cannot afford to waste any piece of their linoleum. One poor measurement could result in them requiring more and could disrupt their budget, and even if they have to squeeze and buy a little piece more, the store has already closed. This is what happens when most people, according to custom, decides to 'put away'[520] their house at the last minute so that their neighbors cannot steal their decorating ideas. For example, why is Miss Millie sewing curtains so late? It is after 12 at night and she threading the sewing machine to acquire her goal of getting those nice window blinds[521] up by tomorrow morning. Then it look like her enthusiasm is being prompted by that anxiety that most of dem Guyanese people does have in these last few hours before daylight. After all, it's like they are entering a competition to see who got de best house.

"*Mammy, yuh done de bed sheets? Ah cud help cut aff de threads aan put dem pun de beds afta?*" enquires Cousin Hazel.

Her mother then points to a closet and describes a bag for Hazel to bring to her. In it is some pieces of cloth already cut according to the sizes of the beds, and her mother explains that all she has to do is sew around the raw edges to make them complete. She also will be making some pillowcases with the smaller pieces. Hazel yawns and takes a seat on the chair just next to her mother. She is now anticipating that this will be a long night as always, as she has to prevent herself from not only nodding, but from falling asleep. Her bed seems to be calling her now, but she has to restrain

---

[520] *Fix up their house*
[521] *Curtain*

herself from laying on that object, but instead is adhering to her mother who is almost done sewing up the sides of two bedsheets.

Then her meticulous mother adds, *"yuh gaffuh iron dem fuss Hazel befoe yuh put dem pun de bed."*[522]

This daughter who is still reminiscing about Tony and is saddened by not seeing him earlier, walks toward a corner in the bedroom to grab the iron board. She is very lethargic now and as she grabs the iron from the closet shelf above, it falls to the ground and her mother sucks her teeth. Hazel knows what that means and quickly steps away from Miss Millie. It is just a few hours before the big holiday and she don't want to get konks up because her mammy's adrenaline rush could result in a flight-or-fight-response. In other words, Hazel's negligence could propel her mommy to anger, and to hit her in either of her temporal lobes with a knuckled up fist even though sheh grown.

Well it look like Jacqueline staying over tonight again and not going to sheh God sister house. She just asked Lenny for the balloons and he just gih sheh a whole bag of them with all sorts of colors. She stretching one of them now and she surveying de whole place with sheh eyes. She living in Cayenne now, but she didn't forget how to decorate "Guyanese style." Plus Ulrick now handing sheh a bowl with some pepperpot that he just thief out he mother pot.

---

[522] *"You have to iron them first Hazel before you put them on the bed."*

222

"Is jus ah lil taste. It gon pep yuh up fuh stay up wid we aan get dis place togetha,"[523] Ulrick says with a charming smile.

Looks like he like sheh as she been suspecting and now he getting a chance to initiate something since Hazel in de bedroom with her mother. He has no girlfriend and although he finds this girl to be a little rude, recently he been liking sheh hot mouth.[524] After all, why not? She is not too bad looking with full lips, a small waist and a rear end that wiggles when she walks that absolutely turns him on. Then the girl has broad hips on top of that and she loves to wear go-go belts with her dungaree pants.[525] This drives him wild, as he imagines her naked sometimes.

"Yuh waan we go aan bathe at de 'blacka'[526] *fuh de new year Jacqueline? Me, you aan Hazel. Lenny yuh cud come tuh aan leh we wash off all de bad vibes fuh de new year."*

Now, allyuh know what he up to ......is want he want to see sheh in sheh bathing suit. At least that's almost to being naked. Freak!!! Imagining all sorts of vain things when Jacqueline near and even far. Wondering if sheh would give he 'ah play,'[527] and then wondering if she would cheat on sheh ole Frenchman fuh he. Lusting, lusting, lusting, as he glances over at her putting the last

---

[523] *It's just a little taste. It is going to pep you up to stay up with we/us and get this place together."*
[524] *Saying rude and abnoxious things*
[525] *Blue jeans, denim jeans*
[526] *A small body of water or creek that is black in color behind Meadow Brook Gardens. It is. said to cleanse you spiritually*
[527] *Give him a 'romantic chance'*

spoon of his mother's delicious dish on her plump and, according to him, "sexy lips."

He then once more walks over to her and gives her a little bit of rum and pepsi.

"Tek ah drink Jacqueline. Is de halidays."

She hands him the empty plate and sips at the drink. Y'all think he ezee!!! He trying to get her drunk.

"Ah wish ah cud 'feel sheh up' tonite," [528] he says to himself, and goes back into the kitchen.

Is late now and somebody knocking at de front door.

"Is who is duh?" a now rejuvenated Hazel asks. [529]

Jacqueline answers the door and it's Carol. Said she went to visit her brother in Lodge Housing Scheme and decided to pass by to wish them a "Merry Christmas." She is beaming with delight and says that her sister-in-law had called for her to come over on her arrival from Holland, and had bought some gifts and money for Carol.

"Y'all place look nice Miss Millie. Ah like how y'all paint it up tuh."

---

[528] *"I wish I could 'fondle her up' tonight*
[529] *"Is who is that?" a now rejuvenated Hazel asks.*

She now walks further into the house and sees Ulrick and Lenny who stops what they are doing to hug her. Hazel is delighted to see her also, since the family has not been to Punchin Yard to visit Cousin Patsy in about two months.

"Ah glad fuh see yuh Carol, aan how dem chirren?" Millie enquires.

"Deh ahrite Miss Millie. If yuh see de gifts dey get. Ah gon go home aan me aan Cousin Leslyn gon wrap dem up becauz all Gavin doing is drinkin up he money. He aan buy we shit..... excuse mih, pardon mih fuh cussin in front uh yuh Miss Millie .... aan if wasen fuh Leslyn, we cudda neva eat. We wudda get 'white mouth.' [530] *Tuh much!!! Ah gon get rid ah he fuh de new year. Ah swear, ah mean it."*

Hazel then embraces her and whispers, *"is ahrite. Yuh like famalee Carol. Is ahrite okay. We deh heh. Yuh gon be ahrite, yuh hear mih. Dhoan run up yuh blood pressure. Is only time wid he,"* and squeezes Carol tighter as if consoling a child in distress.

Meanwhile Miss Millie goes to the kitchen to gather up some food for Carol to take home. She re-emerges and hands Carol a bag ....

"Thank yuh Aunt Millie. Ah gon tell dem chirren dat yuh send dis. Thank yuh. Ah gon go now aan before de year out ah gon

---

[530] *Malnourished looking mouth with white corners*

225

ask mih brotha fuh bring me aan dem chirren fuh visit y'all. Yuh shud see how dey get moe tall in duh lil space ah time dat yuh aan see dem," says Carol and smiles with a perceived joy as how her offsprings has grown and will get even bigger.

She then waves goodbye and gets into the waiting car. See what I told allyuh before …….. things worked out fuh Carol in de end because some relatives return home "announced" and some "unannounced." This story going good, eh? Nice, nice, sweet, sweet Guyana and it's people.

Things coming along now …… Christmas tree lighting up with de nice fairy lights while Hazel and Jacqueline stripping de cotton wool to look like snow on it, as Miss Millie yells for them to ………

"Peep aan see if de nex door neighbas put up dey blinds yet especially Miss Ismay."[531] See because Miss Ismay, according to all the neighbors last year, did have the best blinds …. curtains.

"Donna, shut yuh big mouth" with yuh soliloquy ………. talking to yuhself now. Hahaha!!!"

This is the kind of comic-relief I like around this time as I still question "why?" Why do all that? What? Is it a competition?

---

[531] *"Peep and see if the next door neighbors put up their blinds/curtains yet especially Miss Ismay."*

Just a few more hours to the big day; in the wee hours of the morning and they peeping. Peeping to see who put up they blinds.

On this subject, I asked my own mother why, and she seh, *"is fuh see if dey* blinds *nicer dan me own. Yes, Donna, we dis do dat."*

So, as my queries continued, she said, *"look man. Dhoan ask mih moe questions. Ah come aan meet it suh ,aan ah gon dead aan leff it suh."*[532]

But, of course, she and many other of my country people has long abandoned these customs upon migration abroad. But what I talking bout? Like I forgetting some of them folks in Brooklyn who living in de same building and still peeping. Esther does still peep every year to see if Joan, Sybil, Judith, Norma, Claudette, Roxanne, Sonia, Theresa, Muriel, Arlene, Betty, Wendy, Gem, Glenys, Judith, Lydia, Shanelle, Paula ,Jackie, Verna, Gloria, Annette, Michelle, Stephanie, Carlotta, Bernice, Natasha, Mavis, Karen, Pam, Monica, Pauline and dem other girls blinds …… if they own betta than she own. Then if sheh don't live near to some of them, sheh does jump in sheh car and go by they house to spy. HaHaHa!!!

She got time fuh waste, eh? Some people just can't abandon dem ole ways and assimilate in a new country. Just can't.

---

[532] *"Look man. Don't ask me more questions. I come and meet it so and I am going to dead and leave it so."*

Caught up in a time warp. Is not an entirely bad thing though by holding onto their cultural customs and beliefs even though she; Esther could ketch de plane aan go home for de holidays. Then she could indulge in all that "peeping." Only throwing box haan[533] and not spending de money right. Giving it to Monty every time he give sheh a sad story bout he car need fixing afta he gih sheh lil lovin de nite before.[534] Lie!!! If y'all see he at Pan American office booking he ticket fuh go home and she leff behind. "Peeping" and not seeing that this man lickin sheh up.[535]

So, is what I was saying before we went to the peeping? …… So de fairy lights up by the living room windows, and de Christmas tree got dem lights on too with some cotton wool to look like snow. Plus, Ulrick who still eyein up[536] Jacqueline joined she and Hazel to put up de curtains that Miss Millie just finish.

"Is jus snow pun dis tree Hazel? Wheh de otha deckrations?
Lenny asks.

"Deck-rations" …. he pronouncing that word like Daphne. My Gosh!!! Twenty-six years old and cannot pronounce that word

---

[533] *Box hand or known as 'su su' when people pool their money and take turns at collecting their share*
[534] *After he give her little loving (sex and romance) the night before*
[535] *Robbing her*
[536] *Looking at her lovingly/adoringly*

right as yet. Anyhow, anyhow, as my Jamaican friends would say, "leh we give he a 'blye' or a 'chance' since it's all the merry.

Miss Millie overheard him and emerges from out of her bedroom with a box that supposedly has the *"deckrations."* She looks exhausted as it is almost three in the morning, has been up since seven 'o' clock the day before, and is still delegating.

"Lenny ah comin to see how de kitchen look," Miss Millie yells. Then turns to Ulrick and says, *"leff dem gurls alone. Yuh shud be helpin Lenny."*[537]

She is almost to the kitchen now and nearly tripped on a piece of leftover linoleum that Ulrick was supposed to put away. He so busy admiring Jacqueline that he has neglected his duty of taking the piece of linoleum downstairs.

*"What ah tell yuh. Yuh nearly mek mammy hurt sheh self. Ah did tell yuh fuh **carry** it downstairs,"* shouts Lenny.

A very tired Miss Millie just shakes her head and begins to admire how much the linoleum has enhanced her kitchen floor. By this time Lenny and Ulrick is about to put another piece in the hallway between their two bedrooms.

---

[537] *"Lenny I am coming to see how the kitchen looks." Then turns to Ulrick and says, "leave those girls alone. You should be helping Lenny."*

"It look nice, eh?" Hazel says to Jacqueline and her mother, *"aan ah like de colors. Red aan cream aan de lil green inside. It nice aan suit de Crismus."*

She then goes back into her bedroom, and as if surveilling, watches to see if any of the neighbors on that side had put up their curtains. Then looking a little disappointed by being unable to report to her mother and the others, she goes to the next room, but without avail.

"Like deh gon wait till late, late mammy fuh put dem up, aan ah cyaan even see inside becauz they put sheets up at dey windows aan de ones wid jalousies[538] *close up tight. Is hard fuh see mammy, hard fuh see. We gon gat fuh wait till tamarraw when dey open dey windows wide, then we put we own dem up mammy,"* Hazel complains, while assuring her mother that in just a few hours they will satisfy their curiosity.

Jacqueline is now handing her a piece of garment to hem and cut threads off. This is Miss Millie's new task, as everyone wakes up with new sleeping clothes in the morning. But wait a minute!!! How much more hours are there to sleep since it so late now? Well I guess they will just take a bath, put them on and snooze for about two hours before daylight. Then by this time the neighbors blinds; curtains will be up, and the comparisons will

---

[538] *A louvered window composed of parallel glass, acrylic or wooden louvres set in a frame. They are usually joined onto a track so that they could be tilted open or shut in unison to control. airflow usually by turning a crank*

230

start as to "who blinds betta than whom, and who own come 'from away' and who got lace ones, and who own mek with just cloth and is a 'jimmy swing.'"[539]

Well y'all done know that 'Mouth ah Preh Preh' Doris can't wait fuh morning to come because she is the Senior Reporter in Punchin Yard about people blinds, they furniture if any, how much food they got in deh house, and so on …. and so on. That's Doris' job and no one dare take it away from her, you hear me!!! She dis perch up by de standpipe pretending like she washing sheh grandchildren clothes and 'tek in de scenes.'[540] She likes to mind people business without guilt and with presumption. She going to be dressed up tomorrow in a red kongol and some dress that one of sheh ole time boyfriends or a "fresh ting"[541] that she talking to buy sheh. Don't worry with Doris talking about she ain't got no man. She still got dem residual good looks and she still dis entice men with sheh broad hips and slight parrot toes.[542] That makes her thick legs look a little athletic for an elder. Then she got a nice spicy brown complexion that glows in the sun. But sheh sleeping now and leh we standby fuh sheh drama tomorrow.

Miss Millie dem lights off now. Ah mean de fairy lights by they living room windows and it look like they gon tek ah lil five[543] cause de real action starts in a just a few. Then some people

---

[539] *Not properly made or sewn, looks tacky*
[540] *Take in the scenes or look at the activities around*
[541] *A 'newly found boyfriend or girlfriend'*
[542] *Toes that are turned in the direction of each other when walking or decorticate*
[543] *Going to relax for a little bit*

231

going to be visiting the houses they were invited to all over de place, and if y'all only know!!! This is not de kind of action to miss out on at all. This is 'cultural customs at it's best' for Santa Day. This is the day that everybody been waiting for and when foreign goods like "ice apples"[544] and grapes does deh bout. This is also de day that allyuh gon see who got de best gifts. So go get some rest so that yuh could be nice and fresh when y'all wake up in yuh new pyjamas and nightgowns. Ah yawning now, aan tired ah writing all dis. Ah going to bed tuh.

Oh, aan before ah fuhget........ If any ah y'all see Rastaman Akatunde tell he ah seh save some ital[545] peppapat fuh mih. He did live in America aan dis ilabrate Kwanzaa like me starting pun Boxing Day. He dis 'cook up ah storm'[546] tuh. Ah gone. Dhoan fuhget!!

---

[544] *The term used by most locals for apples*
[545] *A term used for meatless, saltless, non-dairy, and organic food made by Rastafarians*
[546] *He cooks a lot*

232

Christmas Day

It quiet. De place really, really quiet. Everybody inside they house and is nine in de morning, but I know they doing things inside. Yuh would be surprised that some people still fixing up they place. Some start so late in the wee hours of the morning that they lagging back on time and not coming outside until they could show off they house. But Cousin Hazel peeping and sheh doing it really sneaky. She only get two hours sleep but she good to go. She energized from de ginger beer that sheh mother mek and now helping sheh self to a piece of fresh bread that sheh mommy just tek out de oven.

Oh yes!!! Some people does bake early on this morning so that de bread could be really tasty, soft and fresh. They like to even put some butter on it and like to watch it melt into the bread that nice and crusty. Then they eat that and then get another piece for they pepperpot later or my twin sister did like to put some cheese on. Plenty bread bake in this house so we don't have to worry. Why worry, cause is a nice Saturday morning and seven nice big loaves sitting on the kitchen counter waiting to enter the digestive tracks of the people in the household and their guests.

Yes, guests; some invited and some uninvited. The uninvited ones are usually the ones that come peeping to see what new inside the house. They usually like to figure out how much a person spend for de things that they buy, and if they been lying all year around that they didn't have money when they asked them to borrow some. Then some gone warm up yuh sofa to see who foreign-based relatives on vacation gon stop by yuh house or furthermore sit also to listen to yuh radio at the radio announcements. This is because it they don't own their own radio to hear overseas-based Guyanese sending greetings to relatives home, although I must emphasize that not everyone does that. Very rarely indeed. So, with their ears glued to your radio, they would be hoping they hear the voice of an aunt, uncle, cousin, ex-neighbor or classmate, grandmother or grandfather, etc., mentioning their name.

Until today, it is a mental imprint in my head. Not only is it hilarious to see some of their reactions, but also the anxiety and anticipation that fuh sure their names were going to be called. Oh yes, but some were disappointed as they pacified themselves with the food on the plate in front of them and drinks. I was only eleven years old then as I am referring to the year 1971, and could only barely remember that the announcements might have been on Radio Demerara. But what took the cake was that those abroad had these accents that sounded extremely exaggerated over their local accents as if to impress relatives home. Man, yuh shud hear them!!! Some wanted to sound as if born in America, Canada, England or other foreign countries. How kinda impressive and idiotic? Keep yuh pure my sisters and brothers. It's okay to speak perfect English like we were taught but don't fight so hard to disguise your accent. Don't bite yuh tongues tuh. Puh tings!!! But some are the same people who dis send those fancy pictures to make yuh think that they all doing so good. Pictures with them standing dressed up in winter coats and boots by someone fancy car other than their own. Hahaha!!! Be real. It's ok. Not always a utopia while trying to assimilate. Socio-economic change is sometimes a gradual process once you persevere. It is okay and alright. No one to judge, but anyhow those greetings and comic-relief ah did enjoy. Most of ahwe dis[547] elders could remember that day when yuh had to stretch yuh ears to understand .... overstand what those impostors were saying.

Eh, eh, by de way, Miss Cheryl is one who not like that. Not like the uninvited guests and just come to pick up de big pot of pepperpot and some bread from Miss Millie to share out in the yard and fuh Miss Beryl and sheh children next door over the alley. This is because the pot Carol did carry this morning almost half-way done.

"Drinkin rum on ah Crismas mawning

Drinkin rum

Mama drink if yuh drinkin"

Is Gavin at de top of he voice with he buddy Roy who dragging he by he right hand as he stumbling up Carol steps. He

---

[547] *Most of us*

could barely walk and he pissing drunk and loosing he equilibrium. Watch out!!! He almost fall down and he partner who look little sober had to catch he. Ain't been home all night. Leff he woman and chirren and went with he buddies to drink. He like that rum you see. Not even buy them nothing for de holidays and don't look like he care. No, no gifts at all. This is a case of substance abuse and with catalysts of dismantling one's family structure because Carol is thinking of leaving him. The drinking and the domestic violence has been too much for her and the children to bear more and more every day. Hence, she plans to separate from him which would give her children and herself the peace of mind that they need to do better in school as their grades has been affected drastically over the last few months.

Y'all think Gavin cares if we talking bout he because he still singing ……. *"Drinking rum on ah Crismus mawning. Drinking rum. Mama drink if yuh drinkin."*

He stumbling and mumbling, and singing louder again while Sam imitates him, and is singing even louder. Didn't even sit down and now trying to dance with he so-called wife who looking disgusted. Want to kiss sheh too, but sheh pulling away sheh face.

"Tek yuh hand offa mih. Yuh know ah dhoan like how yuh dis smell when yuh drink. Yuh got de nerves fuh waan touch mih.

Yuh went aan 'pick fares'[548] *wid Maylene? Yuh buy anyting fuh me aan dem chirren?"*

Carol then turns around and goes back inside, leaving Gavin and Roy on the front step. Then she comes back outside and rolls her eyes on the man she now detests. Is peeping day, so I know everybody seeing. Taking in all de activities while making mental notes of the events like this one. Then later reciting the details to each other ...... gossip, gossip, gossip!!!

Oh, oh!!! Ethel knocking on Doris door now. Dem two like "Suhrah aan Duhrah[549] and it must be that she carrying news to sheh friend about what she just see and hear. Then she will add in what is not true. Yuh tell she something or she hear something and she will add more; blow it out of proportion. Now that is not good and on this day at that .... still talking bout people instead of enjoying sheh self. That's why last year she did burn up sheh pepperpot that was only supposed to heat up slightly. Then begging de neighbors for some. That Ethel wid sheh 'dry up' self that hardly got any meat on sheh body. Hahaha!!! That's why Andre did leff sheh fuh ah bufianda ooman in August. Ooman with big wide hips. Nuff breasts and a big backside. Said he got more meat now. Filet mignon. Lawd, ah telling yuh!!! See how dem man stay. Now Ethel sad fuh so and pacifying sheself by talking bout other people.

---

[548] *Solicit a woman for sex*

[549] *A phrase used in Guyana to describe two people who partner up to gossip*

"Ah did feel like spittin in de one ah gih sheh. Sheh gettin like Doris aan minein people business tuh much, aan pickin up 'fire-rage'[550] fuh sheh tuh. But ah spare sheh," said Maxine, who dis hardly speak about people and hangout under de tamarind tree. She is commenting about how she had to replace the pepperpot that Ethel did burn. Give her some of her own.

That Maxine that does send sheh son Cyril to play hide-and-seek, and then this frowsy little boy gets out of hand bothering the girls. But, don't leh we talk bout duh. Anyhow, this woman does not like Ethel ever since she stole some of her clothes off de line outside at the back of her house. Nice, nice clothes that Maxine get from England. Must be envy Maxine because sheh lil boy grandmother did buy that little house to save sheh from paying a landlord rent. It buy long, long and in very good condition unlike the other houses. Miss Maxine 'cool aan deadly' and don't tek no nonsense from nobody. Ah never did want to tell y'all that, but I mentioning it now because ah want y'all to know that yuh must never take people for granted. Never judge de book by it's cover cause is true what they say about "still water running deep." These kinda folks are what they also call "silent warriors or weapons" too......another lesson to learn. Anyhow, that's that!!!

Hold up a minute here!!! Wheh Patsy? Ah telling allyuh about Ethel and Maxine and all kinda things and not focusing on we main character here; Patsy, and if she home. Y'all think we

---

[550] *Being instigated to cause trouble*

should send Daphne to knock on sheh door? Ah need a vote on this one. *"Yes?"* .... everybody saying a big *"YES"* to send Daphne. Sharon just come home looking lil tipsy,[551] and look like she hiding from Phillip while she instructing our 'candycane lover' to go look fuh Patsy. Meanwhile Mother Beulah just come outside and beckoning to her granddaughter to come back.

"Ello, ello, ello inside. Inside, inside, inside. Pat, Pat, Pat ... she means "Patsy." Then the word should be pronounced as "Hello" and not like another friend of mine would say it. She then screams *"Ello, ello inside, inside. Candycane, candycane, candycane."*

Daphne screams loud enough to obstruct the hearing of someone standing close to her, and this explains why her grandmother is "HOH" or Hard of Hearing.

She then begins to knock even harder with a doll in her hand. Then harder, harder and harder, and harder. Now the puh doll head look like it want to come off. Now who does give such a grown woman a doll for a gift? Who? ......Mother Beulah, who feel sorry fuh dis young woman; her grandchild. who still like a child and been asking fuh one all year round.

---

[551] *Mildy drunk/intoxicated*

"Ahrite, ah gon get yuh one. Yuh hear mih Daphne, yuh hear mih love" as she consoles her, who at five years old was abandoned by the old lady's daughter.

This is when the mother realized that she was developmentally disabled and did not want to deal with the stigma of *"de chile head aan good."*[552]

"Is 'bad seed' sheh mek deh,"[553] as some of her neighbors said in the scheme. Then is when de mother did tassay. Left, and what bad about it was that it was on December 1st of that year 1944.

"Look motha, ah cyaan deal wid dis. Is ah new month aan de halidays comin aan ah haffa 'mek turnings'[554] *fuh look fuh some money fuh we. Ah going aan hustle aan come back. Mek ah lil 'freck' fuh de holidays yuh hear motha."*

Yeah rite!!! She never returned ….. that Daphne mother!!! Never!!! Went on and started a new life somewhere else and forgetting sheh mother and daughter. Made some more chirren tuh for another man it is said, and never returned to Guyana. Hiding from sheh mother and "abandoned" Daphne.

Knock, knock, knock!!! ……Daphne still knocking and the dolly head just hanging. One more knock with that doll would

---

[552] *The child's head is not sound*

[553] *Was not born physically or mentally able, no good*

[554] *Go places in order to financially advance oneself*

be child abuse on de poor toy. This girl is trying to peep through Patsy window, but de blind too thick and she looking like sheh getting annoyed because nobody not answering. Now all the neighbors up as y'all could guess.

"*Keep de noise down. Yuh like Gavin in de mawnins, aan wuss.*[555] *From day one yuh is ah damn nuisance. Stop knockin pun de ooman door. Yuh aan see sheh aan deh home. Stop de fuckin knockin,*" yells Phillip, as he has already been upset that Sharon disobeyed him and went on a ship, or ships. Also he friend did see sheh in Pegasus "Bow and Arrow" discotheque with one of sheh white customers hugging up.

He continues ……. "*Miss Beulah, yuh granchile is ah fuckin nuisance. Ah new year comin aan none ahwe aan gon put up wid dis shit. Tek sheh outta dis yard. We fed up. Candy canes mih fuckin eye.*"

He then slams his door with anger and total disgust.

But you think Daphne care. Sheh grandmother now on Patsy doorstep tugging at she left arm to come away, and Daphne still banging at de door with the incomplete doll whose head is now lying on the step. De ole lady nearly trip on it and yuh tink de gurl kay?[556]

---

[555] *"Keep the noise down. You are like Gavin in the mornings and worst."*
[556] *You think the girl care?*

"Ah swear ah wudda give yuh ah cut ass heh today if yuh grandmotha did fall aan buss sheh head. Yuh watchin me!!! Yuh tink ah jokin?"

That's Denise who been paying Mother Beulah recently to watch sheh chirren on Saturday nights since sheh mother been refusing lately.

"Tikkay ah come ova dey. Yuh betta move," Phillip joins in while sternly pointing at her with one of his index fingers.

For the first time, Daphne looks scared and follows her grandmother back to their dwelling place as she pelts the doll head in the direction of Denise who refuses to retaliate. It is now easy to make deductions that she will be attending the Boxing night dance tomorrow night with that "regulah" Doris and has to keep her energy.

"Dis aan dat, aan dis aan dat" …… "and so on, and so on." Now the question remains, "where is Patsy?" Miss Cheryl outside now and asking de same question ……..

"Is wheh Patsy? Like sheh 'leff we up '[557] today of all days. Puh ting. Sheh got 'typee.'[558] But is wheh he de Bertie? Lead de gurl on aan neva come bak. Den he lyin auntie always coverin up

---

[557] *"Like she 'gave up on us,' forgot about us"*
[558] *She is longing for and missing her lover badly*

fuh he. Neva cud tell de puh gurl de truth. Gawd, is wheh sheh deh?"

She shouts that last question a little too hard and almost choke on a bone from sheh second plate of pepperpot but ketch sheh self,[559] and shaking sheh head now that full of paper curlers so that she could fix up[560] sheh hair tomorrow night for de ole head dance that Doris invite sheh to. Then thinking now that Patsy could tag along with them, even though she is ah spring chicken.[561]

"Dey dis gat young men deh tuh fuh de ooman dem dat like 'rob de cradle,'[562] yuh know Cheryl, aan some ah dem like olduh ooman becauz dey seh we cud cook aan wash aan keep house betta dan de young gurl dem," Doris had emphasized last Saturday morning on their way to Bourda Market.

She then takes another bite from the plate with the dark juicy substance on the white rice in front of her, and smiles in anticipation of the expectations of tomorrow evening. Glancing at Patsy's doorway, she wishes that this young lady would emerge with some good news, but with all that knocking from Daphne, it is evident that their neighbor is not at home.

---

[559] *Rejuvenate herself, gets better, not choking anymore*
[560] *She could style up her hair tomorrow*
[561] *A young or very youthful person*
[562] *A woman that like to be with young men*

Roy leaving now. He just put he padnah[563] Gavin inside and already we could hear Carol and he arguing. Now it sound like he just fall down from he stumbling, but Roy got to head home to he wife and children also. Hence, he cannot help out with this one as he has assisted Carol before. In other words, he has assisted her countless times to pick up his friend after falling, but today, too much time has elapsed bringing his extremely intoxicated stumbling friend home, as he too, has his wife and children awaiting him to eat what is no longer going to be breakfast, but lunch instead.

"Ah aan pickin yuh up. Yuh see how yuh chirren lookin at yuh? Yuh is ah disgrace aan den yuh walkin in heh with yuh 'two lang haans'..... hands. Nutten fuh we aan is Crismus day. Ah fed up yuh see. Fed up. Den Cousin Leslyn heh aan yuh carryin on same way. Ah fed up. Go to hell."

Her repetition of "fed ups" self-explains how tired she is of the man she met fifteen years ago who has turned into a major disappointment. She is looking now at Cousin Leslyn with bible in hand and who is beckoning to her to let them help Gavin to his bed. A blanket on the floor with a pillow at its headside behind the curtain that not only separates two spaces, but also makes it two so-called rooms. Yes, pick him up because one of the children starting to cry.

---

[563] *Partner*

"Yuh see whah ah talkin bout Gavin. Always pissin drunk aan upsettin dese chirren," Carol utters, while Leslyn struggles even harder to fetch he to the bedroom.

"You're so heavy like lead Gavin. Must be all those drinks in you, " the ole maid complains.

After all, being also both a virgin and unmarried, Leslyn admitted to her cousin just yesterday, that she has only been recently exposed at this house to these kinds of behaviors from a man. She then walks towards their supposed kitchen which is a table with some utensils to assist her cousin in giving the children some of the much awaited pepperpot that Miss Millie sen fuh dem[564] in the wee hours of the morning. They were asleep then and will certainly enjoy this very delicious meal prepared by "Auntie Millie."

"We aan givin Gavin none, Leslyn. Dhoan carry he no plate. He is ah let down," while assisting one of her kids to unwrap his gift, then the outburst ....

"Look, look, if yuh chirren din dey hey, ah wudda tell yuh off some moe. Ah wudda 'buse' yuh out."[565]

"Shut yuh stink mouth Carol, bring mih some peppahpat. Always talkin shit." That's Gavin, and continues ...... *"is de*

---

[564] *That Miss Millie sent for them*
[565] *"Look, look, if your children wasn't here, I would have told you off some more. I would have 'cursed' you out."*

halidays aan ah suppose to have ah nice time. Why ah cyaan eat tuh? Ah dis bring money in heh. Is who dis pay de rent? Me. Look, bring de blasted food."

Such a pity that alcoholism needs to be addressed properly which pivots around this time of the year because it is rarely seen as a major problem. Then there are no AA or Alcohlic Anonymous meetings to attend to assist men like Gavin to conquer his problem. Also, along with the camaraderie and therefore support system that he could acquire in such meetings like in some other places in the world.

Meanwhile the phone rings and Carol answers it. It's a call for Parbattie from her sister in Barrie, Ontario. She then screams outside of her door for one of the little boys playing "cowboy" to give her neighbor the message, but yuh think they taking her on on? In steadily ignoring her, she is too disgusted by what has just occurred in her household to waste her energy in relaying the message. Looking at the reluctant boys once more, she grinds her teeth in annoyance.

"Baw, baw, baw," Terrence yells as he draws his toy gun at Cyril while the other boys are hiding. Dressed in cowboy hats, boleros, and sockets around their waists, they are both drawing guns at each other as they have seen in the movies. Yuh think they studying Carol? They have been waiting since last year to play "cowbai" ...... the cowboy game again with each other. Just who

Carol wants to see ..... Saheed, Parbattie's son, and she yells to him that his aunt is on the phone. But, he too ignores her.

"Go aan tell yuh motha that sheh sistah pun de fone. Hurry up." With telephone in hand, she tells his aunt that Sadeek is ignoring her.

"He aan lisening tuh mih. If Parbattie aan come, yuh gon have tuh call back lateuh Sita cause ah cyaan tie up mih line. De boys excited aan playin cowbai an if yuh smell de sulphur in de yard!!!"

She then hangs up and continues to dive into the bowl of souse that her Meadbrook friends had also given her.

"Miss Mille cud cook, eh?" Beryl from the other yard shouts. *"Sheh is ah nice woman aan dis always 'hook we up'*[566] *when de halidays come roung. Ah tell yuh someting!!! Ah dhoan know whuh me aan dem pickney ah got heh wudda do if it wasen fuh she. We belly full now. De peppahpat delishous aan sheh bread fluffy aan nice. God bless sheh soul."*

She then continues to describe the nice big bowl that Miss Cheryl give her when the big pot arrived this morning with a piece of juicy pig ears inside and a wide assortment of other meats ...... meat fuh so!!! Nuff, nuff meat. She is now licking her fingers,

---

[566] *Always look out for us, our welfare*

much to the distaste of a very "bougie" or bourgeoisie Cousin Leslyn who has just noticed her.

"Ah know whuh yuh mean. She aan Hazel is two God angels. Ah did know dat dey was good people when ah fuss meet dem. When Patsy bring dem aan introduce we tuh dem," Carol exclaims with fondness.

Beryl is sipping on some ginger beer that arrived with the food too, and she just belched as she has just made her way to Carol's doorstep.

"Aaaaaaah, ah enjay dat drink jus now aan it tek out all mih gas."[567]

She then bids farewell to Carol, gets off her stoop, ducks through the fence, and walks up to her front door which is visible to her neighbor. "Merry Crismus," she again yells while closing the door shut to head down the hallway to join her children in her room.

More and more noise in de yard now. All de children coming out one by one. *"Baw, baw, baw"* ...... a familiar sound made as when pretending to shoot around most households as it was common for young boys to receive a cowboy gift. I could recall my own brother getting all dressed up in his cowboy gear, and then loading his gun with caps that were supposed to be like

---

[567] *"Aaaaaaah (an exclamation of relief), I enjoy that drink just now and it took out all my gas."*

bullets but were in fact made of sulphur. Having no brother, he would then head outside to look for the boy next door or other neighborhood boys to play with. In believing that they were in a Western movie, they would turn December 25th into a "Cowboy Town." Allyuh know what I talking about, rite?

That was the norm, as my mother did say earlier, "*ah come aan meet it suh, aan ah gon dead aan leff it suh.*"

Nowadays though, giving young boys and moreso, anyone a gun for a gift is not a good idea. Back then though, it was to romanticize the "cowboy illusion," or as I am thinking, to give these young lads a feeling of manly power; that trigger-happy feeling 'to protect' while the little girls were 'to nurture' and were given dolls; most white dolls because of the scarcity of black dolls in those days. This is what I couldn't understand about the 'color ting.'[568] But anyway, we were very happy with our gifts with extra ones for some of us like doll houses, kitchen sets, and dolly tea sets. Then my sisters and I would have a little tea party with our dolls and were ecstatic throughout the day as we played "mothers" to our little idols. So, all in all, it was customary to give a little boy a cowboy set and a little girl a doll for this day as their major gifts. If not, for one to deprive a child of such gifts, resulted in a form of minute feelings of neglect since they would feel as if not only did Santa forget to include the gifts in the red stocking that they had hung up outside their door the night before, but moreso,

---

[568] *Color discriminatiom*

that their parents or relatives   deliberately did not place such under the Christmas tree.

Hence, this day could be either 'bitter' or 'sweet' for prospective gift receivers; mostly the young ones who were waiting all year round for their wishes to be fulfilled. Could you imagine how Daphne, already riddled by poor cognition would have behaved if her grandmother did not give her that doll? Then given the doll, look at the outcome!!! But at least she was pacified by her caregiver who knew too well her condition, and subsequently, her possible reactions.

Sam dog barking loud, loud, loud. He even growling but not at anybody in the yard. Look like he seeing somebody.

"Shut yuh mouth, yuh mek tuh much naise," he yells at his dog.

But people seh that de dog dis know things. Even when one of the stray cats about to give birth. He quiet now and just bore he self under the tiny bottom house. He is a good guard dog and very obedient, and does what his master says.

As predicted in his barking, shortly after something like a white pick-up truck is pulling up in front of the yard as Miss Charlotte, Ernest mother is outside and looks distraught. She has once more been disappointed by her son who failed to send her the barrel he promised from New Jersey, and we not going to mention that "wutless" Ernest through all his smooth-talking had also promised his very aging and somewhat fragile mother that "a refrigerator inside" …… that a fridge was going to be in the barrel also. Now again, who would believe that? Only she and Daphne her next door neighbor. But anyhow, Miss Charlotte did get some pepperpot out of the big, big pot that Miss Millie and Hazel dem send early this morning and it kind of throw off the little sadness she had from last night. She couldn't fix up sheh house the way she wanted because that no-good son of hers did also promise to send some things to decorate sheh house nice for the holidays. Anyway, thank God for de little throw off[569] she get from sheh grandson and he wife who dis drop by almost every other day.

"Ernest disappint mih again dis year. Ah ain know wheh ah get he from, but praise Gawd mih granson aan he 'betta-half'[570] did get some tings from dey friends fuh fix up mih room. Ernest………" and she begins to sob.

Grandma Tinsy then embraces and pacifies this very sad lady while handing her a handkerchief to sap up the tears that is steadily streaming down her face.

"Is ahrite man, is ahrite Miss Charlotte. Yuh know how he stay. Is ahrite. Gawd dis provide. Yuh gon be ahrite. He aan gon

---

[569] *Used things. In this case decorations, etc.*
[570] *His girlfriend or wife*

tek bread out yuh mouth. All ahwe gon see dat yuh ahrite aan eat tuh."

Miss Charlotte seems to be feeling better already and makes herself more comfortable on the chair that Dookram had brought over for her to sit on.

"*Eh, eh, is who is duh?*"[571] Doris mutters. She then keeps walking further to the front of the yard as she cannot see clearly due to the after lunch sun.

She then quickens her steps and inquiringly says, "*yuh look suh knowin. Wait, is who ah really seein?*" as two men gets out of the truck.

"*Eh, eh, is really you? We din sure if yuh was comin.[572] Yuh look nice……eeeee.*"

It was after the taller and well-dressed one had taken off his sun shades or glasses that she became really excited, and yelled ………

"*Is you Bertie, is really you ah seein?*"

Then at the top of her voice as he followed her into the yard, she screams very loudly………..

---

[571] "*Eh, eh, is who is that?*"

[572] "*Eh, eh, is really you? We weren't sure if you were coming. Yuh look nice ……eeeeee.*"

"Bertie come, Bertie come, Bertie come. Everybady Bertie come. He come."

Well you could guess what's happening now.......everybody coming out they house.....Carol and sheh chirren and Cousin Leslyn, Dookram and he family, Maxine and Cyril, Sharon who is mostly at work and sheh chirren, Denise and sheh chirren, Mother Beulah and Daphne, Miss Charlotte who did go back inside sheh house coming outside again, Bridget and sheh chirren with Little Debbie and Grandma Tinsy, Jason jumping de fence from next door followed by Beryl and sheh chirren, Ethel and sheh daughter, Sam and he girlfriend and stepdaughter, Gwen and sheh chirren, Linette and sheh auntie, the new neighbor Sheila and sheh two daughters and son, and ah think ah got everybody, except Phillip who gone fuh see whuh expensive toys and other things he could thief from people, and Gavin who 'dead asleep' [573] because he too drunk to hear the revelling in de yard.......but where is Patsy? Where is Patsy......which is quite evident to Bertie right now while everyone is hugging he and asking he questions about "away" ..... "New York."

Daphne is staring at the luggage that the driver of the truck has just brought into the yard, then gets up, viciously advances towards one of his suitcases, and yells ecstatically ....

---

[573] *Who is fast asleep*

"Candy canes, candy canes, candy canes, waan, waan, candy canes."

Then how does this developmentally disabled young lady know that Bertie was from abroad, that she suddenly pounces on it and tries to open a piece of luggage, but is restrained by Stanley who just arrives in the yard.

"Ah shudda leh sheh do it,"[574] he suddenly thinks to himself as he realizes that the man that everyone is making a big fuss over is the newly returned boyfriend of the woman that he has been wanting a relationship with for almost two years. He then joins the crowd and carefully peruses Bertie with envy.

"Ah know yuh waan ask we bout Patsy. Sheh aan deh home. Duh same gurl ova deh; Daphne" …… and she is pointing to her now….. *"did rappin at sheh door dis mawning aan sheh din ansha.[575] Sheh rap laang, laang aan still no ansha. Sheh mus be did leff early aan went tuh sheh family dem in Meadow Brook,"* Bridget reveals.

As if he didn't believe, Bertie then attempts to rap at the door once more, but with no avail. He then scratches his head in front of his onlookers, and in his obvious frustration says

---

[574] *"I should have let her do it"*

[575] *"Did rapping at her door this morning and she didn't answer."*

254

"Wonder where she is? How could she leave? Couldn't she guess that I may be coming home from the States?"

He then continues in his salt water Yankee accent …. *"Can't find my babe. Wonder where my sugah is? She must be out of her cotton pickin mind[576] to not be in the crib today,"* as the man who has been pursuing his lover persistently stares at him.

"Is whuh yuh jus seh? We aan understaan,"[577] Ethel asks, as Doris heckles….

"Sheh mean talk leh we understaan. Since yuh come is all kinda fancy words yuh been sehing fuh de last few minutes," as Bertie refuses to interpret what he just said and is confronted with another question ………

Mister, yuh aan bring no 'ice apples' and grapes fuh we? Aan yuh gat any Crismus candy?" Gwen asks with her best friend Linette giggling behind her.

Bertie then beckons to the driver of the pick up truck to pass him a specific suitcase. He opens it and gives his spectators some apples, some big red grapes and candy.

Thank yuh, thank yuh. Dis is ah good suhprise fuh we. De chirren like dat. See how dey jumpin up," Sharon yells while one of her children beams with delight, and as Daphne interrupts,

---

[576] *"She must not be thinking well today"*

[577] *"Is what you just said? We ain't understand"*

255

"candy cane, candy cane," as she is also delighted to see the long red and white sweets.

"Tikkay yuh choke," Denise yells at her because she is stuffing one down her mouth without sucking or chewing on it.

She continues, *"chew it like how Bertie chewing he gum. Only dat he mekkin dem poppin sounds. Is suh y'all dis chew gum in Amerika, Mistah? Duh is ah habit yuh pick up away? It sound annoyin,"* as some people bow their head in agreement.

Talking bout duh mih own mother did return from Chicago in 1969 doing the same thing. Popping gum and talking like a real American after being there for a year. We all were elated upon seeing her but is that blowing of dem bubbles. Lawd, ah telling yuh, that is something ahwe dis Guyanese neva did like. SMH!!!

In defeat at not finding his sweetheart, Bertie leaves the yard, and 'Mouth ah Preh Preh' Doris convinces the crowd that she hates how ………

"Dem Guyanese people dis come home chewin dey gum like dat aan thinkin dey betta dan people. Den he too stingy aan only gih we ahlil bit ah shit. He aan even gih we couple dollas. Wonda what he bring fuh Patsy? Puh gurl," as she walks towards her doorway with a slice of apple in her hand.

Stanley has just tried to interrupt her with ….. *"chewin he blasted cud aan cheap as ah rass."*[578]

"Dhoan fuhget fuh check by sheh wukplace okay," Beryl shouts after Bertie, and resumes to criticize his accent with the others."

"Leh he carry he skunt. Duh is de Bertie? Ah look betta dan he. Sheh cudda choose me. He look like 'Sam Dopey.' *Comin in heh playin all "hoity toity,"*[579] Stanley disgustingly yells. Now y'all know that duh man ain't short short. He de Stanley too lying and insultive.

Tell y'all that Sam dog spiritual. He did know that somebody was coming. Sure enough was Bertie ….. arriving not before Christmas, but on Christmas Day itself to look for his "sugah" ….. his "sugar" or "sweetheart." The sweetheart that he is now desperately searching for.

Now de man that driving he round is ah ole time schoolmate that he did know when attending Charlestown Government School. Now de bannuh can't even understand what the hell Bertie saying. He got to ask he to repeat he self all the time. Then he waan know how come Bertie loose he Guyanese accent suh fass;[580] just in almost three years and trying to talk like

---

[578] *"Chewing his blasted gums and cheap as a rass."*
[579] *Big shotish or like a high society person*
[580] *So fast*

257

an Englishman too. Imitating he cousin that de man just drop off on Louisa Row before they went to Punchin Yard.

"Oi have to find her vury quickly. Oi caunt see why she caunt have waited for me. She must auve gone down that lane. Whah doh you think lad? Oi am thursty and need a cup of "toie"...... he means "tea".... *to quench myoi thurst."*[581]

It's a wonder that he didn't "ashk" ask for a slice of "koie" or "cake" also. Now this is darn foolishness. Now who does want to drink hot tea in Guyana in blazing heat at this time of the day? Then especially if they just come out de cold. I wudda ask for a tall drinka water or some mauby, sorrel or gingerbeer cause is de Big Holiday today. Now y'all see how this fool just leff Guyana fuh ah lil while and acting like he loose he "pure" .... he country's accent.

Then the fellow now looking at Bertie who all dressed up in a tweed three-piece black suit with a inner red shirt, green tye, a black felt hat with a red band around it. Then a black belt and three-toned red, black and white shoes .... matching according to the Christmas theme as he did see a man down 14th Street dressed like that and he decided to be a copycat. Seem like he get vain because all he talking to he friend is about clothes and fashion

---

[581] *"I have to find her very quickly. I can't see why she can't have waited for me. She must. have gone down that lane. What do you think lad? I am thirsty and need a cup of "tea" .... to quench my thirst."*

and only leaving we fuh wonder if is only he clothes in he six suitcases, and not anything fuh Patsy.

Allyuh see how these people dis change and get vain when they leave we shores, and come back modeling pun we? Then if you ask them for a little "throw off," some of them dis tell yuh how hard they wuk fuh it and how cold de place is ….. stingy, stingy, stingy!!! Some don't even want to give a drop of anything, but dis waan yuh to give them all sorts of things like sugarcake, tamarind balls and fry fish to carry back to New York and wherever else they come from. Then they don't even want to give yuh ah 'lil freck' or little money for all de worries yuh tek to gather up the ingredients to make the darn things. Some does even want to ask yuh fuh mek pepper sauce fuh dem and might even go so far as to add black pudding, achar[582] and casareep to the list. That cassareep is to make they peperpot because not every year they dis come home for the holidays.

"I'd like you to get me some mangoes too," Denise aunt from Boston did once tell her in her so-called 'upety' or 'bougie' voice since sheh married to an Irish man.

Well y'all know what? Denise did get de mangoes fuh sheh, and when sheh got to Timehri, she cudn't tek dem on de plane, and y'all think sheh dash them away? ……. All twenty-five of

---

[582] *In the case of 'mango achar' it is made with for example with six chopped green mangoes, blended six cloves of garlic with peppers and salt. Mustard oil for preservation, along with oil. Then fry up everything with lastly the mango*

them ….. she sit right deh with other people who was in de same predicament like she and try to eat as much as sheh could. Then all that sheh couldn't eat, sheh bite them so de customs people couldn't get none. Ah mean no mangoes, none!!!

Then sehing to sheh self, *"leh dey carry dey so-aan-so,"* while a Customs Officer 'adding fire to fury' and telling sheh fuh leff two fuh he.[583]

This is when this woman got ravenous and bite harder, and harder, and harder into the mangoes. Then faster, and faster, and faster in ensuring that she had mangled all of them before she boarded the plane. I actually did know somebody who was a passenger on that plane and they tell mih that she sleep all through the flight like sheh was in a sugar coma. Too much mangoes in sheh system!!! Dem mangoes that sheh mutilated.

Now we could guess what happen to sheh……sheh get colic and sheh blood sugar rise even more when she get back to Boston and then calling and telling Denise that is sheh fault because she panicking now that she could get diabetes. Bareface, downright bareface!!! ….. and greedy. Yes, ah seh suh…. Yes, I said so …… greedy, while Denise still waiting fuh de pair ah shoes sheh promise sheh to wear to sheh good friend wedding.

---

[583] *Then saying to herself, 'let they carry they self-so" …. as in cursing inwardly …. while a. Customs Officer 'instigating things' by begging her to leave two for him.*

260

We gaffin bout [584] de 'mango story' which almost everybody know bout. Is true, some people just said *"yes"* and that they did hear bout stories like that. Then now somebody else in the audience telling mih that dey convinced that ai is ah[585] real Guyanese...... yes, cause I mentioning it in this book.

"Thank yuh, thank yuh mih people. How y'all mean, de 'mango story' will foreva be part of we Guyanese archives with nuff, nuff laff."

Was all caught up in de 'mango story' and forgetting that the "salt-water Yankee" and "English Duck" Bertie looking fuh he ooman. He busy looking back behind he cause Desmond driving and trying to concentrate on de traffic and what he saying at de same time. So Bertie got to be looking back at he suitcases every time they stop at a traffic light that nobody don't grab one because they pile up on one another since Desmond got a bunch of garbage that preventing the suitcases from lying flat. Now who does go to the airport to pick up a friend with they truck smelling like a garbage heap?

Only a *"Dutty Bungle"*[586] my 'yardie sistren' would say, as she has OCD or Obsessive Compulsive Disorder that people does ritual cleanings and everything got to be clean, clean, clean. Some dis even go to the extreme and when they return from the

---

[584] *We are talking about*

[585] *I am a real Guyanese*

[586] *A Jamaican term used to describe a filthy or dirty person*

supermarket like me, they dis wash off with bleach, lysol or another disinfectant, all that they bring home before they put the items in the refrigerator or pantry because they don't want any germs in they house. That's because so many people does be in the supermarket that they be touching things with germs on they hands. A kind of germaphobia, as others dis even arrange they can foods in alphabetical order in they cabinets. Then some again like me, house always smelling of bleach and pine sol. Sounds absurd, but is true. But since then now I editing this manuscript years later, ah dis use natural cleaners. Moreso white vinegar could be substituted.

Me and the lady mentioned above became friends because we both got the same 'so-called' disorder when we met each other at we children Parent Teacher's Meeting. They call OCD a disorder, but is a nice thing to have because we house dis always be clean and nice. No 'duttyness.' Some of de women in Punchin Yard like that too, and all over Guyana and the Caribbean as well. Like to keep they houses 'spic and span.' Look yeh, to hell was OCD!!! Is a good thing to have!!!

Meanwhile, the newly-arrived sweating and fanning heself with the envelope that he boarding pass was in, but it can't help he. That envelope that he think is a novelty because it representing his return home. He buddy just suggested that he should *"tek aff de jacket aan de vess,"*[587] but he not listening. Desmond trying

---

[587] *"Take off the jacket and the vest"*

with he to see that he keep cool and had hinted about three times before that is over 100 degrees, but the fool ignoring he. Why he acting like Maxine and sheh son Cyril on the last dash before Christmas eve day? Remember? Those two was just like he with them inappropriate clothes sweating like a horse in hot, hot Guyana.

"*Chrise man, tek off yuh suit jacket aan vess padnah,*" his friend once more pleads. "*Aan duh ting pun yuh head gat yuh moe hot. De material it mek wid is fuh de cole. Whuh yuh call it? Felt? Ah telling yuh, yuh not use tuh dis kinah weatha no moe. Yuh cud get whuh yuh call it?*"[588]

Bertie then chimes in ……… "*dehydrated,*" then snaps with a very, very angry demeanor, "*bro, yuh not used to dis kinda fashion cuz oi dress like this in the summer in New York too.*"

But while he convincing he to do all this stuff, Desmond using he brain; playing tricky and going round and round, and straying from where they supposed to go……. Meadbrook Gardens. Why de hell they going South by Tiger Bay when they just left Kingston? Also, should be going east up High Street to Durban Street then turn left and keep going to Hill Street. and that would take them to Meadow Brook Gardens.

---

[588] "*Christ man, take off your suit jacket and vest partner,*" his friends once more pleads."
"*And that thing on your head got you more hot. The material it make with is for the cold. What you call it? Felt? I telling you, you not used to this kind of weather no more. You could get what you call it?*"

263

"Whuh kineah shit is duh?" …. Ah saying so, cause I know de place good. See Bertie playin he head ain good[589] by too busy trying to say that ……

"This place looks so strange my brotha. Say what?!!! When did these changes take place? This is off the hook," an amazed Bertie utters.

Then amidst all this, he isn't realizing that he getting conned and it taking too long to reach his destination, and of course, Desmond want those Yankee dollars. He driving round and round some more since Bertie boasted just now, that ………

"America is an awesome place bro. I made some good dead presidents for the time I been there."

So the driver asks him what are *"dead presidents"* and smiles after he realizes that it's money his passenger is referring to. It's been almost two hours, and they are still not at their destination. Now this foolish boyfriend again didn't even think first to stop in by Patsy job to see if she there ….. all on the way to Meadow Brook Gardens, and he tab going up. Wonder how much dollars now? He puffing on his cigars and trying to mek Desmond feel like he was 'ah playah' by talking about how much women like he; attracted to he and want to be with he in Brooklyn.

---

[589] *Acting stupid or insane, foolish thoughts*

He and he wild self with supposedly a reputation now which would not be good news for Patsy.

That idiot better don't let de man overcharge he cause he running he mouth too much and still popping that damn chewing gum. Plus what making matters worse is that he ain't even offer de man a piece of Wrigley nor an ice apple. Always was writing de man and mekkin promises about what he gon bring fuh he, aan pun top of dat,[590] did ask Desmond he size……shirt size, pants size, socks size, shoes size, hat size, belt size, singlet size and even buckta size.[591] Did he bring anything for de man in one of dem six suitcases, ah wonder? Don't tell me he like "wutless" Ernest and Uncle Ovid with they lying ways and false promises. He betta dhoan mek Desmond vex because he will have to pay 'fuh lying between he teeth.'[592] But we gon see though …. we going to see!!! He, that he Auntie Avril dis covah up fuh.[593]

Little Orson mother Eileen outside under sheh bottom house peeping over at Miss Millie and Hazel dem. She busy peeping while de little boy mekkin nuff, nuff noise with he whistle while he playing with he gun. He too small and unlike the older boys in this country, he get instead a water gun to suit he age. No caps with sulphur inside, plus he little hands too small to pull a trigger on a heavy plastic gun. Then he ain't got no waist to put a

---

[590] *And making promises about what he is going to bring for him, and on top of that*
[591] *White sleeveless vest and male underwear that fits below the waist*
[592] *He better don't make Desmond vex because he will have to pay 'for pathologically lying.'*
[593] *Usually cover up for*

holster on. He really tiny too; short and now starting to give he mother rudeness cause sheh just asked he to stop making all that noise with that whistle and he saying *"no."* Now sheh peeping to see de color of Miss Millie blinds and not noticing that a man calling out to her.

Drenching with perspiration, he asks her, *"Is this Hazel's crib?"*

Eileen stutters for a moment and replies, *"crib? Whuh yuh mean by duh Mistah? Is a baby cradle yuh talking bout?"*[594]

"Her house," he replies, then shakes his head while now pulling out a red handkerchief out of his pocket to wipe his face.

A barking dog greets him and obviously is sensing that he is a stranger. The gate is locked and Jeff advances to it as if like a sentry, but without wagging his tail like he would do with familiar visitors.

Bertie realizes that he cannot get any further and yells, *"Hazel, Hazel. It's me Bertie. I am back. I am back. I flew in today."* He has to yell a second time, while the next door neighbor aids him.

---

[594] *"Crib? What you mean by that Mister? Is a baby cradle you talking about?*

266

"Miss Mille, Miss Millie. Y'all gat ah visitah aan he look like he come 'from away.' Miss Millie, Hazel, Ulrick, y'all come nuh!!!."[595]

She didn't mention Lennie's name as she saw him leaving the house about half hour ago. She then turns to the man whom she suspects is from abroad, and shouts over her fence………

"Mistah yuh come 'from away'…… New York, or is wheh yuh come from?"

He smiles and answers, *"New York,"* while Desmond comes out and braces on the truck.

This driver has been looking lustfully at Eileen in her white short pants with legs that look very enticing, and seems not to be concerned as to whether his ex-classmate finds his girlfriend or not, as he has his own interests.

"Well, well, well. Laang time no see. Bertie is you? Eh, eh, yuh look nice bannuh aan yuh get lighta. Yuh look good. Look like ah 'saga bai' now,"[596] answers Ulrick, while ignoring Bertie's question as to if Patsy is there.

After all, he is now consumed into the new arrival's attire; clothes that he has longed for after seeing them in countless

---

[595] *"Miss Millie, Miss Millie. You all got a visitor and he looks like he comes 'from abroad.' Miss Millie, Hazel, Ulrick you all come please' ..... as in pleading.*
[596] *Well, well, well. Long time no see. Bertie is you? Eh, eh, you look nice boy and you have gotten lighter. You look like fashionable ladies man now."*

overseas magazines, on the screen in movie theatres and of course, on other visitors to the country.

"Yeah bro, I am asking you if my 'sugah'[597] is here? Hear me out please."

But you think that Ulrick worrying with he. He just not voomsing[598] on this fellow that just come from America, but again I say on his attire. Meanwhile, Hazel has now managed to shuffle her way to the front door. She notices her cousin's partner; the young man whose absence for almost three years has given Patsy 'nuff, nuff typee'…plenty, plenty 'missing her man' and stress. She is hesitant now as if to be receptive or not, but knowing her, she is much too kind to be hostile.

"Bertie!!! Mammy Bertie come, Mammy!!! Mammy!!! Look he mammy. He come."

She is running now down the stairs towards the front gate to open it for their enquiring and long-awaiting guest, as Miss Millie yells ……..

"Bertie, mih mine tell meh dat yuh was comin. Ah tell Patsy aan Hazel dat de otha day aan dey din belief mih. Oh Gawd, Patsy gon glad. Puh gurl. Sheh praperly did miss yuh aan de ting is, sheh din tek nobody; anotha man.. Sheh leff heh laas nite aan

---

[597] *'Sugar or sweet woman.' A way of calling a woman when her man adores her*
[598] *Not paying attention or reacting to*

ain come back yet. Sheh suppose tuh come tuhday, sheh seh. Come inside nuh," with gesticulations for him to adhere to her, as he reluctantly walks up the stairway.

After embracing the ladies, and being told that Patsy was not at home when Bertie knocked on her door in Punchin Yard, Hazel decides to call Brown Betty's restaurant to see if she is there.

Ring, Ring …… "*Hello, hello Patsy dey? Good aftanoon. Is who ah talkin tuh? Oh Janice, oh ah see. Patsy dey? Ahrite den. Please tell sheh ah call.* [599] Then pauses ………. "*Merry Christmas tuh darling.*"

She looking confused now and looking at Bertie who was just given a plate with some pepperpot along with two pieces of still freshly baked bread. Then studying now how tuh break de news to him, but succumbs.

"*Yuh know yuh cyaan come heh aan dhoan eat some of mih food. Is ah laang time yuh aan 'taste mih haan.' Yuh know everybady seh ah cud cook good?*"[600] Miss Millie boasts.

---

[599] "*Hello, hello Patsy there? Good afternoon. Is who I talking to? Oh Janice, oh I see. Patsy there? Please tell her I called.*
[600] "*You know you cannot come here and don't eat some of my food. Is a long time you have not tasted my hand (due to her ability to cook well). You know everybody say I could cook.*"

Her guest is smiling now and is being joined by Desmond, his long-time friend and chauffeur who is super-excited because Eileen has agreed to be his date tomorrow night.

"De binnie gimme de go ahead fuh tomarraw nite. Sheh ahrite it look like, but ah gon 'suss' sheh out lil bit moe[601]. Den if everyting good, ah gon ask sheh fuh anotha date pun Old Year's nite," while holding on tightly to the paper with her name and address on it.

He then giggles as Miss Millie offers him some food also, while at the same time trying to have a last glance at her through the window before their date.

"Yuh waan peppapat or some souse? Ah gat some nice fresh bread deh tuh aan some gingahbeer aan mauby," she adds.

Bertie just belched. He has not eaten a long time. Hours now since that crook who sitting in front of him been driving he around and dilly dallying[602] all over the place. He sipping some of de gingerbeer now and gets up to go outside after mentioning that he brought some whisky from the duty-free shop at John F. Kennedy Airport. Lenny has just returned after hunting down Brenda to give her a gift.

---

[601] *I am going to check her out/observe her some more.*
[602] *Can't make up his mind like in having no sense of direction when driving*

"Got some noice liquah here lad. Caunt fetch the bloody suitcase boi moiself."[603]

There he goes again!!! With his imitation English accent that he get from he Cousin Neville from Birmingham who stopped in New York and they fly in together today. Only four days that he cousin spent in Bertie apartment and this now Brooklynite laan up[604] in Georgetown talking like he was born and lived in England too. Then he cousin pun de otha side,[605] all caught up in he vanity that he not even stopping Patsy boyfriend from mekkin a fool of heself.

Neville mek de trip to New York to go shopping. Said he wanted the latest in the United States. Emphasized that he wanted the latest fashions in Manhattan. Had Bertie up and down in the streets looking for the clothes he cudn't get in London, and then he got the nerve to be trying to compete with women in the streets of New York. Said he dress better than theirs, and that they cyaan step like he[606] with he hair well done up and he make-up looking flawless. Then Bertie looking up to he like he ah super model, and trying to talk like he in he over-exaggerated cockney with that feminine tone.

---

[603] *"Got some nice liquor here lad. Can't fetch the bloody (a profanity used in England) suitcase by myself."*

[604] *Arrive*

[605] *Imitates the other sex, gay*

[606] *Can't compete with him/like in dressing like him*

271

"*Is whuh y'all gat deh?*" [607] Cousin Hazel asks as Jacqueline stares questioningly at Bertie and his friend.

Meanwhile, Lenny with bag in hand is about to take the bottle of whisky out, and glances at Jacqueline as though to tell her that she is not entitled to none. Theirs is an ongoing and silent feud stemming from her Cousin Linda and the cruelty meted out to her by her teacher. After all, it is he who caused Teacher Callender to be flogging her cousin badly because of his numerous and fictitious complaints in his quests to be the teacher's pet ... "*cachar*"...[608] and he neva did become de teacher pet. Instead, Miss Callender turned on he after 'peeping he cards' [609] after realizing what he was up to.

"*Oh, is liquah,*" as she moves closer to see. Hazel then reads the bottle and says, "*ah gon tek ah lil taste. Mammy yuh waan some?*" Bertie then cautions his friend that he has to go easy on the drink because he is the driver, while Miss Millie mentions ....

"*Ah aan waan duh. Allyuh gon taste mih 'Aunty Desmond' wine?*" It cure good. Ah dis always mek it fuh de holidays."[610]

---

[607] *"Is what you all have there?"*

[608] *"An informer"*

[609] *After 'realizing what he was up to'*

[610] *"I don't want that. You all are going to taste my 'Aunty Desmond' wine? It is cured good. I usually make it for the holidays."*

272

Ulrick hears her, emerges from his room, then heads to the kitchen and brings some glasses to the living room where everyone is seated. He is now giving their guests, sister and brother a choice between the two drinks ... the whisky and the Aunty Desmond wine.

"Mek y'all choice. Ah gon put both drinks heh. Ah gon get some ice from de fridge. Hole on."

Bertie then succumbs to Miss Millie's wishes and pours himself some of the Aunty Desmond wine.

"Duh is mih name-sake," Desmond declares.

By that remark he means that this wine has the same name as him; got that name from the ole folks even before he was born.

"Ah had enuf uh duh every haliday. Ah gon tek de farin whisky dat mih fren bring heh," Desmond insists.[611]

Bertie nods his head in agreement and then urges Cousin Hazel to check-in with Brown Betty again to see if Patsy had showed up for work. She calls and again, the supervisor assures her that his girlfriend was not scheduled for work today.

---

[611] *"I had enough of that every holiday. I am going to take the foreign whisky that my friend bring me,"* Desmond insists.

"Sheh seh Patsy wasen suppose tuh guh in deh tuhday. Yuh know whuh? Ah gon call Carol aan see if sheh tun up. If sheh deh home now."[612]

Then Desmond interjects, *"what about sheh "chuch?"* ..... he means "church." *We cud check deh cause some people dis go tuh chuch on Crismus day."*

Hazel off the phone now and upset because Carol tell sheh that not only *"Patsy ain deh home,"* but also that Hazel owes her for the telephone call. Now who charges people for incoming calls? Only Carol, and sheh serious bout it too.

"Hazel yuh owe mih five dallas fuh dis call. Leh Bertie pay fuh it. He got Yankee dallas.[613] *Tell he whuh ah seh aan whuh ah dis charge, cauz ah know he rite deh sittin in yuh house. Dhoan feel no way. Is nah you ah vex wid. Is he who waan fine out wheh he ooman deh"* ...... as if Bertie knows about her phone charge.

"Oh, bye de way, de chirren like de peppapat aan de black cake" ...... then a *pause*..... *"aan de gingahbeer. Oh, aan please tell Auntie Millie whuh ah seh. Tell sheh we gon come aan visit ah day."*

---

[612] *"She says Patsy wasn't supposed to go in there today. You know what? I am going to call Carol and see if she turn up. If she is at home now."*

[613] *"He has American Dollars."*

274

She then hangs up, leaving Hazel to deliver her message to Bertie who is about to go searching for his sweetheart again.

"Is whuh chuch sheh dis guh tuh? Ah gon tek mih time aan drive, aan if we aan see sheh deh, we gon go by de car park aan check."[614]

Take he time, eh? Yeah, rite!!! All that Desmond studying is to drive round and round again and to eat out[615] Bertie pocket. By de time he done is going to be plenty money …….. "dead presidents" changed up into Guyanese money outta Bertie pocket …… into he own. Darn scamp!!! Never wanting to take the short way to get to the destination, and like Doris did say about sheh porknocker boyfriend who did not only put de gold teeth in sheh mouth, but did buy sheh de 'jingles' on sheh hand ……

"Ketch ah packoo, buss he back,"[616] and this is exactly what this heartless driver is doing…..using, using, using, all de way!!!

"Like if people dis pick up money in America," my mommy used to say. *"If dey only know how dis place hard."*

Then she would go on to talk about the cold and how hard yuh dis have to work here, and how some people had they good

---

[614] *"Is what church she goes to? I am going to take my time and drive, and if we ain't see her there, we are going to go by the car park and check."*
[615] *Financially exploit*
[616] *"Catch a fool and use him/her for material things or money"*

275

lives back home and shudda never come to this place in this rat race; my stance also, as it becomes even more robotic running up and down the subways because parking too expensive on the job or city streets. Then when the winter comes de place cold, cold, cold and yuh still have to get out there aan grine[617] for a daily living. De road slippery and cars can't drive properly and yuh slipping and sliding in de snow when yuh walking. Then de road looking like de ice in yuh fridge like de day when ah was carrying Jahkeda to school and we had to hold unto de fence. Then other parents in de same predicament like we but we waan carry de lil ones dem fuh get a lil learnin,[618] and not stay at home because de blasted School Board refuse to close de schools. Talking bout dey waiting fuh de school Superintendent to shut dem up.

Everybody walking because de cars going to cause accidents by running into each other. All this people haffa go [619] through and Bertie come home showing off about he money, and not telling the truth that the place ain't no 'bed of roses.' That it damn cold; cold like de damn ice in we refrigerators. Lie?!! No, that not no Lie!!! Then yuh coat better be warm and yuh boots better be good to walk in de snow with them things to grip de ice or else ..... yuh fall down, fall and buss yuh head. They must be warm tuh or yuh toes get frostbite. Yes, is true and ah have another story to tell y'all .... a true story.

---

[617] *And grind for or work hard*

[618] *We want to carry the little ones to get little learning/schooling*

[619] *People have to go*

Is about Glenys ….. who did running to catch de bus by Avenue D and Nostrand. The B-8 bus. Running with all sheh might and look like de bus driver was going to pull off from de stop. Ow, bap, bap she go!!! People running to help sheh. She sprawl on de ground and by now all sheh things all ova de road from sheh handbag. Now I and some other people examining sheh cause she look now like she unconscious, but …. Praise the Lord!!!

Glenys eye open and somebody call de ambulance fuh come and examine sheh. Now this was a 'big lady'[620] with a pair of boots that did too smooth at de bottom that did sheh a real injustice. Couple days later ah did see sheh pun Utica Avenue and sheh seh that how sheh son buy sheh some Lugz boot …. kick out sheh foot and show mih. Now dat's what ah talkin bout!!! As little as it look, yuh boots is important too. No cheap boots …. cause it going to throw yuh down.

Ask Bertie Aunty Avril. Sheh gon tell yuh. She been working as a home health aide all sheh life in America; working with dem white folks tekkin care of they grandmothers and grandfathers, and sometimes their children. About ten different employers for the thirty odd years she been living in that country and even had two jobs at once sometimes. Now does complain about sheh bad back and knees from lifting de patients. Doing nurse work and getting underpaid and could hardly take vacations. Wish she could come home like Bertie but got mortgage to pay,

---

[620] *An elderly woman*

car note and other bills, and this fool home showing off and dis only pay sheh $30 a week for de bedroom in sheh house pun Ocean Avenue in Brooklyn that can't offset her major expenses. Despite that, sheh nice and helping he out. Then de thing is that sheh Jewish employers giving sheh pay without taking out taxes which is good now but she worried that it could hurt sheh later as she get older because it is going to affect her pension.

But, let we get back to where these two fellows going and leh we pray that they find Patsy …….. Desmond now looking at he gas level in this beat up truck and it look like he going to have to fill up the tank soon. Yes, while he running up de mileage on this wild goose chase that he has created himself by not making shortcuts to their destination. A real con-artist in he own way and without consideration for Bertie pocket. But wait, let's see how much this tab is going to be. Blasted trickster!!!

Only thinking about he self. Then now he going to try and scheme some more since he just invited Eileen out; Little Orson mother, while sheh thick red legs still in he head, and he licking he lips now in anticipation to kiss her as soon as possible. Y'all think he ezee?!!! But, wait a little bit, as sheh got a reputation of not only going with married men, but is "ah Doris" in sheh own way. Ah don't mean with de gossiping, but de tricks. Sheh has proven to them that "ah red ooman aan ole car does done man money."[621]

See that house sheh living in next door to Miss Millie and sheh chirren? Is a man buy it fuh sheh. He was Sybil from Prashad Nagar husband who did own a store on Robb Street, and sheh break de two of them up …. a home wrecker. He was pun sheh like hot potato[622] when he meet sheh in a party in Tucville. He knew that he had an instant crush on her when they eyes did meet. All nite he wanted to dance with sheh while she flirted with other men. Yuh see Eileen goes for the highest bidder and never did tun ah straw in sheh life.[623] See, is sheh mother grow sheh up suh. Now this thirty-eight year old young woman get lazy and uses sheh head on men.

"Yuh red, aan dem men wud pay fuh get yuh mih daughta, aan walk roung de place wid yuh aan show yuh off fuh yuh nice face, good body aan complexion,"[624] her mother would say.

Though long deceased, Eileen would never forget that statement and other words from that lady who was mixed with Portuguese, Black and Indian saying ………

---

[621] *A saying in Guyana referring to a light-skinned woman who feel they are financially entitled and.* *use men directly down to the last dollar*

[622] *Vigorously pursuing her*

[623] *Never made an effort in life like working*

[624] *"You light-skinned, and those men would pay to get you my daughter and walk around the place with you* *and show you off for your nice face , good body and complexion," her mother would say*

279

"*Yuh gaffa use yuh head mih chile. Dey stupitey ova we, aan gon gih yuh anyting yuh waan cauz dey waan chirren wid good hair aan nice complexion. Dey dhoan waan no black face ooman.*"

Simple as that!!! As presumptious and factitious as these words may seem, this was the thought-processing of many, many of both young and older men and ladies, tarnished by colonialism. Then what took the cake is that "if yuh black yuh haffa stay back," reigned here and also neighboring countries like both Brazil and Venezuela, as others entertain the same mindset too against people of darker skin colors. But, let's see what's happening with the two friends who looking fuh one ah dem gurlfriend.

They driving and driving, and they just left Smith's Church Congregational Church on Hadfield Street where Patsy step-sister was baptized. She got very well acquainted with the members there and visits from time to time, but since she living far, dis only attend sometimes like on auspicious occasions such as these. They are almost near the church. Could see it, but no cars or bicycles in the distance so that mean nobody at the church today. They getting closer and in front now, but Bertie still adamant about looking inside and nobody there...... empty chairs, empty pulpit, no choir, no piano playing, nobody there. Even de ladies in the back pew not yelling and shouting with Miss Eulene almost looking like she going to faint from all that hollering she be putting down. Word is that sheh went to a clap-hand church in Washington, DC, and come back home with de Holy Spirit.

So every Sunday sheh dis show sheh self[625] as the most self-righteous person in de church heckling after Pastor Andrews as Bertie remembers that in the past when he had accompanied Patsy there for a Service on this said nite. That explains the emptiness within the confines of this church as Miss Eulene and de choir members not in here today. He yawning now and getting tired, and looking worried. He look like he waan cry but he buddy gon laff at he.[626]

"Is wheh sheh deh ah wonda?" Desmond enquires.

"Hope she's not with the 'fam' in the country, cause that's quoite[627] a far way, blood,"[628] Bertie quickly responds.

"Fam" and "Blood?" My American friend is telling me that "fam" means family and that he doesn't know what the word "Blood" means, but Jacqueline who been to England once saying that it means the same as "fam" ….. so we learn something today. See how Bertie got the American language and the English cockney all mixed up, and only God knows if this going to sit well with Patsy because that puh gurl come from de country; the rural

---

[625] *Jumping up, singing out loud and so on as if in showing off*
[626] *He looks like he wants to cry but his buddy is going to laugh at him*
[627] *Quite*
[628] *The British way in referring to a relative with the same bloodline or very close acquaintance*

area and it is hard enough for her to understand de town people much less him.

Oh God, we gon need an interpreter here, but let we concentrate on finding sheh at first. All that jargon is nonsensical and only fuh mek he look like people.

"He playin he head ain good," Stanley did say when he pull off with that fool that still driving he around looking for de girl that basidee ova he; confused over he.

They now in Brickdam and Bertie quiet as ah whistle [629] and not talking. But wait a minute heh? Is whuh I jus write deh?[630] "Quiet as a whistle?" ...... now who dis know that a whistle quiet? Now, is wheh mih[631] country people get that from? Anyway, now I older and it just sink in that duh statement ain't got no logics. Well .... "is so ah buy it, and is so ah sell it." Ha ha ha!!! Oh shit, ah almost choke pun de cherry ah was jus eating how de laff got mih.

Bertie now again ...... he guessing to he self where he girlfriend at and if Aunty Avril give sheh de news that he talking to a few chicks in New York. He wondering if Patsy herself got somebody here, but nobody telling he nothing.

---

[629] *Supposedly very quiet; not saying a word, non-verbal*
[630] *Is what I just wrote there?*
[631] *Is where my*

"That Hazel, her brothers, Miss Millie and those people in the yard must be keeping secret for her," he is thinking.

He yawning again now and hoping that he not going to get a 'shockatock'[632] and he feeling drowsy from all that pepperpot, Aunty Desmond wine and the black cake he just ate in Meadow Brook, and wishing he in Patsy bed because he no longer has a place of his own in Campbelville. Done gave that up about three years ago when he left here; Guyana, for de nice house that he Aunty Avril got on East 43rd Street in Brooklyn. He is smiling now because he has crossed hurdles to what he perceives as a *"betta loife"* …. "better life," as he is thinking in cockney too. That idiot!!! He has two jobs also and has been able to save a lot of money in two different banks. But what makes it worse is that Desiree from the Bronx who deeply in love with he give he some money night before last and does cheat pun sheh boyfriend Randolph to meet up with he sometimes.

Y'all see whuh ah talkin bout? Then lying to he auntie that he can't give sheh more money to help pay de bills in de house. Don't worry, it gon ketch up wid he.[633] Now he conscience tormenting he about how"" he been cheating on Patsy, and he comforting himself with the ole saying, 'eye nuh see, heart nuh

---

[632] *A very bad surprise*
[633] *It is going to catch up with him*

bun,'[634] and delegating to Desmond to drive more faster and let they go back to Punchin Yard.

"*Ah waan ask yuh someting, Bertie. Why is it dat yuh neva move de gurl outta deh?* "[635]........ as Desmond interrupts Bertie's quiet thoughts.

Then raises his voice, "*as yuh seh yuh love sheh. Gawd man sheh aan even gat ah tailet inside aan sheh gaffuh bathe in de yard. Yuh aan see no wattuh ain in de house?*[636] *Duh place ain suh 'catholic' fuh live in aan yuh deh in America suh laang? Gawd man!!! Why yuh din help sheh fuh move out, eh bannuh?*" Desmond adds.

No word from Bertie, as he is tapping his two legs with his hands. He is becoming very upset as is quite evident after *suckin he teeth*[637] about two times.

"*That's for me and her to discuss okay bro. Just drive on, and I wonder what my tab is?*"

He becomes silent again and refuses to talk to his driver until they arrive at his so-called girlfriend's dwelling place. 'Push comin tuh shove'[638] and he has to find his lady; his "sugah." Its

---

[634] *If you don't see your lover cheating, no need to worry for your heart to hurt/burn*

[635] *"I want to ask you something, Bertie. Why is it that you never moved the girl out of there?"*

[636] *"You ain't see no water ain't in the house?"*

[637] *Manipulating his teeth in annoyance*

[638] *Time running out. Time to take action.*

after five and she should be home now, but Ethel who still perched up outside yells ………

"S*heh aan come home yet. Daphne wid sheh crazy self did run up deh ah lil while ago aan sheh aan come out. Carol dis hear sheh inside unless sheh tip-toeing*" ……….

As Doris intercedes, "*you is de fault Bertie. Sheh did complainin dat sheh din hearin from yuh. Owh, we prayin dat sheh inside*" with hands akimbo as if to agitate him so she could tell him off. Yes, give him a piece of her mind.

After all, Patsy has been seen jumping the fence next door more often recently and scrambling quickly into her lil cubby hole[639] that she calls home. Of course, there has been too many enquiries as to if her man is coming home this Christmas which embarrasses her.

"*He been comin since year before de laas, aan fuh 'thy kingdom come,'*[640]*dis is de third year aan now he showin up,*" Stanley said four hours ago. "*Ah mad tek he gurl.*"

Remember I did tell allyuh at de beginning of this book that he been pursuing this man girl a long time now, but sheh not succumbing to his persuasions because sheh man was abroad.

---

[639] *A very small living space*
[640] *"For heaven's sake"*

Now he home. Home after almost three years. Thank God!!! Hallelujah!!!

"Lawd, whuh dhoan happen in ah year, Donna, dis happen in ah day," my friend Lena would say.

Bertie knocking, he knocking, he knocking hard hard....... *"It's me baby, it's me Bertie. Are you there Patsy, honey? Open, open please sweetheart."*

Some people hearing he loud knocking and they coming outside now. Even Miss Beryl hearing he from the other yard, and of course y'all know who? Daphne, Daphne of all people, of course.

She screaming and heckling after him .... *"open, open, open"* .... and as we all know by now, she adds, *"ah waan candycanes, candycanes, candycanes, open, open, open."*

That was all this young lady wanted to hear. That someone was knocking on that door that she was unsuccessful with her neighbor not answering earlier. Then with an audience, she in sheh royal blues.[641] She yelling and screaming and now standing next to Bertie, and getting into the fighting mode as usual and she just shove Desmond one side.[642] He is shocked and gets out of her way very quickly. There is no need for Bertie to knock any longer cause

---

[641] *In her profuse madnes, acting insane*
[642] *To the side, out of her way*

she is doing all the knocking for him. Then she suddenly makes a dash and runs over to her place of abode much to her grandmother's amazement and the other onlookers, and returns with her doll who is now completely beheaded. Y'all think sheh was bluffin?[643] No, that doll head off long time now and she don't care.

Sheh really did mean to do it, and now she knocking and knocking with that damaged doll and yelling again, *"open, open, open. Ah waan candycanes, candycanes,"* and knocking at the one window that she almost broke the glass.

She looking in keenly now and like sheh noticing something. She pointing now and yelling, *"inside, inside, inside, open, open, open."*

She squinting sheh eyes and now everybody including Bertie looking cause it look like this young woman, even though developmentally disabled has some cognition to know that something ain't rite; that somebody in there. So what y'all think sheh doing now? …. Kicking de front door as if sheh want to kick it down so it could open up. See, that's what she did see the police doing a time when they went to Phillip house and he didn't want to open de door.

---

[643] *Pretending not to want to act up*

287

She getting mad now. Kicking again with all sheh mights and acting hysterical until Miss Cheryl shouts ....

"Stap!!! Is whuh wrong wid yuh? If de gurl in deh yuh gon mek sheh dhoan waan come out. Stop de stupitness," as Daphne squints her eyes again in trying to comprehend those words, and has become quiet.

"Gawd, yuh mean dis is whuh we gaffa put up wid fuh nex year? Miss Beulah yuh gaffa put dis gurl some whey,"[644] she says to the very emotionally and physically exhausted grandmother who has been showing recent signs also of poor tolerance and low coping mechanisms.

Daphne suddenly stops as she senses that Miss Cheryl dhoan play[645] and runs so fast down the little flight of stairs with both anger and fright straight into the arms of her grandmother, that she almost throw sheh down. Thank God that Bridget son Orin hold sheh up. This ole lady is now seventy-eight and don't have de constitution[646] to handle no falling down on top of all de stress she going through. Plus if anything happen to sheh, Daphne mother not going to come back to take care of her since she done

---

[644] *"God, you mean this is what we have to put up with for next year? Miss Beulah you have to put this girl somewhere"*
[645] *Cannot be played with or manipulated, has no tolerance for bad behavior*
[646] *The strength or immune system for fatigue*

288

prove that she is ah 'fifth wheel tuh ah jackass coach.'[647] Useless, useless, useless!!!!

No, never coming back!!! Done left de girl with sheh mother since she was five years old and hauled ass; went away to 'only God knows.' But all everybody know is that she abandoned de little girl and left her with her grandmother all these years. No looking back. Gone!!! Gone with the wind and ain't even say when she gon return and where to. Not a letter. Nothing!!! Nor no money either. Leff her daughter fuh punish[648] with sheh mother while somebody did say, like I mentioned earlier, that sheh mek otha chirren in another country.

Well is how I stray off so and stop focusing on if this door gon open, even though I been promising allyuh that I not gossiping at all in this book. See how easy it is to get caught up in de 'peeping and de gossiping?' Easy, but we all mean well and agree that is constructive criticism. Is a "Guyanese ting" and all ahwe dis do it[649] even in other parts of the world and elsewhere cause we are the only English speaking country in South America, in case nobody didn't know that. Yes, we are. Had gained independence from the British on May 26, 1966. As a matter of fact big preparations had taken place on that said day in 2016 for the 50th Anniversary of our Independence. Ah did want to go, but

---

[647] *The fifth or spare wheel to a coach or other vehicle that is rarely used. Have no uses for, unreliable*
[648] *Left her daughter to punish*
[649] *All of us usually do it*

ah have this book to complete, but nuff, nuff, nuff Guyanese went home for de celebrations and we could bet we last dollar that it was very nice. So I decided from ever since to take on this project of writing as paying tribute and homage to mih country and people.

Ah hope y'all gon like it cause is like bringing back sweet memories with sweet nostalgia of our great land .... with its motto, "One People, One Nation and One Destiny." Nice rite? Ah like dem words.....cause we is ONE..... six races and ahwe dis is "one." One.... like de people in Punchin Yard. Full of cohesiveness and even though teeth aan tongue dis bite,[650] they dis hold hands for de sake of survival. Y'all hear mih? For de sake of survival, and they doing a good job at it. With "unity is strength" and they proving that this theory is true and correct.

Shoo, shoo!!! Quiet, quiet!!! Eh, eh, look like we gon mek some headway now. Sam just tek up a ladder he get from the next yard and carrying it round to the back by Patsy side. Bertie following he and he gesticulating to de man that looking desperately for he lover to keep quiet. Sam up now pun de ladder and he peeping inside. See whuh ah seh ...... see what I say ... nuff, nuff .... plenty, plenty peeping in dis book. Nuff, nuff action, but look like we getting somewhere with this one.

---

[650] *When teeth and tongue bite, it causes pain and this relates to also two people not getting along*

Sam whispering something to Bertie and we cyaan hear.[651] He coming down now so Bertie could climb up and look inside. The man on the ladder peeping inside and now turning looking at we with he eyes big open in surprise. He looking crazy now and banging hard at de window. Look like he waan get inside. Meantime, Stanley who vex up[652] since this man arrived from America, trying to restrain Daphne who done get agitated again, and want to go and help Bertie to go inside Patsy house.

She yelling from afar ...... *"open, open, open, candycanes, candycanes, candycanes,"* and getting more boisterous.

Stanley little training as a security guard now kicking in and he just wrestled sheh to the ground, while Miss Beulah and Granny Tinsy praying for this child that getting worse and worse every day, and secretly fuh Stanley to pass he security exams. See whuh we jus see? He good with de practical in restraining Daphne, but de theory; de written exam he not doing good with. But dem two ole people know how to pray. They is prayer warriors and ah bet y'all that de next time he sit that security guard exam, he going to pass. Ooooh chile!!! Bless his heart. Cause they might have to sprinkle he with some holy water too. Ha ha ha!!! Jokes fuh so!!!

See why I like writing. Drama fuh so!!! Cousin Hazel cracking up with laughter on sheh sofa ova there. Yep, Cousin Donna loves to write with drama. Ha ha ha!!! If only ah could

---

[651] *And we cannot hear*

[652] *Who very annoyed*

write this book in full creolese, but ah gotta cater[653] for other people who not Guyanese. Cause ah want them to enjoy it too ….. learn bout we, and I repeat ….. we sweet, sweet Guyana and its people.

Oh skites!!! ……Oh my!!! So while I did distracting y'all with Daphne and sheh stupitness and mekkin dem jokes, Bertie done get de window open and he inside. Now everybody waiting to see whuh gon happen. Doris got sheh hands akimbo again and did waiting sheh turn at de standpipe to wash sheh dishes, but abandons de basin with de cups and plates, and sheh other utensils and rapping now on Patsy front door next to Carol own in they dilapidated cottage.

"Eye nah see, heart nah bun Patsy." Then continues, *"if yuh inside deh give he ah chance nuh. He aan comin out, suh ah know yuh in deh,"* Doris yells.[654]

There is silence now. Real silence and we aan seeing Bertie nor he gurl. De t still close but it sound like two people talking. Now there is silence cause yuh know how we know? Gwen just went pon top de ladder and peep inside.

"Eh heh, eh heh, ah seein."

---

[653] *I have to cater*

[654] *"If you don't see a partner cheating on you, then your heart will not hurt. If you are inside there give him a chance please. He ain't coming out, so I know you in there"*

292

That's nosey Gwen!!! Who people seh lately getting like Doris and Ethel now. Sheh betta watch sheh self!!!! Cause people dis despise people who like to meddle in other people affairs. Now, sheh suggesting from her actions to the crowd that the couple is doing something, and winks her eyes while satisfying her curiosity. Bet y'all sheh did think they making love ….. but no. De man just hugging up he woman.

Stanley overwhelmed with jealousy yells, *"time longah dan twine. He only come fuh pompazet he self.*[655] *Got de gurl shame in deh. Is me who love sheh. Ah gon gih he ah laang rope. Whuh yuh just seh Bertie? Come out aan seh it. Carry yuh stink mouth. One ah dese days 'push gon come to shove' aan sheh gon know who really love sheh. Only deh heh aan "flammin."*[656]

Steuuuupse!!! Lord, is whuh is dis? …. look like Christmas day in Punchin Yard gon turn out into a fight between de man who been sooring Patsy for all these years and de so-called lover and boyfriend who just fly in today from America. Plus Stanley like de binnie so much that he not playing ….. he aan tekkin leff.[657] Poor ting …. puh ting, he can't stomach Bertie returning. It messing with he head bad, bad.

---

[655] *"Time is always available. He only come to show off himself."*
[656] *"And pretending to be better than others"*
[657] *He ain't tg left; as in being deserted romantically*

293

"Patsy, Patsy. Come out nuh. We waan see yuh. Is Crismus," Gwen yells, while Bridget concurrently says.........

"Patsy, Patsy, come leh we see yuh nuh. Come get de peppahpat dat yuh auntie mek aan de black cake. De bread fresh aan nice. Come out nuh gurl. Leh we enjoy we self. Yuh only lack up yuhself in deh. Yuh man come. Leh we celebrate."

Still......no response!!! Somebody now at de window plooking outside and it look like Bertie. A shadow next to he and we could now assume that is Patsy. Now he ex-classmate Desmond outside with Bertie georgie bundle.[658] Ah mean, he six suitcases, and still aan get paid yet fuh going and pick he up at the airport and driving he around town to look fuh Patsy. Well we ain't going to say nothing bout dis one because he don't deserve de amount of pay that he been mumbling to he self just now that Bertie owe he. Anyhow, de door still close and Patsy not pickin sheh teeth.[659] Not even looking outside, but as we could see, sheh standing beside sheh man. From how it look like now, they looking like they hugging up and looking at the commotion that Stanley creating outside.

---

[658] *His belongings, suitcases*

[659] *Patsy not saying anything or budging. Not looking outside or opening the door*

He bhuseing out[660] and just throw a brick at the window. He is very upset and shouting to de top of his voice ……. "*dhoan worry wid he. He come fuh put yuh in 'swing up' like if he love yuh.[661] He ain gon marry yuh. Look how laang he tek fuh come bak home. If he did miss yuh, he wudda come heh ah laang time now.*"

The crowd is now waiting for the the couple to respond while Desmond, the taxi driver, is waiting patiently with Bertie's luggage outside their front door and for his payment as well. He looking restless now and Stanley now telling he………

"*In dis hard guava season he need to pay* yuh. *Is Crismus yes, but tings still ruff wid all ahwe. All dis time he in deh, yuh shudda tief he tings.*"[662]

His neighbors cannot believe what this security guard just said. Doris in they face and she stupsing up she mouth in disagreement with these two men as Desmond just grinned at Stanley's suggestion. Ethel looking too like sheh going to set fire to fury[663] and just then, Patsy's door opens up.

---

[660] *Using profanities, cursing*

[661] *"He come to lie to you like if he loves you."*

[662] *"In this hard guava season (severe hard times) he needs to pay you. Is Christmas yes, but things   still rough with all of us. All this time he in there, you should have thief/stolen his things."*

[663] *Escalate and instigate the anger*

"Well, well, well is whuh ah seein heh?"[664] Doris yells as the crowd's attention is focused on a beaming Patsy. Bursting with joy and anxiety, she is exhibiting her left hand to her onlookers, while Bertie endorses her delight with ....

"she really likes it. Bought it at a jewelry store in Manhattan. "Oi" ..... he means *"I"*..... *knew she would like it. Gotta show my babe that oi care for her, not jiving."*

He is hugging her even closer now and is refusing to let go of this woman whom he has not embraced for so long, while she seems confused at his strange accent. He begins to kiss her now, much to the annoyance of Stanley from his facial expression, and whose despise is steadily increasing for this now-fiance of the woman whom he has grown to admire or even moreso, is now madly in love with.

Ethel glances at this now deranged competitor and senses that his mood is getting worse and almost neurotic. She turns to the crowd and says, *"but look at dis one heh Stanley. Ain gat ah pot tuh piss in aan ah window fuh throw it out.'*[665] *Look leh we go inside aan leff dese two lovers alone. See allyuh tamarraw."*

Patsy then nods her head in agreement, as she once more is displaying the sparkling object on her left hand finger that she has desperately been longing for. The women are now taking turns

---

[664] *"Well, well, well is what I am seeing here?"*

[665] *"Has nothing in life; material things like even something as simple as a potty to even urinate in and his/her own dwelling place with a window to dispose of it.*

at hugging and congratulating her after promises from the couple for a get-together tomorrow in de yard. Meanwhile Desmond has just unloaded Bertie's six pieces of luggage into the house with all de tings sheh did waan fuh Crismus and has one more job to do ……tek dem to Auntie Millie and sheh family to done up de balance of de day.

GLOSSARY

Aah	-	Ah
Aan	-	And
Ah	-	A
Ai	-	I
Ain	-	Ain't
Allyuh	-	All of you
Bai	-	Boy
Bannuh	-	Young man, fellow or guy
Bout	-	About
Chirren	-	Children
Cyaan	-	Cannot
Dat	-	That
Deh	-	There
Dem	-	Them
Den	-	Then
Dey	-	They
Dhoan	-	Don't
Din	-	Didn't
Dis	-	This
Dis do	-	Usually do or Does
Dis get	-	Gets
Duh	-	That
Dun up	-	Done up, finish up
Eh Eh	-	An exclamation, no

Faas	-	Fast/inquisitive
Fren	-	Friend
Fuh	-	For
Gih	-	Give
Gon	-	Going to
Guh	-	Go
Haan	-	Hand
Heh	-	Here
Laas	-	Last
Leh	-	Let
Lil	-	Little
Mek	-	Make
Mekkin	-	Making
Mih	-	Me
Nuff Nuff	-	Plenty, plenty
Nuh	-	No
Oi	-	I (in British cockney)
Ooman	-	Woman
Pon/pun	-	On
Puh	-	Poor (as in sympathy)
Roung	-	Round
Seh	-	Say
Sheh	-	She or her
Suh	-	So
Tek	-	Take
Truh	-	True
Tuh	-	To

Waan	-	Want
Wheh	-	Where
Whoan	-	Would not
Whuh	-	What
Wid	-	With
Wonta	-	Wouldn't
Yuh	-	You
Yuh dis	-	You usually

About the Author

DONNA MILNER

Born a twin in my native Guyana, South America in the early 1960s, I grew up in a family with three siblings and my parents Mavis and Roy Parris in Georgetown, the capital. Almost sixteen of my years was spent in the military base Eve-Leary, Kingston, as my father was a Police Officer. There most of the children of the top cops felt isolated and were even jeered for attending private catholic high schools and other learning institutions as those that critiqued us referred to us as being in a "bubble." It is then that I realized that there was another side of the fence and that myself and siblings needed to assimilate more with the larger society. It is in doing so that I made deductions of some and the catalysts to their circumstances. Then one day I visited a tenement yard and the stark reality did hit me about the socioeconomic inertia and extreme poverty that existed in my country for some families. My heart truly cried as I felt more than empathy and knew that one day I must literally advocate for the persons dispelling the bourgeoisie ideologies labelling them as so-called underdogs.

So, as I departed from Guyana for the United States in 1983, I not only became nostalgic for my country but kept thinking about how some are coping economically. Then as I became a Rastafarian in 1984, my blood boiled for "equal rights and justice." That same year I returned home and got wedded to William Alfred Milner who has influenced the title of this book with his frequent utterances with regards to business … "man ah tek blows today" with reference to how much profit he had made, etc. That remark remained with me and I said to myself one day that I will call this book "Punchin Yard" signifying blows or punches especially amongst Guyana's grassroots populations and like entrepreneurs. William has passed on three years now but I will forever be grateful for the knowledge he has imparted upon me. After attending college and university, I had an awakening of how much I had liked writing with of course how avid my dad and mom was, siblings and even my own offsprings. So with accolades and everything, I concluded that nothing else mattered but just to write.

So one day in Miami, FL, I searched in an old bin and found a tattered essay that I had written in an English 2 class in New York City more than twenty years ago. It was about Old Year's night there, and hence almost like a prophesy to fulfill, the birth of this book as paying homage to my country's people as a Dawta of the Guyanese soil.